JANET
EVANOVICH
AND
PETER
EVANOVICH

THE
BIG KAHUNA

REVIEW

First published in Great Britain in 2019 by
HEADLINE REVIEW
An imprint of HEADLINE PUBLISHING GROUP

First published in paperback in Great Britain in 2020
by HEADLINE REVIEW
An imprint of HEADLINE PUBLISHING GROUP

1

Cataloguing in Publication Data is available from the British Library

ISBN 978 1 4722 6624 8 (A-format)
ISBN 978 1 4722 6094 9 (B-format)

Printed and bound in Great Britain by Clays Ltd, Elcograf S.p.A.

Headline's policy is to use papers that are natural, renewable and recyclable
products and made from wood grown in well-managed forests and other
controlled sources. The logging and manufacturing processes are expected
to conform to the environmental regulations of the country of origin.

HEADLINE PUBLISHING GROUP
An Hachette UK Company
Carmelite House
50 Victoria Embankment
London EC4Y 0DZ

www.headline.co.uk
www.hachette.co.uk

THE
BIG KAHUNA

THE
BIG KAHUNA

Janet Evanovich is the No. 1 *New York Times* bestselling author of the Stephanie Plum series, the Lizzy and Diesel novels, twelve romance novels, the Alexandra Barnaby novels, and *How I Write: Secrets of a Bestselling Author*, as well as the Fox and O'Hare series.

Peter Evanovich is Janet's son. He has been part of the Evanovich writing team since the beginning of the Plum series.

Raves for Janet Evanovich:

'As smart and sassy as high-gloss wet paint' *Time Out*

'Romantic and gripping . . . an absolute tonic' *Good Housekeeping*

'Chutzpah and sheer comic inventiveness . . . The Evanovich books [are] good fun' *Washington Post*

'A laugh-out-loud page-turner' *Heat*

'Making trouble and winning hearts' *USA Today*

'Evanovich's characters are eccentric and exaggerated, the violence often surreal and the plot dizzily speedy: but she produces as many laughs as anyone writing crime today' *The Times*

'Among the great joys of contemporary crime fiction' *GQ*

'Plum is not just a smart private eye but a heroine with a sense of humour' *Daily Mail*

BY JANET EVANOVICH

The Stephanie Plum novels

One For The Money	Fearless Fourteen
Two For The Dough	Finger Lickin' Fifteen
Three To Get Deadly	Sizzling Sixteen
Four To Score	Smokin' Seventeen
High Five	Explosive Eighteen
Hot Six	Notorious Nineteen
Seven Up	Takedown Twenty
Hard Eight	Top Secret Twenty-One
To The Nines	Tricky Twenty-Two
Ten Big Ones	Turbo Twenty-Three
Eleven On Top	Hardcore Twenty-Four
Twelve Sharp	Look Alive Twenty-Five
Lean Mean Thirteen	Twisted Twenty-Six

The Knight and Moon novels

Curious Minds (with Phoef Sutton)

Dangerous Minds

The Fox and O'Hare novels
with Lee Goldberg

The Heist

The Chase

The Job

The Scam

The Pursuit

The Big Kahuna

The Diesel and Tucker series

Wicked Appetite	Wicked Business

Wicked Charms (with Phoef Sutton)

The Between the Numbers Novels

Visions Of Sugar Plums	Plum Lucky
Plum Lovin'	Plum Spooky

And writing with Charlotte Hughes

Full House	Full Speed
Full Tilt	Full Blast

1

Kate O'Hare's favorite outfit was her blue windbreaker with the letters *FBI* written in yellow on the back, worn over a black T-shirt and matching black Kevlar vest. She had reluctantly relegated the outfit to the back of her tiny closet, which now overflowed with an assortment of designer clothes and resort-casual beachwear. The designer clothes and beachwear were all acquired during her recent stint of undercover work. Tools of the trade, she told herself. Unfortunately, it was Nicolas Fox's trade. He was a brilliant con man and a world-class thief. She'd arrested him two years ago, and he'd charmed his way out of a lifetime in prison by offering up his unique talents to help the FBI take down the worst and most elusive criminals.

Now she had the impossible job of acting as his handler. When conventional police work couldn't get the job done, the

FBI set Fox loose to run questionably legal cons and undercover operations on out-of-reach bad guys.

Some days Kate wondered whether she was managing Nicolas Fox or he was managing her. Today was one of those days. It was noon, and she was standing in the middle of the Beverly Hills Saks Fifth Avenue dressed in black slacks, a black-and-white striped shirt, red suspenders, white gloves, and a black beret. Her face was painted completely white, except for her bright red lipstick. She was surrounded by a sea of similarly dressed men and women, possibly hundreds of them. It was a flash mob of mimes, and they were all doing classic mime stunts, trying to get out of invisible boxes and climb invisible ladders, struggling not to get blown away by nonexistent wind.

"This is ridiculous," Kate said to the mime standing next to her. "In fact, this has got to be the most ridiculous, humiliating plan you've ever devised. And that's saying a lot."

The mime next to her was Nick Fox. "You have a short memory," he said. "Dressing as mimes can't compare to some of the humiliating situations we've experienced together. And besides, this is all your boss's fault. He gave us this case. I merely came up with the brilliant plan to solve it." He silently threw an imaginary lasso at Kate and pretended to pull her in to him.

"Get a grip," Kate said. "Not gonna happen."

A growing crowd of shoppers and sales clerks had gathered

around the flash mob. Kate scanned the room. The entire store, including two security guards, was entranced by the spectacle.

"Think about it," Nick said. "In the last five years, three high-end jewelry stores have been robbed in New York, Chicago, and Las Vegas while onlookers were distracted by flash mobs. It's actually pretty brilliant. Anonymously organize a flash mob over the Internet, and you've got a crew of a hundred people unwittingly helping you commit the crime, all without having to split the money a hundred ways. It's perfect. And it's designed to be a surprise piece of performance art, so participants are encouraged to keep the time and place private."

Kate narrowed her eyes and stared at Nick. "I get that. What I don't get is how you happened to be on the guest list of the best-kept secret in Los Angeles. And why you think this mob is going to cover for another robbery. I'd better not find out you're somehow involved in this."

"I'm hurt. It's as if you don't trust me. We're supposed to be partners on this assignment."

"You're a world-class con man. Of course I don't trust you."

"Yeah, but you like me, right?"

Kate blew out a sigh. "Yes. Mostly."

Nick flashed a crooked grin at Kate. Even with the white-face makeup, Kate had to reluctantly admit, he had a great smile, and Nick Fox was outrageously sexy in his tight-fitting black mime pants and black-and-white striped shirt.

"It's noon," Nick said, "and the flash mob is supposed to

dissipate in three minutes. If it's going to happen, it's going to be soon."

Kate looked over at the Graff jewelry counter. A pair of Manolo Blahnik–clad feet poked out from behind the counter, toes up.

"Crap," Kate said. "Man down at Graff."

Nick and Kate pushed their way through the traffic jam of mimes and stared at the woman stretched out behind the counter. She was lying on the floor, breathing but not moving. She had on a red bandage dress, a name tag identifying her as Beth the Fine Jewelry Manager, and a tranquilizer dart stuck into her thigh. The counter was open with the key still in the lock.

Kate pulled the dart out of Beth's leg and felt for her pulse. "She seems okay," Kate said, "but she should get checked out. Why isn't there better security here?"

"The security guards are watching the flash mob."

"Call for medical assistance and then call security."

Nick placed the calls and gestured across the room at a young female mime wearing a black minidress and striped knee socks. "Well, that's something you don't see every day."

Kate rolled her eyes. "The minidress? Seriously."

"No." Nick pointed to the 110 carats of pink, yellow, green, and blue diamonds on the woman's wrist. "A mime wearing a fifty-five-million-dollar Graff watch."

"How do you know it's a fifty-five-million-dollar watch?" Kate asked.

"It's the Graff Diamonds Hallucination watch. It was unveiled at Baselworld in 2014 and is the most expensive watch ever created. It was on loan to the Beverly Hills Graff this month. Let's get a closer look."

Kate placed the dart next to the unconscious woman and tagged after Nick. "Weren't you on vacation in Switzerland during Baselworld in 2014?"

"You know, I think I might have been. Strange coincidence, no?"

"No," Kate said.

"You aren't going to ask me if I was contemplating snatching the watch, are you?"

"No again," Kate said. "I already know the answer."

The woman in the black minidress turned, stared directly into Kate's and Nick's faces, and took off running toward the exit. Kate pushed aside several mimes and plowed through a crowd of onlookers. Nick was right behind her as they burst out of the store, onto Wilshire Boulevard. They pulled up short when the female mime jumped into a white Econoline van parked on the street, and the van took off down Wilshire.

"This is a role reversal for me," Nick said, hands on hips, catching his breath. "Usually the beautiful woman is chasing *me*."

Kate thought he might be referring to her as the beautiful woman, but she wasn't willing to put money on it. She yanked the valet out of a red Ferrari idling in front of the store. "FBI. I'm commandeering this vehicle."

Nick jumped into the passenger seat, gave the valet ten dollars, and mimed a thank-you. "Mimes aren't supposed to talk," he said to Kate. "It's all about storytelling using your body language."

Kate held her white gloved middle finger up to Nick and pressed her foot down on the accelerator. She chirped her tires, and went from zero to seventy miles per hour in three seconds.

The van took a hard left onto North Camden Drive, bounced off a parked car, and swerved wildly before regaining control. Kate rounded the corner and caught up to the van just as it turned right onto Santa Monica Boulevard.

"Well, you caught up to them," Nick said. "What's next?"

The back doors to the van burst open, and two mimes armed with semiautomatic AR-15 rifles took aim at the Ferrari. Kate veered to the right, and a stream of bullets struck the left side of the car. The mimes took aim again and Kate swerved left, leaving a bunch of fresh bullet holes in the right side of the car.

Nick looked at the holes. "I'm pretty sure these weren't here when you borrowed this car. I hope your insurance covers commandeering."

The van swung a right onto Rodeo Drive and accelerated past the Ralph Lauren and Vera Wang storefronts, cutting around cars, blowing through traffic lights, and barely missing people attempting to cross the street. Kate was less than a car length behind it. She had one hand on the wheel, and the other on the horn.

She turned to Nick. "Are you wearing your seatbelt?"

Nick tightened his seatbelt. "I'm not sure I like where this is going."

Kate pressed the accelerator to the floor, and the Ferrari lurched forward, and rammed the back of the Econoline. The impact set off the Ferrari's airbags and sent the two gunmen tumbling around the back of the van.

Nick beat down the airbags and looked out over the bullet-hole-riddled hood of the Ferrari at the crushed front end. It was locked onto the rear of the van, which careened wildly down Rodeo Drive, towing the Ferrari behind it.

Pedestrians were screaming and scrambling to get out of the way.

"It's like they've never seen two mimes driving a Ferrari in a high-speed chase with international jewel thieves," Nick said.

"Let's try to slow this freight train down," Kate said, slamming her foot on the brake.

Nick looked out at the wheels of the car. The brake pads were smoking, and burnt rubber from the tires lined the street behind them. The Econoline was slowly losing speed, but its momentum still carried it forward.

"In zero point two miles, you will have reached your destination," the Ferrari's computer announced.

Nick looked down at the map on the touch screen. "It looks like this car was programmed to find the Beverly Wilshire hotel before you commandeered it. By the by, you know that Rodeo Drive dead-ends at Wilshire Boulevard, right?"

Kate still had her hand on the horn. "Holy shit pickles. Hang on." The van and the Ferrari, still locked together, sped through the intersection of Rodeo and Wilshire, pinballing off cars. They jumped the curb and plowed through the Beverly Wilshire's outdoor dining area, demolishing a dessert cart but miraculously avoiding hitting any guests.

The two vehicles crashed through a plate glass window into the hotel lobby, and finally came to a halt just in front of the concierge desk.

"You have reached your destination," the Ferrari announced and burst into flames.

Kate and Nick jumped from the car, rushed to the van, and pulled the three dazed mimes to safety before handcuffing them. Hotel staff rushed in with fire extinguishers and worked at getting the blaze under control. Police cruisers and fire trucks screamed in the distance.

"When you think you're going to die, it really puts things in perspective," Nick said, wiping away a stray bit of cheesecake from Kate's cheek . . . the last remnants of the now-deceased dessert cart. "Money doesn't mean too much if you don't have love in your life."

Kate drew in close to Nick, reached into his jacket, and pulled out the Hallucination watch. "That explains why you pocketed this fifty-five-million-dollar watch."

Nick grinned at Kate and ate the cheesecake from his finger. "What can I say? It's my nature. I see things of great beauty, and I must have them."

2

Nick and Kate paced outside the corner office of Carl Jessup, special agent in charge at the FBI's Los Angeles field office. They'd been kept waiting for twenty minutes. The wait wasn't a good sign. When they finally were allowed entrance, they sat across the desk from Jessup for a good thirty seconds, staring into the fifty-something Kentuckian's craggy face, before he broke the silence.

"So, what do you two knuckleheads have to say for yourselves?" Jessup said, more a condemnation than a question.

Kate leaned forward. "Long story short. We captured the mega-successful criminals you wanted taken down, and we saved the world's most expensive watch from being stolen."

Jessup held up his hands and looked over at Nick. "And your take on the morning's events?"

"I'd prefer to skip right to the good stuff," Nick said.

"The 'good stuff'?"

Nick nodded. "You know. The part where you tell us how the mayor took a giant bite out of your ass and how you told him we're a couple of loose cannons and how if we screw up just one more time it will be our badges. But, secretly, you think we're the best damn cops on the force and wish you had a hundred others just like us."

"You're not a cop, and you don't have a badge," Jessup said. "You're an asset we recruited to help us in situations that require finesse and discretion. You're lucky you're not in jail."

"Yessir," Nick said. He looked over at Kate and silently mouthed, "Best damn cops on the force."

Jessup shook his head in disgust and turned to Kate. "You demolished a million-dollar Ferrari, shot up Rodeo Drive, and set a five-star hotel on fire."

"Chasing down dangerous felons," Kate said.

Jessup wasn't buying it. "In the past year alone of undercover work, you've destroyed three sports cars, a helicopter, and a ten-million-dollar yacht."

"Don't forget about the city bus," Nick said while Kate kicked at him under cover of Jessup's desk. "The one she totaled trying to arrest me."

"And a bus," Jessup said. "The point is you two are like a herd of bulls in a china shop. That's why I've added a new team member. He follows the rules. He fills out his paperwork on time. He doesn't destroy buses or Ferraris or hotels."

Kate worked at keeping her composure. "With all due respect, sir, I don't think we need a third team member."

"With all due respect, O'Hare, you *deserve* this team member."

"He's going to drive me crazy, isn't he?" Kate said.

Jessup smiled for the first time. "Yeah. And that's not the best part. I have a real humdinger of an assignment for you and Nick and your new partner. You're going to love it."

Nick turned to Kate. "I think he's being sarcastic."

"Maybe a little," Jessup said. "Mostly I'm being cautious while I'm reevaluating your worth to us. I'm giving you a job that should require a minimum amount of your *special* talents. And, hopefully, it will not lead to explosions, grand theft auto, scaring the daylights out of half the population of Beverly Hills, and screwing up my year's budget." Jessup handed Kate a thin manila folder. "It's a missing persons case. Richard Wylde. He's the owner of a Silicon Valley software artificial intelligence start-up, and he disappeared last week. Worth over a billion dollars, so you can imagine a lot of people, including his wife, are looking for him."

"Kidnapped?"

Jessup shook his head. "No sign of foul play. He had his pilot's license and was last seen taking off in his private plane from John Wayne Airport."

"Crashed?" Kate asked.

"No evidence to support that either."

Kate silently groaned. The only thing worse than a Silicon Valley billionaire was the wife of a Silicon Valley billionaire.

11

"In other words, he's probably holed up with some bikini model in a Mexican luxury resort. And you want us to hold his wife's hand for the next two weeks until he runs out of bodily fluids and decides to come home."

Jessup smiled again. "Like I said. It's a real humdinger."

Kate sat in the driver's seat of her blue Buick LaCrosse sedan, reading the Richard Wylde case file while she waited for the new partner to show up. Jessup had refused to divulge his identity. Said he didn't want to spoil the surprise. Nick was in the passenger seat, texting and checking emails.

Kate finished reading and put away the manila folder. "What's with the texting? I've never seen you so tethered to your cellphone."

"I'm amusing myself while you do official government business. This case isn't exactly an intellectual challenge for me."

"This is true," Kate said. "I don't need you to help me babysit some billionaire's wife. You're attached to this hideous job because Jessup doesn't trust you to be left unattended."

"Completely unfair," Nick said. "You were the one who stole the Ferrari."

"I commandeered it. Big difference. *BIG*."

"Fortunately, as luck would have it, the wife might be a prospective client."

Kate narrowed her eyes. "You have clients?"

Nick read an incoming text and typed a reply. "What's wrong with having clients?"

"You do realize it's considered illegal in most circles to steal from your clients."

Nick put down the cellphone. "You're going to love this."

"I highly doubt that. But go ahead anyway."

"I found a way to use my entrepreneurial talents without breaking any laws," Nick said.

"Oh boy. This should be good."

"It took a while to come up with it. At first, I thought I'd form a foundation. You know, the kind that raises money for worthy causes by having me fly around in private jets all over the world and throw kick-ass parties. I was going to call it the Don't Not Stop Not Helping People Fund."

"Catchy. The scariest part is that this was the idea you rejected."

"Turns out there isn't so much money in not stopping not helping people." Nick leaned in toward Kate. "If you want to be a visionary business magnate you need to follow the money."

"And the place you followed it to is . . ."

Nick smiled. "I'm a social media influencer influencer."

"What?"

"I influence social media influencers. Turns out there's a lot of Instagram models and social media personalities who need some help getting top dollar for their YouTube videos and from their corporate sponsors. That's where I come in."

Kate started to talk, stopped, then started again. "So, you're basically an agent for other con men."

"Exactly. And the best part is that it's completely legal-ish."

"Good grief," Kate said. "Could this day get any worse?"

Nick grinned and pointed at the driver's side window. Kate looked over and jumped when she saw the smiling baby face of Cosmo Uno.

"Jinkies," Kate said, hand on her heart. She rolled down the window. "What the heck, Cosmo?"

"Hello," Cosmo said through the window. He opened the rear door, slid into the backseat, and adjusted the headrest. Cosmo was five foot four inches tall on a good day, and he practically disappeared into the backseat of the Buick.

Kate and Cosmo shared a cubicle wall in the FBI headquarters on Wilshire. Kate spent very little time there. Cosmo spent all of his time there. He ran background checks and did research for other agents. And he lived vicariously through Kate as she chased down bad guys. He had a recurring dream that he morphed into Kate, and Kate had a recurring dream that she was lost in a maze of people-sized hamster tubes, trying to escape from Cosmo Uno.

"No," Kate said. "Don't tell me."

"Yep," Cosmo said. "I'm your new partner. Are you surprised? Special Agent Jessup said you'd be surprised. You're surprised, aren't you? I can tell just by looking at you." Cosmo paused, waiting for a response. He held up his hands and shook them, jazz hands style. "Surprise!"

Kate barely squelched a grimace. "If my head suddenly exploded, I couldn't be more surprised."

Cosmo looked at Nick. "Holy criminy, what's he doing here?"

"He's part of the team."

"For real? Wow. Nick Fox. I'd know him anywhere. He's famous. I heard a rumor he got a deal, but I never thought it would be like this. Like, he's one of us now, right? Right? Oh man. You chased him forever. He was a total obsession for you for years. You had pictures of him all over your cubicle."

Nick grinned. "All over her cubicle? Pictures of me?"

"Wall to wall," Cosmo said. "Some of them had holes, like she stuck pins in them. I thought that was a little sick, but what do I know? I mean who am I to judge, right? Am I right?"

Kate pulled out of the underground garage into traffic. "He's on loan as my snitch," she said to Cosmo. "Let's not make a big deal about it. And Jessup wouldn't be happy if this arrangement got out and became common knowledge."

"Okay. My lips are sealed. I'm zipping my lips. ZIP! Did you see that? Did you see me zip my lips?"

"*Snitch* is such an ugly word," Nick said. "I prefer to think of myself as a consultant."

"Sure, I get that," Cosmo said. "It's your cover. Your cons always involved a cover. Kate always said your covers were genius."

Kate stopped short for a light, throwing everyone against their seatbelts. "I absolutely did *not* say anything about Nick Fox being a genius. And you're grossly exaggerating about the pictures in my cubicle."

"What kind of consultant are you?" Cosmo asked Nick. "I bet it's sexy. Like not politically incorrect sexy but cool sexy. Like slick-new-car sexy, right?"

"Right," Nick said, handing Cosmo a business card.

Cosmo read the card. "Nicolas Nacky. Social Media Influencer Influencer."

"Seriously?" Kate said. "You're going by the name *Nick Nacky*?"

Nick reached around and shook Cosmo's hand. "My extra-close friends call me Nicky."

Kate exited Wilshire Boulevard onto Interstate 405 North and began to climb through the Santa Monica Mountains toward the San Fernando Valley. It was the middle of the day, so the normally horrible traffic was moving along at a decent pace.

Cosmo fidgeted in his seat as they made the slow ascent toward the top of the Sepulveda Pass. "It looks like we're headed to the Valley. Have you noticed how it's always at least ten degrees hotter in the Valley? My core temperature runs hot. It's just how I am. Always hot. That's why I hardly ever go the Valley. You know why? Because it's hot."

"We're not going to the Valley," Kate said. "We're going to Santa Barbara." She tossed him the manila folder. "Richard Wylde has his second or third house there. That's where we'll find his second or third wife."

Ten minutes later, Kate turned left on Ventura Boulevard

and made her way through the strip malls and residential neighborhoods of Sherman Oaks, Calabasas, and Oxnard. Cosmo finished reading the case folder and leaned forward from the backseat, poking his head between Kate and Nick. "I've never met a billionaire. Or a billionaire's wife. What do you think they're like?"

Kate turned to Nick. "She's your prospective client. What are they like?"

"I haven't met them in person, but he's a pretty interesting guy," Nick said. "Pretty much everyone in Silicon Valley calls him the Big Kahuna."

"Why?"

Nick shrugged. "Who's to say? I'm not really an expert on kahunas. He's kind of the under-the-radar Elon Musk of unicorns. Spends most of his time working or surfing."

"'Unicorns'?"

"Privately owned companies worth at least a billion dollars."

Kate looked at Nick. "What makes his business worth that much?"

"He owns a company called Sentience. The artificial intelligence software he's developing is supposed to be state-of-the-art, revolutionary stuff."

Kate turned north along Route 101, and the brilliant blue Pacific Ocean came into view. "What about the wife?"

"She's his third. Twenty years younger. Actress turned Instagram model."

Cosmo perked up. "Really? I've never met an Instagram model either."

"They're just like you and me," Nick said. "They put on their pants one leg at a time, except before that they take a picture of themselves in their underwear and post it on the Internet."

3

The town of Ventura disappeared into Kate's rearview mirror, and they began the roughly thirty-minute drive along the coast to Santa Barbara. The highway was literally wedged between cliffs and ocean in places and seemed far removed from busy, frenetic Los Angeles.

Kate exited Route 101 into the village of Montecito and wound her way up into the foothills of the Santa Ynez Mountains. A mixture of contemporary and Spanish Colonial–style mansions dotted the hillside. The Big Kahuna's forty-acre ranch was near the top of the road, hidden behind an ornate cast iron gate.

Cosmo rolled down his window and surveyed the property. "Zillow says it's worth thirty million. I just checked on my cellphone."

Nick nodded. "This area of Santa Barbara is called the

Golden Quadrangle. It's one of the wealthiest communities in the United States. Oprah. Ellen DeGeneres. Rob Lowe. They all have homes here."

Kate pressed the intercom at the gate and held out her FBI credentials to the camera. "Agent Kate O'Hare to see Victoria Wylde."

Cosmo leaned over Kate and waved his identification as well. "And Senior Agent Cosmo Uno."

Kate released the intercom button, and the speaker crackled in response. "Call me Vicky. The door's open. I'm in the back by the pool with my useless limp dick of a lawyer." The intercom turned off for a few seconds before crackling back to life. "And bring the tray of mimosas with you from the kitchen. I'm running low on mimosas."

"She sounds delightful," Cosmo said.

Kate slowly turned to look at Cosmo. "'Senior Agent'?"

Cosmo fidgeted in his seat. "Technically, I started a week before you. So, technically, that kind of makes me the lead." He paused, waiting for Kate to say something. "Of course, it's only a technicality."

Kate took the wallet from Cosmo's hand and held it open for him to see. "Technically, you just identified yourself as an FBI agent using a Blockbuster premium membership card." She handed the wallet back. "So, you're in charge the next time we need to rent a VHS tape. And, by the way, Blockbuster closed all its stores but one."

"Good thing I've still got my card," Cosmo said. "It's not like there aren't any."

The gate swung open, and Kate drove through, meandering along a cobbled driveway and parking in front of a fifteen-thousand-square foot, two-story, red-roofed house. Kate opened the front door, and they all made their way through a sea of modern furniture and surfing memorabilia to the sliders leading to the pool deck at the rear of the house.

Cosmo stopped in the kitchen and picked up a giant silver platter holding twenty crystal flutes, all filled to the brim with orange juice and champagne. "I guess Vicky really likes mimosas," he said, trying hard not to spill as he walked toward the pool. "Do you think they're all for her?"

"Some of them might be for her horse," Nick said.

Kate looked sideways at Nick. "Pardon?"

"I might have forgotten to mention some small details about Mrs. Big Kahuna," Nick said. "You know how some Instagram models specialize in photographing themselves making duck faces while wearing bikinis or doing yoga in the supermarket?"

"Not really," Kate said.

"Well, anyway, it's a social media fact that you can only make so many duck faces before people start to get bored with them."

"Shocking."

Nick nodded. "I know. That's why you need to be constantly reinventing yourself to find the hole in the selfie marketplace.

It's what makes the difference between an Instagram model and a super Instagram model."

Kate opened the slider door and stepped out onto the pool deck with Nick and Cosmo. "And which is Mrs. Big Kahuna, regular or super?"

The tray of mimosas slid from Cosmo's hands and crashed to the floor. A white horse with a horn attached to its head was standing in the pool with Victoria Wylde. A weaselly looking photographer jumped around taking pictures from every possible angle.

"That's weird. Why is Mrs. Wylde swimming in a silk nightgown?" Cosmo asked.

Kate raised her hands. "There's a unicorn in a swimming pool drinking a mimosa, and you think it's weird she's wearing a nightgown?"

Victoria Wylde stepped out of the pool, walked over to Cosmo, stared down at the spilled drinks, and shook her head. Cosmo, for his part, was trying unsuccessfully to look everywhere except at the thin piece of wet silk clinging to her enormous silicon-enhanced breasts.

The photographer approached and offered Vicky a towel.

"This is Larry. My worthless lawyer slash photographer," Vicky said.

Larry handed Nick and Kate a wrinkled business card. It read "Larry, Esquire. Attorney-at-Law."

"You know most people wouldn't hire a lawyer with no last name," Nick said. "But it works for you."

Vicky dried her bleached-blond hair with the towel and looked Cosmo up and down. "You can take a selfie with me for a hundred dollars. For two hundred, I might throw in a wardrobe malfunction."

Cosmo looked over at Kate for help. "I don't know. The daily stipend for field agents is fifty dollars per day, and I already bought a coffee and an egg salad sandwich this morning. Okay, okay. Let me start from the beginning. I suffer from low blood sugar, so unless I start my day with an egg salad sandwich, I tend to sweat excessively." He paused to check his armpits. "And that's why I'd have to fill out a Department of Justice form J19, Request for Additional Funds, except that I don't have any with me."

Vicky wrinkled her nose. "Gross."

Cosmo looked over at the horse in the pool. "You seem to be doing all right. Why do you need the money?"

"I just do it as an homage to my fans. Before I met the Big Kahuna and settled down, I was a famous actress."

"Really?" Cosmo said. "Would I have seen you in anything?"

"Probably. I had some pretty big hits. Did you see *Bi-Curious George*?"

"I don't think so. What was he so curious about?"

"Mostly boners," Vicky said. "How about *Whack-a-Doodle*? It made a really big splash in the indie market."

Cosmo shook his head. "That doesn't sound like something I'd be interested in."

"Your loss." Vicky turned to Kate. "So, moving on. What

do I have to sign in order to have my husband declared legally dead?"

"I don't know that he is dead."

Larry and Vicky looked at each other.

"He doesn't have to be actually dead," Larry said. "Just legally dead, per se."

"I'm a little confused," Kate said. "Don't you want to find your husband?"

"I'm not in any rush. Right now, I have a bit of a cash-flow problem and a two-hundred-page prenup that gives me diddly-squat unless my husband dies while we're still married, so I kind of need a death certificate more than a living Kahuna."

"I'm not really allowed to declare him legally dead until I'm sure he's actually dead," Kate said.

"Well, there are other interested parties," Vicky said.

Larry nodded vigorously in agreement. "Yes. Surely you must realize there would be other interested parties, per se."

"Tell me about the other interested parties," Kate said.

"My husband is the owner of a business worth a billion dollars. His son, Hamilton, will inherit the whole thing minus what's left to me. That is, unless the vultures who've invested in the company don't steal it first."

"Is that a possibility?" Kate asked. "Could the investors stage a takeover?"

"Do bears poop in the woods?" Larry asked.

"Do you think one or more could be responsible for your husband's disappearance?" Kate asked Vicky.

Vicky shrugged. "The Big Kahuna was acting a little crazy just before he disappeared. Kind of jumpy. Always looking over his shoulder. Plus, he's a good pilot. It wasn't like him to leave without filing a flight plan."

"How about the son?" Kate asked.

"Hamilton? I've only met him once," Vicky said. "He's been living the dream in Hawaii ever since dropping out of college. That is, if your dream is starting every day surfing the perfect wave and ending it with a big bowl of weed. Comes off as pretty harmless. Didn't even question when his father married me. Said if his father was happy, he was too. Still, people will do a lot of crazy stuff for money."

"Tell me about the vultures," Kate said.

"Take your pick. Investment bankers. Thousand-dollar-an-hour lawyers. Some firecrotch hottie Czech venture capitalist who invested a ton of money in Sentience last year. Olga something or other. She's the worst of the bunch."

Larry tapped his watch. "We're a little behind schedule. I need to upload the photos from the morning session to Instagram," he said over his shoulder as he scurried into the house.

Vicky rolled her eyes and followed Larry. "Look, I really need to wrap this up. Just call me when you have a dead Kahuna so I can collect my inheritance and afford a lawyer who doesn't end every other sentence with *per se*."

Nick, Kate, and Cosmo watched the sliders close and walked around the house back to the car.

"Why didn't you tell her you were Nick Nacky, the world-famous social media influencer influencer?" Kate asked Nick. "I thought she was a prospective client?"

"In the first place, she's a nut at best. At worst, she murdered her husband. I do have some standards."

"And in the second place?"

Nick flashed the crooked grin at Kate. "When's the next time I'll have a chance to look for a missing kahuna? It just got interesting."

It was midafternoon by the time Nick and Kate dropped Cosmo off at the FBI field office on Wilshire Boulevard. It was decided that he would tend to the day's paperwork and do Internet research while Nick and Kate checked on the Kahuna's plane.

By the time they made their way to John Wayne Airport in Orange County, thirty-five miles south of Los Angeles, Cosmo had left Kate three voicemails and sent four texts. She listened to the first voicemail in the airport parking lot.

"Hello, it's Cosmo. I filled out my form J1707, Daily Field Report, and form J453, Expense Report, but they require you to countersign attesting to their accuracy. No rush, but when are you planning to get me *your* J1707 so *I* can countersign? Also, we really need to get them submitted as soon as possible. Okay, so I'm running background checks on Vicky and Hamilton right now. On *48 Hours*, it's always the spouse, right? Just kidding. I'm a trained FBI agent and don't base my investigations on a TV show, no matter how good. But, let's face it. It's always the spouse. And, also, *48 Hours* is really good." He paused. "This is Cosmo. Call me back."

The rest of the messages were all Cosmo asking if she received the first message.

"Do you think someone murdered the Big Kahuna?" Nick asked Kate as they walked into the private-flights terminal.

Kate shrugged. "Murdered, kidnapped, accidentally crashed his plane, having an affair, vacationing off the grid in his favorite surf spot. Who knows? He was last seen taking off from this fixed-base operator in his private plane. Hopefully, we can narrow down the list of possibilities after talking with the FBO manager."

The private terminal consisted of a small, tasteful lobby and some interior offices. A couple of pilots milled around the coffee machine, waiting for their passengers. An unaccompanied trolley filled with Disneyland bags waited by the doors leading to the tarmac.

Kate showed the woman behind the reception desk her identification. "I'm looking for the operations manager. We have a few questions about a departure from this terminal three days ago."

"I'm Angela Rook, the operations manager. Is this about the Big Kahuna? You're the second person today to ask about that flight."

Kate glanced over at Nick. "Who else was asking?"

The woman behind the desk opened a drawer and fished

out a business card. "A couple of guys who looked like corporate types and a pretty redhead who looked like she was in charge." She handed the card to Kate. "Olga Zellenkova."

Kate took the card. "What did they want?"

"Well, it was a little odd. They were looking for the Big Kahuna. They told me he'd disappeared with a Cessna Citation, and the plane was titled in the business name. They wanted my help to declare the aircraft legally lost at sea."

"What did you tell them?" Nick asked.

Angela shrugged. "Nothing other than what you could learn from FlightAware and other publicly available information. At two forty-five P.M., a Citation X aircraft with tail number N733BK took off from this FBO. There's absolutely no evidence that the plane crashed, so there wasn't really anything I could do to help them."

"So N733BK is registered to Sentience?" Kate asked.

"Yes. But everyone at the airport knows the Big Kahuna is the owner. He's kind of a charmer. Besides, a plane painted with a robot riding a surfboard stands out, even in L.A."

Kate nodded. "And he was the pilot?"

"Yes. He always pilots his own plane. Usually he has a copilot, but this time he flew solo. No passengers or copilot."

"Are there any records of his flight path?" Kate asked.

Angela scrolled through the computer screen. "Air traffic control lost track of him over the Pacific Ocean, ten minutes into the flight. That shouldn't happen unless the GPS transponder was destroyed or disabled."

"I'm assuming there were no distress calls?"

"None. It's like he just disappeared."

Kate shook Angela's hand. "Thanks for your time. We'll be back in touch if there are any more questions."

Nick walked with Kate out of the terminal. "I might have disabled one or two transponders in my past, back when I was in the semi-legal business of smuggling antiquities. They're pretty fail-proof unless it's intentional, and there's only one reason to tamper with them . . . to cover your tracks."

Kate rolled her eyes. "There's no such thing as semi-legal. And I seriously doubt the Kahuna is leading a secret life as a smuggler. Not everyone steals for a living."

"What's wrong with smuggling? Han Solo was a smuggler. Han Solo saved the Republic from Emperor Palpatine. Everybody loves Han Solo."

"Not me. Not Princess Leia."

Nick moved closer to Kate. "Are you sure? Princess Leia changed her mind about Han Solo after one kiss."

Kate bit her lower lip. Her number one rule of undercover work was don't get romantically involved with charming con men who looked like Han Solo. "Not going to happen. But that must have been some kiss."

Nick nodded. "Game changing."

4

Nick and Kate huddled over the round glass dining table in her father, Jake's, small casita. The casita was actually a converted detached garage at Kate's sister's house in Calabasas. Jake had moved there to spend more time with his grandchildren, play more golf, and generally live the good life of a retired career military officer. Turned out you could take the man out of Army Special Forces, but you couldn't take the Special Forces out of the man, and Jake had a hard time staying retired.

Jake pulled up a chair, and they all studied a map of the world, spread out on the table. Jake had drawn a circle in black pen with Los Angeles at the center and a diameter of seven thousand miles.

"The range of a Citation X is thirty-five hundred miles," Jake said. "So this is the potential search area."

The circle covered most of North America and half of the Pacific Ocean.

"That narrows it down to pretty much everywhere," Kate said. "Including the bottom of the ocean. We can't ignore the possibility of a plane crash."

Nick shook his head. "Vicky told us that the Kahuna was acting strangely before he disappeared. We think he disabled his transponder shortly after takeoff. I'd bet good money he's not dead. He's off the grid, hiding from someone or something."

"This sounds awesome," Jake said. "I'm in."

"No," Kate said. "You're definitely out. Megan will kill me if I get you involved in this."

Jake rubbed the close-cropped hair on the back of his head. "Yeah, that doesn't really work for me. So I'm in."

"I like it," Nick said. "Your code name can be Gunny. We could use a crusty drill sergeant type with a heart of gold to round out the team."

"*Gunny* is a nickname for a gunnery sergeant. I was a lieutenant colonel when I retired."

"A lieutenant colonel. Even better," Nick said. "Just like George Peppard's character in *The A-Team*. If I bought you a white safari jacket and some black leather gloves, do you think you could chew on a cigar and periodically say 'I love it when a plan comes together'?"

"Not happening. Except for the cigar part."

"Good enough," Nick said.

Kate blew out a sigh. "Fine. You're in, Dad. Please try not to shoot anybody or blow anything up."

"Sure," Jake said. "Not a problem. What's first on the agenda?"

"We pay a visit to the Big Kahuna's business partner, Olga Zellenkova," Nick said. "I googled her. She owns a venture capital company that invests in Silicon Valley start-ups. Also owns the entire second story of an office building in Sherman Oaks, not too far from here. She's Czech and splits her time between L.A. and Prague. Her LinkedIn profile credits her as being on the board of directors for Sentience as well as a couple of San Francisco Bay area biotechs."

Fifteen minutes later, Kate pulled into the parking lot of a nondescript three-story redbrick office building and walked through the front doors with Nick and Jake. They rode the elevator to the second floor and stepped into the deserted lobby. "Zellenkova Private Equity" was written in large block letters on the wall behind an empty reception desk.

Kate peeked around the corner. All the offices and cubicles were dark and unoccupied. "Hello. Anybody here?" The only answer was a faint mechanical whirring coming from the back of the space.

Jake looked around the office as they walked toward the whirring noise. "Am I the only one with the heebie-jeebies? This place feels like a ghost town."

Kate, Nick, and Jake peered into a small conference room. Two men in suits were shredding stacks of papers through an oversized document shredder, while a curvy late-thirty-something woman with wavy red hair reaching halfway down her back, wearing a tailored pencil skirt and white blouse, stood and watched.

Kate knocked on the door. "Olga Zellenkova? I'm Special Agent Kate O'Hare. I was hoping to ask you some questions about the disappearance of Richard Wylde."

The redhead looked up. If she was surprised to see Nick, Jake, and Kate it didn't register on her face. She walked slowly out of the conference room, closed the door behind her, and shook Kate's hand.

"You'll have to excuse us. We're doing a little spring cleaning."

Kate looked through the glass door at the stacks of documents covering the conference table and the garbage bags of shredded paper that filled the room. "Looks like more than just a little."

Olga smiled at Kate. "I invest in private equity. Knowing how to keep a secret is a prerequisite."

"I'll take your word for it," Kate said. "I'm an FBI agent. I don't have a lot of use for secrets."

Olga looked Nick directly in the eyes and smoothed her hair. "How about you? You don't look like an FBI agent. You look like trouble."

"I'm more of an independent contractor," Nick said. "Let's just say that I have a healthy appreciation for a good secret."

Olga winked at Nick. "I'll bet." She turned to Jake and looked him up and down. "Who's Mr. Buzzcut with the hard body and Special Forces tattoo? Don't tell me. He must be an independent contractor too."

Jake crossed his arms but didn't say anything.

Olga turned back to Kate. "I'm guessing he's the strong, silent type who lets his actions speak for him." She removed a lipstick from her pocket and applied it to her lips. The smile was gone. "I have a couple independent contractors like that on my payroll too." She paused. "Anyway, how can I help?"

"We were at John Wayne Airport this morning and were told you were conducting your own investigation into Mr. Wylde's disappearance."

"Not exactly. He crashed the company plane into the Pacific Ocean. I own ten percent of Sentience, so I own ten percent of that plane and ten percent of the Big Kahuna's big ideas. It's tragic what happened to him, but I need to protect my investments."

"Let me guess. You want me to declare him legally dead."

"That would be helpful."

"It's still an open investigation," Kate said. "I don't think he's dead. I think he's scared of someone or something. I think he's in hiding."

"I have a very expensive Washington lawyer who has a letter signed by the deputy attorney general that says otherwise. Trust me. By tomorrow morning, your boss will have talked with his boss, and the investigation will be closed. The Kahuna is already dead, at least on paper. You just don't know it yet."

"I don't care who sends a letter to my boss. It's not closed until I say so."

Olga shook her head. "You don't know when to quit. Be smart." She walked Nick, Kate, and Jake back to the elevator. "Just sign the paperwork and move on," she said as the elevator door closed behind them.

"What do you make of that?" Kate asked once they were in the parking lot.

Jake hopped into the backseat of the car. "Pretty sketchy. She's a relatively young investment banker with access to hundreds of millions of dollars, shredding documents in a sham office."

"She's no investment banker," Nick said. "I know another con man when I see one, and my gut tells me that she's good at her job. She made us immediately. I don't think she knows where the Kahuna is, but she's definitely involved in his disappearance."

Kate started the car. "Well, she got one thing right. I don't know when to quit."

Kate woke up early the next morning in her Spartan one-bedroom apartment, tied her shoulder-length brown hair into a ponytail, and went for a run. By the time she got back, Nick was waiting in the kitchen, fiddling with her cellphone and eating her last yogurt.

She snatched the half-eaten yogurt and cellphone out of his hands. "Jinkies. How the heck did you get in here again without tripping the security alarm? And didn't we have a major discussion about boundaries just last month?"

Nick put the spoon in his mouth and ate whatever yogurt was left before Kate snatched that away as well. "What about your bathroom? Is that off-limits too?"

"It includes my entire apartment and everything in it. Especially the bathroom. What did you do?"

Nick pointed to himself. "Me? Nothing."

The bathroom door crashed open and Cosmo walked gingerly into the room, massaging his stomach. "Don't go in there. It's totally polluted. Did I mention I have an irritable bowel? What's for breakfast? I can't eat anything with gluten or I get diarrhea."

Nick reached into a box of Cap'n Crunch cereal and pulled out a handful. "By the by, Kate, you got a text from Jessup. He wants to see you in his office first thing this morning. That's why I invited Cosmo to breakfast. He has some pretty interesting news about Zellenkova Private Equity."

Kate smacked Nick's hand, sending Cap'n Crunch scattering across the room. "You can eat my yogurt and you can use my bathroom, but stay away from my Captain Crunch." She turned to Cosmo. "What have you got?"

"So, I stayed up all night researching Zellenkova Private Equity. It invests exclusively in Silicon Valley businesses. Mostly tech, but also biotech."

"I'm guessing there's more."

"Okay. Here's the good part. According to the Securities and Exchange Commission, Zellenkova owns ten percent or more of three different unicorns. Sentience, the Big Kahuna's company. Kranos, a biotech developing cancer drugs. And Waterloo, an Internet security start-up."

Cosmo smiled at Kate, then at Nick, then back at Kate. "Hello. Don't you read the financial news?"

"Not unless I have to," Kate said.

Cosmo shook his hands back and forth. "Okay, okay. Kranos was founded by a woman named Irenka Radcliffe. She died in a car crash three weeks ago. Waterloo was owned by Peter Travis. He committed suicide two months ago by overdosing on his insulin medicine."

Kate looked at Nick. "Two dead and one missing-presumed-dead billionaires in the past two months can't be a coincidence."

"There are around five hundred billionaires in the United States," Nick said, "but the ones connected to Olga Zellenkova seem particularly accident prone."

Cosmo gathered up some stray pieces of Cap'n Crunch from the table and popped them into his mouth. "I checked with Homeland Security. Olga has an iron-clad alibi. She was out of the county in Prague when Irenka and Peter died. There's absolutely no evidence of foul play."

"It also doesn't make financial sense," Kate said. "Without the Big Kahuna leading Sentience, the business would be worth a fraction of what it is today. Zellenkova Private Equity stands to lose money if the Kahuna is dead. Why kill the goose who lays the golden egg?"

"We won't get any answers from Irenka Radcliffe or Peter Travis," Nick said. "We'll have to find the Big Kahuna, preferably before Olga or Vicky. They've both made it clear they'd prefer a dead Kahuna to a living one."

"This is more complicated than Jessup envisioned," Kate said. "He thought he was going to bury us for a while on a missing-persons case that was probably bogus. As it turns out, we seem to have stumbled into a crime that's appropriate to our commission."

"We should tell him," Cosmo said.

"I'll take care of it," Kate said. "Do you have anything else? Were you able to contact the Kahuna's son?"

"I tried to call him a couple of times. He finally answered the phone, sounding totally baked. When I told him that his father had disappeared, he said, 'Don't worry about it, dude. Let the universe handle it. He'll turn up eventually.' Then he told me he had to go because he was playing Xbox and hung up."

"I guess I should count my blessings that he isn't pushing me to declare the Kahuna dead too," Kate said. "It doesn't sound like he's interested in taking over his father's business anytime soon."

Cosmo gathered a few more pieces of cereal into his hand. "There's no gluten in Crunch," he said. "Okay, maybe a trace from cross contamination, but I don't count that. I could probably eat this whole box and not have an issue. Maybe some bloat, but everyone has bloat. I mean, who doesn't have bloat?"

"I need a fast shower and change of clothes," Kate said. "Go outside and wait in the hall. I don't trust either of you in my apartment."

"Can I take the Crunch?" Cosmo asked.

"Yes! Anything. Take the Crunch. Just get out of my apartment."

"One last thing," Cosmo said. "You might want to give the bathroom a moment."

5

Jessup sat on one side of his desk. In front of him was a letter signed by the deputy attorney general strongly suggesting he declare Richard Wylde lost at sea. On the other side of the desk were Nick, Kate, and Cosmo with Jake's search map.

"Let me get this straight," Jessup said. "You want me to ignore a directive from the deputy attorney general so you can search an area over thirty-eight million square miles for a person who is, likely, either at the bottom of the Pacific Ocean or else downing tequila shooters in Los Cabos. And the reason I should let you do it is so you can chase some hunch that somebody is killing Silicon Valley billionaires for an unknown reason."

"I told you he'd get it," Nick said.

Jessup shook his head. "Just for the sake of argument, let's assume there's a kernel of a mystery buried somewhere in this. You don't have a clue where to look. His wife and business partner aren't going to help, and his son thinks the Kahuna will magically turn up."

Kate glanced at the map, the seven-thousand-mile-diameter circle, and the location where the Kahuna's plane went off the grid, one hundred miles off the coast of Los Angeles.

"We just assumed Hamilton was so wasted, he didn't care that his father was missing," Kate said. "What if he told us the Kahuna will eventually turn up, because he already knows where he is?" She drew a line connecting L.A. to the last known location of the plane and continued the line west to the border of the circle. It passed through 2,500 miles of Pacific Ocean before coming within fifty miles of the Hawaiian Islands.

"The Big Kahuna's son lives in a small town on the north shore of Maui," Cosmo said. "It's called Paia, and it's within the flying range of the Citation X. There are dozens of private air fields in that area left over from the sugar plantation era. A plane could easily land unnoticed there."

Kate nodded. "It makes sense. From what Vicky told us, it sounds like Hamilton and his father care about each other. If the Big Kahuna was scared, maybe he went to hide with the one person he thought he could trust."

Jessup sighed and slid the letter from the deputy attorney general into his desk drawer. "You have three days to find the Kahuna. That's as long as I can pretend to misplace this letter. After that, I'm pulling the plug."

Kate stood, gathered up the map, and hurried Nick and Cosmo out of the room before Jessup could change his mind. "Three days. No problem."

"I can't believe I'm sending you three on an all-expenses-paid trip to Hawaii on some wild goose chase while I'm stuck here in this office, dodging phone calls from Washington," Jessup said as Kate exited.

"Yep. It's a real humdinger," Kate said, and closed the door behind her.

"Let's try to get on the next available flight to Maui," Kate said to Nick once they were out of earshot of Jessup. "Three days isn't a lot of time, and I want to hit the ground running." She turned to Cosmo. "Check the Maui airports to see if any of them have a record of the X landing."

Cosmo's upper lip had begun to bead with sweat. "Okay, okay. Let's not panic. I'll get all the forms and reports and paperwork we're going to need and pack them into my big suitcase. I should probably also check in with human resources." He smacked his head. "I almost forgot. We're going to need vouchers from accounting. Lots of vouchers."

"I heard accounting is running low on vouchers," Nick said. "You'd better get them now before they run out. You can meet us at LAX at three P.M."

"Gotcha. Three P.M. I'll call you once I have the vouchers so you don't worry."

Nick watched Cosmo disappear into a maze of cubicles.

"So, once we get to Hawaii, have you given any thought to what comes next?"

"We stake out Hamilton and follow him around Maui until he leads us to the Big Kahuna."

Nick laughed. "That's your plan?"

"What? It's a classic." Kate crossed her arms. "It's how I caught you."

"Have you ever been to Paia?" Nick asked.

"No. Why?"

"It's a small town of three thousand people, made up of big-wave surfer types, bohemian types, artist types, and other assorted back-to-the-earth types. There are people there from all over the world, of every possible different culture, religion, and background. But you know what type there isn't in Paia?"

Kate pointed at herself.

"Bingo," Nick said. "There are zero take-no-prisoners, make-no-apologies FBI types in Paia. And even if you do somehow manage to blend in, there's no way you're going to stake out Hamilton."

Kate narrowed her eyes. "I've been on hundreds of stakeouts. I can stake the heck out of just about anything."

"How about a herd of Black Angus cattle? Because that's where Hamilton lives—in a one-bedroom cottage in the middle of a two-hundred-acre pasture overlooking the Pacific Ocean. Trust me. What you need is a plan with subtlety."

"You mean I need a first-class grifter type who can cozy up to Hamilton and con him into revealing where we can find his father?"

Nick smiled. "Bingo."

"Well, then, it's lucky I know where to find one of those."

"No problem. I'll have the entire thing organized by the time our plane is in the air."

Kate stared at Nick. "You're being unusually cooperative. What's up?"

"Did I mention I have this teensy problem with one of my most important clients that we need to solve before I can leave town? It shouldn't take more than an hour or two. And, before you ask, I already know what you're thinking. Yes, it's absolutely one hundred percent legal-ish."

Kate shook her head. "No. Not happening."

"That's too bad. It's going to be awfully hard to be on my A game in Hawaii when I have my mind on clients."

"I'd think staying out of jail would be enough motivation."

"Good point. Jail sucks." Nick draped an arm across Kate's shoulders and hugged her into him. "How about professional courtesy? Curiosity? Doing a friend a solid? Paying it forward? A bag of burgers?"

Kate sighed. "No, no, no, no, and those burgers had better come with bacon and cheese fries."

"That was easier than I thought," Nick said. "I thought you'd hold out for dessert too."

Kate smiled. "What can I say? It's my nature. I see bacon, cheese, and all-beef patties tucked between toasted sesame seed buns and I must have them."

Kate and Nick were parked across the street from a modest circa 1970 split-level ranch house with a small but well-cared-for yard. A wood-paneled station wagon was in front of the single-car garage.

Kate finished her burger, crumpled the empty burger bag, and threw it into the backseat. "This is where your most important client lives? Don't tell me. Let me guess. It's either the Partridge family or Marcia Brady."

Nick retrieved a Loro Piana white button-down shirt, a black Armani sports jacket, and designer sunglasses out of his backpack. He stripped off his T-shirt and changed in the car. "How do I look?"

Kate thought he actually looked pretty good. Not as good as he did without the shirt, but pretty good. "Like Jerry Maguire."

"Excellent. Nicolas Nacky dresses for success." He grabbed a manila envelope stamped "Top Secret" out of the backpack and handed it to Kate. "So, when Mrs. Kowowski answers the door all you need to do is flash your FBI badge, hand this to her son, and tell him, 'Be careful. The Badger is on the move.'"

Kate opened the envelope and removed the contents—three

cards with pictures. Miss Scarlet, the conservatory, and the lead pipe. "Who is Mrs. Kowowski? Why do you have an envelope marked 'Top Secret' containing board game parts? And also, what the fudge?"

"Mrs. Kowowski is my client's grandmother. Because Clue is an awesome game. And I kind of told her that her grandson, Greg, is a secret agent working for the government."

"Okay. Why?"

"She was threatening to kick him out of the house unless he got a real job."

"And secret agent is what you settled on?"

"At the time, it seemed like a good idea," Nick said.

"Wouldn't it be easier to just get a job?"

Nick walked with Kate to the front door. "Greg's a good guy, but he's had kind of a tough life. Parents died when he was just a kid. He isn't what you'd call 'employable' in the traditional sense. Do you consider playing video games twelve hours per day a job?"

Kate rolled her eyes. "No."

"Strange," Nick said and rang the doorbell. "Neither does Mrs. Kowowski."

An older woman answered the door. Her hair was cut utilitarian short. Her skin was pre-cancerous. She was wearing a faded cotton caftan and fluffy pink slippers.

Nick removed his sunglasses. "Good morning, Mrs. K. This is Special Agent Kate O'Hare. She has urgent business with Gregory. The fate of the world could be at stake."

Mrs. Kowowski took off her reading glasses and squinted at Kate. "Are you really a government man?"

Kate showed her FBI identification to the woman. "Yes, ma'am."

"And you have urgent business with my Gregory?"

Nick stepped forward. "She's not really at liberty to say, Mrs. K."

Mrs. Kowowski nodded toward the basement door. "He's down there, like always."

Kate peered down the stairs. An eerie electric glow emanated from the otherwise dark basement. "I'm not going to get sucked into an alternate universe by some poltergeist if I go down there, am I?"

"Alternate universe, yes. Poltergeist, no," Nick said.

Kate and Nick walked down the stairs and into a basement apartment. The walls were wood paneled. The carpet was orange shag. A scraggly looking twenty-something with a five-day-old beard, the worst case of bed head Kate had ever seen, and mustard-stained dinosaur pajamas was playing a video game in front of an eighty-five-inch high-definition television screen.

"What's he playing?" Kate asked.

"Fortnite Battle Royale. It's a live-action game where you compete with up to a hundred other players to be the last one standing. It has over 125 million people actively playing and earns hundreds of millions of dollars each month for its developer, Epic Games."

Kate looked at the television. The scraggly twenty-something's avatar was busy using a pickax to mine some kind of metal. "This is your important client?"

"He has ten million YouTube subscribers and has made more than a million dollars so far this year."

"Just to watch him sit around and play video games?"

"Not exactly. That's only fifty percent of it. You also need to be able to goof around and crack jokes," Nick said. "YouTube pays around ten dollars per every thousand views, so you need to broaden your appeal to as many people who like to watch free crap as possible. The most popular online gamers have fifty million or so subscribers and can earn more than ten million dollars per year."

"Sounds ridiculous."

"Did I mention people like free? Anyway, that's when it came to me in a flash of social media influencer influencer genius."

"I can't wait to hear all about it."

"L.A. is filled with good-looking out-of-work actors who are great at goofing off," Nick said. "And it's also overflowing with dysfunctional millennials living in their parents' basements playing Fortnite. By themselves, neither could scrape together enough to buy a cup of ramen noodles, but put them together and you have social media gold."

Kate looked at Greg. Except for the rapid-eye movement and fingers working the PlayStation controller, he was almost catatonic. "He doesn't exactly seem like the life of the party."

"That's why I hired an actress and outsourced the goofing around." Nick opened a bedroom door. A cameraman was filming a pretty girl-next-door type, wearing stretchy lululemon yoga pants and a sports bra one size too small for her breasts, pretending to play Fortnite, while a clone of Greg Kowowski's gameplay was live-streamed onto her television.

She stopped playing, walked over, and waved a stack of papers at Nick. "I've been trying to reach you all day. This script is awful. The writing is horrible, and the jokes are worse." She handed one of the pages to Nick and pointed at a sentence she'd circled in red pen.

Nick studied the page. "What's the problem?"

"Are you kidding me? It doesn't make any sense. I mean, come on. *Blort* isn't even a real word. It just rhymes with *Fort*."

Nick googled *blort*. "It's a blend of *blow* and *snort*, or a snort of liquid out through the nose in response to something unexpected." He pointed to the script. "You must have missed the part where you're supposed to take a drink of milk then blow it out your nose when your avatar gets bushwhacked by zombies. Then you say . . ."

The actress reread the script and smacked her forehead. "Fortnite. More like Blortnite." She took back the pages from Nick. "That's actually pretty good. It might even be Twitter hashtag worthy," she said and turned to the cameraman. "I don't want to half-ass this thing. Can somebody get me a gallon or two of milk, so I can practice my blorting before we go live?"

49

Nick closed the bedroom door. "Sorry about that," he said to Kate. "You have to put out a lot of fires when you're in the high-octane world of professional online gaming."

Mrs. Kowowski walked down the basement stairs, carrying a platter of peanut butter sandwiches and oatmeal cookies. She put the tray on the couch next to her grandson, looked around the room, and used a broom handle to fish out a pair of tighty-whities from a stack of clothes lying in the corner. "Gregory!" she shouted. "How many times have I told you? Put your dirty clothes in the hamper."

Greg twitched, jumped out of his seat, and put his hand to his chest. "Judas H. Priest. You scared the heck out of me, Grandma." He paused to take a bite out of one of the sandwiches. "She's always sneaking up on me," he said to Nick and Kate.

Mrs. Kowowski hit him on the back of the head. "It's almost noon, and you're still in your pajamas."

Nick nudged Kate. "Thanks for the sandwiches, Mrs. K., but we should probably be going. Agent O'Hare has to catch a flight in a couple hours."

Kate handed the "Top Secret" manila envelope to Greg. "Watch your back. The Badger is on the move."

"Thank you for your service, FBI lady," Greg said. "Your country owes you a debt of gratitude." He nodded solemnly and saluted Kate. "I'll take it from here."

Mrs. Kowowski shook her head, followed Nick and Kate

back up the stairs, handed Kate an oatmeal cookie, and let them out of the house.

"Do you think she bought it?" Kate asked once they were back in the car.

Nick shrugged. "It's a long shot, but Greg's the classic underdog. She wants to believe."

Kate looked at Nick. "I've noticed you like the long shots. And the underdogs."

"Are there any other kind of shots worth taking?"

"Anyway, that had to be the weirdest part of the past forty-eight hours," Kate said. "And that's saying a lot considering that I just blew up a Ferrari in the lobby of a five-star hotel."

Nick smiled. "At least you got a cookie out of it. And the day isn't over yet."

6

At 3:15 P.M., Kate and Nick were sitting in the first-class cabin of their five-hour Hawaiian Airlines flight direct to Kahului, Maui. Kate had booked four economy tickets a couple of hours earlier, but an overly friendly flight attendant moved her and Nick to the comfortable leather seats in the front of the plane, leaving Jake and Cosmo to fend for themselves in economy.

Nick finished his heated nuts, wiped his face off with a warm wet towel, and settled back into his seat. "There's just something about heated nuts. Why do people even bother with room-temperature nuts?"

Kate thought about Jake and Cosmo back in economy. She suspected they didn't have any nuts, let alone warm ones. "Look," she said to Nick. "I enjoy warm nuts as much as the next person."

Nick raised an eyebrow. "Really?"

Kate punched him in the shoulder. "What I was about to say was why are we sitting in first class, being waited on hand and foot? Even the pilot came out and greeted us personally. What did you do?"

"I suppose you wouldn't buy that I used my frequent flier miles."

"No."

"I might have told the airline I was planning to propose."

Kate stared at him. "Excuse me?"

"Being engaged is central to my plan to find the Kahuna."

"Are you sure it wasn't just central to your plan to get a free upgrade?"

"Just a happy coincidence. We have only a short amount of time to cozy up to Hamilton and convince him to tell two complete strangers where to find his father. You can bet we're not the only ones looking, so we need an edge—something to tilt the scales in our favor."

"I'm not sure how posing as a newly engaged couple is going to help."

"Trust me," Nick said. "People like to feel like they're in the presence of true love." He made a head motion toward the two flight attendants talking and watching them. "That's why we got the upgrade. That's how we're going to make a connection with Hamilton."

"I love my job. I love my family. I believe in commitment and taking responsibility for the people you care about. I'm not sure I believe in true love, at least not in a Disney princess kind of way."

"I don't know about Disney, but the ancient Greeks thought there were four kinds of love. *Storge,* or familial love. *Philia,* or friendship. *Eros,* or romantic love, and *agape,* or unconditional love. Sounds to me like you're already batting .750 in the love department. All you're missing is a little passion. And who knows? That too just might someday sneak up on you, like a thief in the night."

"You don't have any particular thief in mind, do you?" Kate asked. "Because the last time somebody snuck up on me, I put him in a choke hold."

Nick grinned. "Good to know." He spread out a map of Maui on the tray table. "There are two areas on Maui where the best resorts are located, Lahaina on the western side and Wailea on the southern side."

"Do you think the Big Kahuna is staying in one of them?"

"Possibly. I reserved a room for Cosmo at the Four Seasons in Wailea. He can pose as a tourist and snoop around. Maybe we'll get lucky and find the Kahuna lounging by the pool or eating dinner at the hotel restaurant."

"What about Dad?" Kate asked.

"I have him at the other five-star resort on the island, the Ritz-Carlton, near Lahaina. There are several popular surf spots on that part of the island. According to Cosmo's research, the Big Kahuna likes to surf. He might not be able to resist trying one of them out."

"That leaves you and me."

"Right. We're masquerading as a newly engaged couple, looking to move to Paia. I arranged a nice place for us to stay on the property that abuts Hamilton's farm." He handed a couple sheets of paper to Kate. "I also took the liberty of preparing our backstories."

Kate read through the first page. "You've got to be kidding."

"What?"

Kate pointed at the paper. "My name is Rain. No last name. Just Rain. My occupation is candlemaker. We met on a communal farm, and it was love at first sight when you saw me riding my tractor topless through a hemp field."

"Those were some good times," Nick said.

Kate continued reading. "What the heck? You're a big-wave surfer named Nicolas Lodeon. Why do you get a last name and a job that doesn't involve hot wax?"

"Hamilton's cottage overlooks Peahi. It's a really famous surf spot. The locals call it Jaws because the waves are huge and deadly. Hamilton surfs it almost every day, so it's a good opportunity to meet him on his own turf where he'll feel more comfortable. Do you know how to surf?"

"No."

"That's why you're Rain, the candlemaker."

"Good grief. I'm going to sleep. Wake me when they serve the hot fudge sundaes or big, chewy cookies or whatever dessert they serve in first-class."

Kate woke up four hours later, just as the airplane was

beginning its descent into Maui. A plate of long-cold chicken and rice sat on the tray table in front of her. Two empty sundae glasses were in front of Nick.

"Did you eat my ice cream?"

"Who, me?"

"*Someone* ate it."

"You were asleep and it was melting. Would it help to smooth things over if I offered you my heated nuts?"

"Absolutely not. Keep your heated nuts to yourself."

Nick reached into his pocket and pulled out a small blue jewelry box. "Then how about this?"

"Oh crap," Kate said. "This better not be what I think it is."

Nick slid it over to Kate. "Only one way to find out."

Kate cracked the box and peeked inside. "It's a diamond ring," she said.

"I've been saving it for just the right moment, like our pretend engagement."

"It's huge."

"Miss Manners recommended I spend three months' salary."

"You don't have a job or a salary," Kate said.

"Yeah. It was a real bargain, practically a steal."

Kate fully opened the box and examined the ring. "It looks familiar." She turned to Nick. "What the heck? This is the Crimson Teardrop diamond."

"Our first date," Nick said. "You hit me with a bus when I was trying to borrow it from the Roland Larsen Kibbee museum. Then you arrested me, threatened me with prison, and forced me into a life of indentured servitude working for the FBI. The rest is history. Romantic, right?"

"You consider that our first date?"

"At the very least, it's a pretty good 'how we met' story."

Kate snapped the box shut. "I should be mad, but truth is, it beats out topless tractor riding."

By 5:30 P.M. the plane had landed, Jake was in a Jeep Wrangler driving west to Lahaina, and Cosmo was in a Toyota Prius driving south to Wailea. Nick and Kate were standing in the airport's long-term parking lot, staring at a partially refurbished 1978 Mr. Freezy ice cream truck with off-road tires and a surfboard rack mounted to its top.

"Tell me again why you didn't just rent a car from Avis?" Kate asked. "Where did you find this thing?"

"Craigslist. The previous owner said it was slightly haunted so he gave me a really good price." Nick ran his hand over the decals covering the sliding window on the side of the truck advertising Fudgsicles, Tasty Pops, shave ice, and assorted other ice cream novelties. "This van is the real deal. It's the gold standard of bohemian transportation."

"You bought a haunted ice cream truck from some guy on Craigslist?"

"*Slightly* haunted. Of course, he also tried to sell me some peyote, so there's a remote possibility it might be just an ordinary ice cream truck."

Kate opened the driver's door and slid onto the

wood-beaded driver's seat while Nick threw their luggage in the back with the ice cream freezers. She turned the ignition. The truck backfired, belched black smoke, and they were on their way, traveling east on the two-lane Hana Highway toward Paia. The civilized two-lane road slowly grew progressively less civilized, leading them through green, if a little scrubby, pastures and into bohemian chic Spreckelsville, where a mixture of old-moneyed Hawaiian families and new-moneyed L.A. celebrities called home. The ten-thousand-foot-tall ancient shield volcano Haleakala loomed in the distance.

"Paia is the next town," Nick said. "Hamilton lives just about ten miles past it in Haiku-Pauwela."

Kate slowed down as she passed a sign saying "Welcome to Paia. Do Not Feed the Hippies." Unlike Spreckelsville, the town was more bohemian than chic, with an eclectic mixture of coffee shops, natural food stores, yoga studios, surf shops, tattoo parlors, new age boutiques, and even a colorful Buddhist shrine. Glimpses of white sand and the blue waters of Paia Bay peeked through alleyways separating storefronts. Locals and tourists mingled together, chilling out in low-key restaurants and meandering through the streets.

"It has a good vibe," Kate said. "It's like stepping back in time forty years ago before the world sped up."

Nick nodded. "It's a little sleepy at this time of the year. In the winter, the swells are larger and can reach as high as eighty feet. That's when the top echelon of professional surfers and thrill seekers come to town."

Kate drove about a mile to the other side of town, where the highway dipped down to Hookipa Beach. Expert windsurfers and kitesurfers rode the waves, defying the laws of gravity, while a small crowd of onlookers watched from the sand.

"It's one of the best windsurfing spots in the world," Nick said, "but there are dangerous rip currents and the occasional shark attack, so it's not for beginners."

Just past the beach, the road curved inland, passing through lush green gulches thick with jungle and pastures covered in tall, swaying guinea grasses. On the right of the highway, rural side roads led to the misty mountains and rolling hills of Upcountry Maui and the agricultural communities of Kula and Makawao.

Nick pointed to a one-lane dirt road nestled between two steep gulches on the seaward side of the highway. "This is our turn. The place we're staying is a mile down."

Kate bumped along the road, which quickly degenerated into little more than a glorified cattle path. A feral pig and her three babies bolted across the road, and disappeared into the jungle on the other side.

"I'm not sure this road is ice cream truck appropriate," Kate said. "In fact, I'm not even sure this road is Jeep Wrangler appropriate."

"No matter. I think we've arrived," Nick said, pointing at a makeshift sign fifty feet in front of them that read "Park Here. Pedestrian Access Only."

Kate stopped the truck, got out, and looked around. "I

know people always say 'We're in the middle of nowhere' when they're lost, and most of the time it isn't true. But we are literally in the middle of nowhere."

Kate and Nick followed the pedestrian path through a grove of bamboo before emerging onto a small patch of land fronted by an eighty-foot cliff overlooking the Pacific Ocean and the white-capped waves of Peahi. A small white-domed canvas structure, decorated in Buddhist prayer ribbons and peace symbols, was perched on the cliffside. "You rented us a tent?" Kate said.

"Technically, it's a yurt." Nick pointed at a small cottage, three hundred feet away, on the other side of the gulch. "And it has a direct line of sight over Hamilton's place."

Kate opened the flap and peeked inside. It smelled heavily of sage incense, and the walls were covered in the owner's original artwork, mostly watercolor paintings of her nude husband. An ancient television and DVD player sat on a wooden bench that was backed against one of the walls.

"It looks small for two people," Kate said.

"It has a big bed."

"That's great. For your sake, I'm hoping it also has a big couch."

Nick winked at Kate. "Gotcha. Saving yourself for our pretend marriage. That's hot."

"Good grief. Do you have any more surprises for me?"

Nick sat down on the bed. "You don't like surprises?"

"I like normal surprises, like a birthday party or my aunt coming over to visit."

"Would you consider my repacking your suitcase a normal surprise?"

Kate opened her luggage and dumped the contents on the bed. "What the heck?" She held up a colorful full-length maxi dress. "What is this?"

"It's flowy and comfortable. The saleswoman at Free People said it was all the rage in bohemian chic fashion. It's how Rain, the candlemaker, dresses."

"Where am I going to keep my gun?" She sorted through the rest of the clothes. "Seriously. All I'm seeing are fringy blouses, baggy cardigans, and cut-off shorts. Where are my jeans? Where are my T-shirts?"

Nick looked at the pile. "What about these jeans overalls?"

"You've got to be kidding."

"They looked great on Demi Moore in *Ghost*," Nick said. "And they have plenty of pockets and places to hide a gun."

Kate narrowed her eyes. "Where are my clothes?"

"Don't worry. I asked Steven and Willow to pick them up at LAX and take them back to your apartment."

"Who are Steven and Willow?"

Nick pointed at a painting on the wall of a forty-something man wearing nothing but a cape, hands on hips, chest out, looking off into the distance. "That's Steven. He and his wife, Willow, own this yurt. You house-swapped with them."

"What?"

"Funny story," Nick said. "They're staying in your place while we stay in theirs."

"Hippies are living in my apartment?" Kate blinked and stared at Nick. "And they have my clothes?"

"I wouldn't worry too much." Nick flipped his chin toward the paintings on the walls. "I don't think they much believe in clothes."

"Naked hippies are staying in my apartment?"

"I thought about letting them stay in Jake's place, but I didn't want to make a bad first impression on my pretend future father-in-law."

"This plan better work." Kate poked Nick in the chest. "Because if I don't nab a kahuna, there's going to be one more ghost haunting that ice cream truck." Kate shoved a pair of military-grade thermal-imaging binoculars at Nick. "You have the first watch over Hamilton's place. Wake me up if you see anything unusual."

"Absolutely."

Kate changed into a pair of loose-fitting tie-dyed pajamas with crochet trim. "I look ridiculous. Do you get some weird kick from making me crazy?"

Nick opened the yurt's flap, turned around to face Kate in the open door, and flashed her a crooked smile. "You have no idea."

7

It was 2 A.M. when Kate woke up to relieve Nick and take the second watch over Hamilton's house. She walked outside into the cool night air and listened to the sounds of trade winds blowing through the grasses. Except for a faint light from Hamilton's place, a sliver of moon, and a thick blanket of stars, it was pitch-black. "Nick?"

"Over here."

Kate followed his voice to a bench overlooking the ocean. "Anything happening?"

"Hamilton came home by himself around eleven P.M. The light is still on, so it looks like he hasn't gone to sleep yet." He handed the binoculars to Kate. "Also, there's a yacht anchored offshore. It's been there for at least two hours. I was able to catch a glimpse of the stern, and it looked like the name is *Carpe Diem*."

Kate looked at the yacht through the binoculars. It was about fifty feet long, and it was bobbing like a top on the massive waves of Peahi. "It doesn't look like a comfortable place to spend the night."

"It's not. It's probably the worst possible choice to anchor."

Kate watched as a motorized raft was dropped into the water from the side of the yacht. "Two guys are in a Zodiac, heading this way." She focused the binoculars. "At least one of them has an assault rifle."

"It's probably a safe bet they're not looking for Steven and Willow," Nick said. "There's an old footpath, near where we parked, across the gulch. It leads to Hamilton's farm. What do you think?"

Kate grabbed a couple of flashlights from the yurt. "Let's go. We probably have ten minutes or so before they reach shore, and another ten before they figure out how to scale the cliff."

Kate and Nick walked back through the ironwood trees and shone their flashlights into the gulch. "Is this the right place?" Kate asked. She pointed at the "Park Here. Pedestrian Access Only" placard.

Nick focused his light on a small opening in the jungle. "This is it." He peered down through the opening into the gulch. "I think."

The path led Kate and Nick through a series of switchbacks

before flattening near the bottom. Except for the sounds of a small stream and an occasional frog, it was eerily quiet. As they crossed the water, Kate looked to her left. A narrow waterfall cascaded over an eighty-foot escarpment to the tidal pools in the valley below. Down where the valley widened and emptied into the ocean, Kate could see a spotlight scanning the rocky beach.

"The Zodiac found a landing spot," Kate said. "We've got to hurry."

Nick and Kate scrambled through the brush, up the steep bank on the other side of the gulch, hopped a cattle fence, and emerged into a field covered in four-foot-high guinea grasses and about a hundred sleeping cows.

A couple of cows in the distance startled awake, mooed a couple of times, and trotted away from where they had been sleeping near the cliff. A few seconds later, a rangy twenty-something with shoulder-length blond hair, wearing only board shorts and Crocs, appeared in the doorway of the cottage, looked out toward the cows, and scanned the field.

Nick looked at Kate. "Who needs an alarm system when you have cows?"

"That must be Hamilton," Kate said, pointing at the rangy twenty-something. "He looks jumpy."

Hamilton aimed a handheld spotlight in the direction of the cows. The beam danced back and forth across ohia trees, cows, and pasture before finally coming to rest on two men.

One was tall and lanky, the other shorter with a round face. They were both dressed in black paramilitary uniforms and held assault rifles.

"Dude," Hamilton said, his voice carrying across to Kate and Nick.

He catapulted himself off the lanai and bolted full speed toward the gulch on the other side of the property, with the two gunmen in pursuit.

"Stop," the taller one shouted, taking aim and firing off several rounds at Hamilton.

Hamilton reached the gulch, leapt down the embankment, and disappeared into the jungle.

The shorter gunman peered into the darkness. "What do you think, Jasper? Should we follow him?"

Jasper shook his head and threw up his hands. "*Do riti. Sprosté kozy.* We'll never find him now." He fired a couple rounds in the general direction of the cows, sending them scattering. "Let's search his place, Horace." They walked back to the house and went inside.

"What do you think they're looking for?" Kate whispered as she listened to the sounds of the little cottage being ransacked.

Thirty seconds later, the noises stopped. Jasper and Horace walked outside onto the lanai.

"Nothing," Horace said. "But my gut tells me the old man was here. I just know it."

"Well, even if he was, neither of them are coming back

anytime soon. We might as well just make sure he's not hiding in the fields and call it a night."

"It's pitch-black, and there must be two hundred acres to search. How are we going to do that?"

Jasper walked over to the little carport on the side of the house, picked up a couple of ten-gallon jugs of gasoline, and handed one of them to the shorter gunman. "Burn it, Horace. Burn it all."

Horace grinned, put down his gun, and took the canister. "I like burning things. Maybe this night won't be a total waste after all."

Nick looked at Kate. "It's the dry season. I don't want to be sitting in the middle of this field when it goes up in flames. I think it's time we skedaddled."

Kate drew her gun. "We can't just let them start a massive wildfire."

"We're outgunned," Nick said. "And we have no place to hide once the bullets start flying."

"Then let's even the odds." Kate looked back toward the gulch. "Plenty of hiding places in there."

"How are you going to get them into the jungle?"

Kate stood up and used her cellphone to take a picture of Horace and Jasper. The flash illuminated the dark pasture for just a second, but it was enough to get their attention. "Smile, assholes," she said before ducking back into the tall grass.

The gunmen whipped around, looked in the direction of Kate's voice, and dropped the gasoline jugs.

"Now what?" Nick asked.

"We run."

"That's your big plan? Run?"

"Let's leave bushwhacking hired killers to me. I don't tell you how to catch kahunas, do I?"

They sprinted across the field, stumbling on the uneven ground, slipping on cow patties. They reached the gulch and made their way to the bottom while a spray of bullets cut through the vegetation all around them. They took cover behind a large koa tree near the waterfall.

"All we want is the cellphone," Jasper shouted from above. "We don't want to hurt you."

"Why do these sorts of guys always say they don't want to hurt you?" Nick said. "It's such a cliché. Of course they want to hurt you. That's the first thing they teach you how to do in hired-goon school."

Kate could hear Jasper and Horace crashing through the jungle and cursing, as they slowly made their way down the embankment.

Kate activated the flashlight app on her phone, and threw the phone into the open clearing near the waterfall. "Come and get the phone," she shouted at them. "It's by the waterfall."

"Bait?" Nick asked her.

"Yep. You can't catch a fish without bait."

Horace and Jasper finally reached the bottom of the gulch. They cautiously walked up to the light and retrieved the cellphone.

"Probably just a couple of dummies in the wrong place at the wrong time," Jasper said.

Horace nodded. "It's a shame we'll have to kill them."

Kate stepped from behind the tree and aimed her gun at Jasper. "Yeah, that *would* be a shame. Drop your weapons."

Horace and Jasper looked at each other. "She can't shoot both of us," Horace said.

Jasper shrugged. "Then we each have a fifty-fifty chance. You know, Horace, I've always been lucky when it comes to killing." He raised his gun, opened fire, and Kate ducked back behind the tree.

"Well, that didn't work out like I'd hoped," Kate said. "Time for plan B."

"What's plan B?"

"First, we wait for one of them to run out of ammo."

"And then?" Nick asked.

"Then I shoot the guy who's still got ammo, and you whack the other guy with your nineteen-inch, three-pound Maglite. Plan B."

"It's friggin' dark in this stupid gulch. How am I supposed to see some idiot replace his clip?"

"Good point. I'm changing plan B." Kate stepped out from behind her tree, arms in the air, gun still in one hand. "Hey!" she said. "Can we talk?"

Jasper and Horace moved forward out of the shadows, and Kate shot Jasper first and Horace second.

Nick rushed at Horace and smacked him square in the face

with the Maglite. Horace fell backward into Jasper, and the two of them tumbled into the stream and over the waterfall edge.

Kate ran to the cliff and peered over the side. Jasper was clinging to a small ledge about twenty feet down, and Horace was clinging to Jasper. "They're okay," Kate said to Nick.

The ledge gave way, and the two gunmen fell, disappearing into the darkness before splashing into the water below.

"Whoops," Nick said.

Kate aimed her flashlight at the pool at the base of the waterfall. Horace and Jasper dragged themselves out of the water and collapsed on the side of the bank.

"They're alive, but they're going to need a whole bottle of Extra-Strength Advil when they get back to the ship," Kate said.

"Buttercup, you shot them and knocked them off an eighty-foot waterfall. I think they're going to need the whole pharmacy," Nick said.

"I shot them both in noncritical body parts. You were the one who got carried away and smashed your Maglite into Horace's face and knocked them off an eighty-foot cliff."

"I was just following instructions," Nick said, trudging after Kate as she fought her way through the underbrush to the top of the gulch. "You told me to whack him with my Maglite."

"That was before I decided I had time to shoot both of them."

"Has anybody ever told you that you're lacking in communication skills?" He stopped and picked up Kate's cellphone. "Lucky for you they dropped this."

They reached the grotto of ironwood trees and the ice cream truck.

"Good old Mr. Freezy," Kate said. "Haunted or not, I'm happy to see it here."

8

At 8 A.M., Kate woke up to the sound of Nick singing "Mr. Blue Sky" in the outside shower. She got out of bed, changed from her tie-dyed pajamas into denim overalls and a white T-shirt, and checked her cellphone. There were three texts. The first was a selfie of Cosmo enjoying a mai tai during check-in. The second was a selfie of Cosmo's view from his lanai. The third was a selfie of Cosmo at the breakfast buffet.

Nick walked into the yurt, wearing board shorts and a fitted Billabong rash guard. "Got up at sunrise and walked back to Hamilton's place. It's still a mess, and I'm guessing he's not planning on coming back for a while."

"We know he's a surfer. Maybe Dad will spot him at one of the surf spots near Lahaina. Meantime, let's track down the owner of the *Carpe Diem* and see if we can figure out who hired Horace and Jasper."

Her cellphone buzzed and she squelched a grimace at the caller ID. It was Cosmo.

"I thought I was going to get your voicemail," Cosmo said. "Did you get my texts? You didn't respond, so I wasn't sure you got them." He paused to catch his breath. "The Four Seasons Wailea is awesome. There's a guy who walks around poolside and gives you fruit Popsicles and spritzes you with Evian water. It's all free, even the spritzing. I've probably been spritzed at least ten times since I got here. I never knew how much I liked getting spritzed, but there you have it."

"That's great, Cosmo."

"I just thought you'd want to know."

"About the spritzing? It sounds terrific."

"Oh, it is. You've got to try it," Cosmo said. "But I meant about Vicky and Larry. They're here at the hotel. I saw them at the breakfast buffet."

"We'll be right there," Kate said and ended the call.

"And?" Nick asked.

"Vicky and Larry are at the Four Seasons. Cosmo spotted them. Maybe Vicky has something to do with Jasper and Horace."

"Possibly," Nick said.

"But you don't think she's the type to hire hit men?"

"I don't think she's the type to hire Czech hit men. Olga Zellenkova, on the other hand . . ."

"How do you know they were Czech?"

Nick shrugged. "I don't, but they were cursing in Czech last night."

"You speak Czech?"

"Just the curse words. For some reason, I tend to get cursed out a lot."

Kate hooked her thumbs into the overalls. "I can't imagine why."

"Whether Jasper and Horace work for her or not, she didn't fly all the way to Maui just for a vacation. She's here for the Kahuna."

"Hamilton's in the wind, so there's no sense sticking around here," Kate said. "Let's get in our haunted ice cream truck and drive to Wailea."

Kate and Nick walked through the ironwoods and found Mr. Freezy still parked near the sign.

"Maybe it's only haunted at night," Nick said as Kate got into the driver's seat.

Kate turned the ignition and waited for the backfire before bumping down the dirt road on her way to the main highway. Once they'd turned toward Paia, Kate tilted her head and adjusted her rearview mirror to get a better look at the back of the truck. "Did you hear that?"

"The creepy moaning coming from the freezer chest in the back? Yeah, I heard it."

Kate pulled over to the side of the road. They got out, walked to the back of the truck, and stared at the freezer chest.

The compressor wasn't running, and the lid was ajar.

Kate rapped on the lid. "Anybody home in there?"

"It could be a ghost," Nick said. "I hear if you get too close they might eat your face."

Kate flipped the lid open, and they stared in at Hamilton.

"Hey, bud," Hamilton said, looking up at Kate.

"Hey, yourself. What are you doing in our ice cream truck?"

"Mostly getting carsick. I was ready to hurl when you stopped. You're the newbies in the yurt, right?"

"Right," Kate said.

"I live across the gulch from you. Had kind of a rough night and needed a place to crash." He paused. "I'm, like, famished. Do you have any French toast? We should stop in Paia and get some French toast."

"We're on our way to Wailea."

Hamilton headed for the jump seat. "Great. They have French toast there too."

Kate got in the driver's seat and pulled back onto the highway. "We heard gunfire last night. Is everything okay?"

"These two barneys tried to kill me and trashed my house. That's why I hid in the chest." He looked around the truck. "This is a sweet ride, unless you're in the back in a freezer chest." He held out his hand to Nick. "I'm Hamilton Wylde."

Nick gave him a fist bump. "Nick Lodeon." He gestured toward Kate. "This is my fiancée slash lover, Rain. I don't like to brag, but she's the best darn candlemaker in Hawaii."

Kate gripped the steering wheel with both hands and stared straight ahead.

"She gives real tense vibes. Does she want some weed?" Hamilton asked.

"Do you want some weed, Sweetie Poo?" Nick asked.

Kate forced a smile. "I'm good."

"Maybe after the French toast," Nick said to Hamilton. "Why'd they want to kill you?"

"I think they were looking for my dad. He's in trouble."

Kate turned her head toward the back. "Do you know where he is?"

"Top secret, dude. That's, like, on a need-to-know basis, and you don't need to know."

Kate drove through Paia, passed the airport, and turned south on Route 311 toward the resorts in Wailea.

"Can you drop me off in Kihei?" Hamilton asked. "There's a killer diner right in town."

Kate drove into town, followed Hamilton's directions to the diner, and idled Mr. Freezy in the parking lot. "Maybe you should stay at our place until at least Friday, just in case those two guys come back," Kate said.

"Friday. Good thinking, dude." He got out of the truck and scratched his stomach. "What day is it today?"

"Wednesday."

"Awesome," Hamilton said. "Can you pick me up later? I'll be hanging out at the Kalama Beach Park all day."

"We'll be back at five," Kate said.

Kate pulled out of the parking lot and drove down South Kihei Road. "At least, we know the Big Kahuna is still alive and likely hiding in Hawaii. Now all we have to do is convince Hamilton to tell us where."

"Before Horace and Jasper find him."

"Or Vicky."

Kate took a hard right onto Wailea Alanui Drive and descended the winding road with its grassy median separating her from oncoming traffic into the resort community of Wailea. The street was lined with flowering bushes, tropical trees, golf courses, multimillion-dollar condos, and five-star resorts.

"This is the hot tourist section, at the moment," Nick said. "Some old-timers prefer Lahaina, but Wailea has arguably the best beaches, the best weather, the best shopping, and the newest hotels."

Kate turned into the Four Seasons Resort and parked in front of the porte cochere. A valet dressed in white hurried over to her, opened her door, and smiled. "Welcome to the Four Seasons."

Kate and Nick got out of the truck and handed the keys to the valet. "Please be extra careful with my haunted ice cream truck," Nick said. "It's one of a kind."

The valet nodded solemnly, just as if he drove haunted ice cream trucks every day. He turned the key in the ignition and the truck backfired. A group of Chinese tourists ducked and were engulfed in a cloud of black smoke, before the valet chugged away toward short-term parking.

"Holy schnikes," Kate said as she walked into the hotel. "This is where I want to go on my pretend honeymoon."

The vast open-air lobby, constructed almost entirely from natural stone, was filled with contemporary artwork and tropical floral arrangements. A gentle ocean breeze blew through the lively little bar in back, toward the immaculate reception desk and hotel entrance.

"I kind of thought we'd go on an African photographic safari for our honeymoon," Nick said. "Botswana is amazing, and we could go to Kenya afterward and climb Kilimanjaro."

"It sounds like you've put a lot of thought into our pretend marriage."

Nick moved in a little closer to Kate. "Let's just say I have a rich fantasy life. You'll find out all about it on our pretend wedding night."

Cosmo ran up to them from the other side of the lobby. "Isn't this place great? Why are you wearing overalls? Vicky's in a private cabana by the pool. Have you had breakfast? I ran out of sunscreen. Why are you wearing overalls?"

Kate took a deep breath. "The place is great, we'll go to the gift shop later and buy you some sunscreen, and I'm dressed like this because I'm undercover."

Cosmo stared at Kate. "As a groupie for a Seattle grunge band?"

"I'm a hemp-farming candlemaker."

Cosmo nodded. "Oh, of course. That makes more sense. You're a dead ringer."

78

Kate shook her head at Nick. "Let's just go see Vicky."

Cosmo led them down a flight of stairs. An enormous glass-tiled pool sparkled in the morning sun, while attendants in white shirts brought towels to the growing throng of guests settling into the surrounding lounges and cabanas.

Kate scanned the pool deck. "Where's Vicky?"

"There are three pools. She's at the Serenity Pool in a cabana," Cosmo said.

The Four Seasons' Serenity Pool was located a short walk away in a private, quiet area of the resort with amazing views of the island of Lanai. A sign reminded guests that they needed to be at least twenty-one years of age to use the pool and the two hot tubs. Vicky was sitting at the swim-up bar, in a barely there bikini, nursing a mimosa and taking selfies.

She was scrolling through the pictures on her cellphone when Nick, Kate, and Cosmo sat down across from her on the dry side of the bar. Vicky gave them a finger wave and showed Cosmo one of her bikini shots. "What do you think? Is it a hottie or a nottie?"

Cosmo looked at the picture. "It's a nice bathing suit, but it's giving you a wedgie. I can't wear anything that gives me a wedgie on account of my hemorrhoids."

Vicky moved the picture to her saved folder. "It's supposed to look like that. It's a Brazilian cut thong. It goes with my Brazilian wax job. Men get them too. You should try it," Vicky said to Cosmo. "It'll make your junk look bigger."

"I don't know," Cosmo said. "On the one hand, I'd like to

have bigger junk, but it also might make my hemorrhoids bigger." He turned to Kate. "What do you think?"

"Okay. Switching subjects," Kate said, turning to Vicky. "You don't seem very surprised to see us. Don't you want to know what we're doing here?"

"Probably the same thing I'm doing. Looking for my technically dead husband."

"At the Four Seasons?"

"Hamilton used the emergency credit card his father gave him to book an oceanfront suite. Visa called the house to confirm it wasn't a fraudulent charge. Anyway, I figured it was for his father, since Hamilton almost never uses the card."

"If he's staying at the Four Seasons, he probably isn't dead, even technically."

Vicky sighed. "I guess. I bribed a guy in Reception for the Kahuna's room number and sent Larry to watch his suite. There's no sign of him, coming or going. He hasn't even gotten room service since we got here last night."

"It's still possible he might be dead then," Cosmo said. "I mean, just saying. Or he could just be in a coma. Or he could have brought some granola bars with him. I do that sometimes. It's always good to have a granola bar on hand."

Vicky put her hand on Cosmo's arm. "Bless your heart. You're sweet to suggest he could be dead."

"Only one way to find out," Kate said. She got up and ushered Nick, Cosmo, and Vicky out of the bar and back into the hotel. "Where's the Kahuna's room?"

Vicky led them through a maze of elevators and corridors to the fourth-floor ocean-view rooms. "He's over there in the corner suite, but where's my worthless lawyer?"

Nick picked up a shiny Italian loafer, lying in front of the Kahuna's half-open vandalized door. "Size nine. I think Larry may have been taken, per se."

Vicky scrunched up her nose. "Who would want to kidnap Larry? I'm pretty much the only person who can stand him. And I can't stand him."

"Two mercenaries tried to kill Hamilton last night," Kate said. "I think they were looking for the Big Kahuna. Nick thinks they may be working for Olga Zellenkova."

"Firecrotch stole my Larry? What a witch."

Kate pushed open the door and peered inside. The room had been ransacked, but there was no sign of a struggle and no personal belongings in the closets or bathroom. She picked up a couple of twenty-dollar bills left on the entertainment center. "I don't think the Kahuna was here when they took Larry. He left a tip for housekeeping, like he was checking out."

Vicky looked around the room. "Crap. We just missed him. Now I have two missing losers to look for."

9

Kate and Vicky waited in the lobby for hotel security, while Nick and Cosmo talked with the concierge about whether anybody had seen Larry or the Kahuna leaving the hotel.

"You don't really want the Big Kahuna dead, do you?" Kate asked.

Vicky adjusted her bikini top. "Of course I want him dead. We're married. I wouldn't mind killing him myself."

"I get it." Kate gestured toward Nick. "We're only pretend engaged, and I want to kill him half the time."

"What about the other half?"

Kate looked across the lobby at Nick in his board shorts and skin-tight rash guard. Vicky followed her lead and looked Nick up and down.

"I know what *I'd* like to do to him for the other half," Vicky said.

Kate worried that her thoughts ran in the same direction.

By 11 A.M., Kate and Nick had deposited Vicky back into her private cabana, left Cosmo behind to babysit, and were in their ice cream truck driving toward the western side of the island.

"I called Dad and asked him to meet us in Lahaina Harbor," Kate said. "Cosmo did some digging and found out that the *Carpe Diem* has a berth there."

Kate drove back through Kihei, turned left, and drove along the Honoapiilani Highway toward Lahaina. The Pacific Ocean was directly to her left, and the dry, arid land of West Maui was to her right. "It's amazing how many different climates there are in Hawaii," Kate said as they approached the little town. "When we woke up this morning, we were in the rainforest."

Nick nodded. "Lahaina means *cruel sun* in Hawaiian, probably because of how little rain the region gets each year. It was one of the biggest whaling towns in the Pacific. Today, the main industry is tourism, but it still has a funky old Hawaiian sea town vibe."

Kate drove slowly along Front Street. Ahead of her, restaurants, art galleries, souvenir shops, and crowds of tourists lined both sides of the road. She turned left, just past an enormous banyan tree occupying an entire city block, onto Hotel Street and parked by the harbor.

Jake walked over to them and stared at the ice cream truck. "As I live and breathe, it's a full-on hippie-mobile." He looked at Kate. "And what the heck are you wearing?"

Kate slid a sidewise glance at Nick. "There was a mix-up with my luggage. Some doofus switched my bag at the airport."

Jake shook his head. "Well, I guess so."

Kate handed Jake her cellphone so he could see the picture of Horace and Jasper. "I took this last night. These two mercenary types showed up at Hamilton's house and tried to kill him. We think their boat might be here in the harbor."

"I might have seen them this morning in Lahaina Town," Jake said.

"What were they doing?"

"Just limping up and down Front Street, checking out all the coffee shops and breakfast places. They looked like they should be in an ICU bed."

"They kind of accidentally on purpose fell off an eighty-foot waterfall last night."

Jake smiled. "I'm sure they had it coming. They should consider themselves lucky you didn't shoot them."

"No. She did that too," Nick said.

Jake nodded. "Impressive."

Kate scanned the harbor, looking for the *Carpe Diem,* and found it tied up on the north side in an end berth. A sign out front advertised it as a charter.

"According to Cosmo, it's an old Hatteras fifty-two-foot

motor yacht that's been retrofitted to take tourists on underwater adventures," Kate said. "It looked better at night in the moonlight."

They stood watching from a distance for a while, and when no activity was observed they moved closer and boarded the boat. The small salon's original furnishings had been replaced with more utilitarian bench seating. Stairs led up to the cockpit, and to the right of those stairs a thin trail of blood led toward a steep set of stairs to the cabin down below.

"I'm not liking the blood trail and the smell coming from the belowdecks cabin," Jake said.

"I'm thinking it smells like Larry," Nick said.

They crept down the stairs and stopped at the bottom. A fifty-something man with a potbelly and white hair was propped up in the corner with a captain's hat lying next to him and a bullet hole in his head.

"I've got a new theory," Nick said. "I'm thinking the smell might belong to this guy."

Jake examined the body. "He's been dead for a while. At least half a day. I'm guessing your guys hijacked the boat and killed the captain once he wasn't useful to them anymore."

"Not good," Nick said. "It's only a matter of time before Horace and Jasper discover that Larry isn't useful to pretty much *anybody*."

Kate looked up, just as Larry tumbled down the stairs, crumpling in a heap at the bottom.

"Too late. We already figured that out an hour ago," Jasper said from above and slammed the cabin door shut.

Larry sprang up and dusted off his shiny pants. "I'm okay."

Kate drew her gun. "Let us out before I get mad," she shouted at the door.

"Sorry," Jasper said, throwing the dead bolt. "You're just going to have to get mad. You might want to do it quick-like, though, on account of Horace plans to take this boat out into the channel and set it on fire."

The engines started, and the boat moved slowly through the harbor before accelerating into the open ocean.

Larry lifted his head and sniffed the air. "I smell gasoline, per se."

"They're dousing the upper deck," Kate said.

Jake climbed the stairs and tried the door. "Yep. It's locked."

"Stand aside," Kate said.

She fired two rounds into the door and paused while Jake examined the damage.

"Not good," Jake said. "The rounds penetrated the wood but then went flat. The hatch has a metal core. I've seen these doors before. They're fairly common and are engineered to stay locked, even in a Category Five hurricane. We're not breaking through."

Kate looked around the room. It was essentially one large open space with a small galley kitchen at the rear, a small bar up front, and a sitting area in the center featuring a glass bottom for watching sea turtles, reef fish, and other marine life. There were two small portholes on either side. They were much too small to climb through.

"We're going to have to turn it up a notch," Kate said. "I'm going to start at a Category Six and take it to a Category Ten real quick."

Nick looked at Jake. "I've seen Category Six Kate in action. It involves possible loss of life and catastrophic property damage."

Kate tapped the glass bottom with her gun butt. "Here's our escape route. How does everyone feel about a little swim?"

"That seems like a really bad idea," Larry said. "We're trapped down here. The boat will sink, and we'll drown."

"Would you rather be burned alive?"

"Good point."

"I'm sure this is high-impact glass," Kate said. She looked over at her father. "You were in Special Forces no one even knew about. You know forty-three ways to kill a man with a fork. What do you know about this?"

"I know if you keep hammering away in the same spot it will eventually break. Six or seven well-aimed shots would be a good start. Then I'd suggest the large cast iron fry pan on the galley stove to finish the job."

"Sounds like a plan," Kate said. "When we finally break the glass, water is going to rush into the cabin really fast. We'll have to wait for the cabin to completely fill before we'll be able to get past the rushing water and swim through the opening. It's going to be dark and you might be disoriented once you're under the boat, so just follow the bubbles to the surface."

"There are flashlights on the kitchen counter," Nick said. "They look like they might be waterproof." He tossed flashlights to Jake, Larry, and Kate and kept one for himself.

Kate drew her gun and discharged seven rounds into the window. A spider web of hairline cracks radiated out from each of the bullet strikes. Nick stepped in with the fry pan and whacked away at the cracks. He backed off, Kate fired five more rounds, Nick two-handed the fry pan against the glass, and the spider web turned into a solid mass of fractures. A trickle of water bubbled up through the fractures.

"One more good whack should do it," Kate said. "Is everyone ready?"

Nick struck the glass again, and the window shattered completely and gave way. Water exploded into the room. After half a minute, the cabin was already half filled with water and the boat was starting to sink. In another half minute, the water was so high that only Kate's head was above it.

"This is it," Kate said. "Everybody take a couple deep breaths and dive."

Kate waited for Larry, Nick, and Jake to make their way through the window. She followed them out into the dark water, and immediately saw that Larry was panicked and struggling without his flashlight underneath the hull. Nick swooped in, grabbed Larry, and dragged him out from underneath the boat and up toward the surface.

Kate breached the water, inhaled a deep breath of air, and helped Nick support Larry while Jake searched the sinking, smoldering boat for the emergency raft.

"The good news is we're alive," Kate said. She looked off into the distance at a small boat speeding toward the harbor. "The bad news is we're offshore in shark-infested waters, and Jasper and Horace took the Zodiac."

"Found the raft," Jake yelled.

He was bobbing in the water with what looked like a huge yellow brick. He pulled the cord, and the brick exploded into an inflatable raft. Jake and Kate scrambled in and hauled Larry on board.

"He took in a lot of water," Jake said. "He's not breathing."

Nick climbed into the raft and watched while Jake started CPR on Larry.

"I never realized you were such a strong swimmer," Kate said to Nick.

"Summer camp," Nick said. "I had to swim across a lake to get to the girls' side."

Kate had no doubt that was true, but she suspected there was also boot camp rescue-and-survival training somewhere in his history. He'd kept his head underwater, and he knew exactly what he was doing when he went after Larry.

Larry coughed out what looked like a gallon of water and shot straight up into a sitting position. "I'm okay."

Nick watched the *Carpe Diem* sink beneath the waves and disappear. "Good thing Cosmo brought extra forms for destruction of personal property."

"Unfortunately, this raft didn't come with paddles," Kate said. "We're going to have to hand paddle."

Larry started to paddle toward shore. "You saved my life," he said to Kate. "I make a solemn oath that I will find a way to repay you, even if it takes the next twenty years. Even if I have to follow you to the ends of the Earth, per se."

"Gee, as amazing as that sounds, I didn't really save you. Nick was the one who dragged you out from under the boat."

"Yes, but you were the leader."

"Maybe you could just tell me what happened with Horace and Jasper, and we'll call it even," Kate said.

The look on Larry's face showed no intention of calling it even.

"They were searching for the Kahuna," he told Kate. "When they couldn't find him in the hotel room, they figured Vicky and I might know where to look next."

"What did you tell them?"

"That we had no idea," Larry said. "They took me to meet with some redhead named Olga, and I told her the same thing."

"I'm guessing that didn't go over so well."

"She told me she believed me, but her employers hated loose ends and liked to keep things neat and tidy. That's when she told Jasper and Horace to get rid of me, permanently."

"Interesting," Kate said as she paddled. "So Olga is working for someone else."

"Whoever it is must be pretty dirty if he needs to hide his identity behind Zellenkova Private Equity," Nick said.

Larry kept paddling. "I'm in. Whatever it is that we're doing. I have to be there for you," Larry said to Kate. "A life for a life, per se."

Kate paddled harder. "Why is Olga Zellenkova so desperate to find the Kahuna?"

Nick scanned the horizon. The Lahaina Harbor was still far away, but a couple of small boats seemed to be headed toward them. "There's only one person on Maui who might know. What do you say we go load him up with French toast and see what we can find out?"

It was 5 P.M. by the time Kate parked the ice cream truck at Kalama Beach Park. She was exhausted. Even with the help of a rescue boat, it had taken the better part of the afternoon to get back to Lahaina. She'd met with the Coast Guard to direct them to the wreck and the body of the *Carpe Diem*'s captain. She'd met with the local police and given them descriptions of Horace, Jasper, and Olga. And she'd had the longest car ride of her life, transporting an eternally grateful Larry back to Wailea. Jake had found his own way to his room at the Ritz-Carlton.

"What if Horace and Jasper come back to the Four Seasons, looking for Vicky and Larry?" Nick asked.

"I talked with hotel security. They're going to keep a close watch. So long as they don't leave the resort, they should be fine."

Kate and Nick got out of the truck and walked around the park looking for Hamilton. There wasn't a sandy beach, but the park had picnic tables and pavilions, tennis courts, a soccer field, a playground, great ocean views, and just about everything else you'd need for a family outing. Hamilton was hanging out at the enormous twenty-thousand-square-foot skateboard park, eating a shave ice and holding a tote bag.

"Hey, man," he said, "look what I got. It's a kick-ass PlayStation and Call of Duty. I traded some weed for it."

"We've been looking all over for you," Kate said. "You were supposed to meet us in the parking lot at five o'clock."

Hamilton looked up at the sun. "What time is it now?"

"Five-thirty. Don't you have a watch?"

"Why would I have a watch, dude?"

Kate smacked her forehead with the heel of her hand. "I don't know. How about so you could be on time for things?"

"That sounds, like, super stressful. I'm all about managing my stress." Hamilton offered his spoon to Kate. "Do you want the rest of my shave ice?"

Kate took a deep breath. "Sure."

A crowd of kids had gathered around the ice cream truck by the time they returned. Nick pulled out a water-soaked twenty-dollar bill and sent them to the food court.

"That was nice of you," Kate said as she got into the driver's seat. "You have a soft spot for kids, don't you?"

Nick smiled. "Maybe. If I did, would it make me boyfriend material? Would I be Mr. Right?"

The truck backfired and Kate exited the parking lot, leaving behind a cloud of smoke. "Not even close. You're more of a Mr. Right Now."

Nick relaxed into his seat. "I can live with that."

"Good grief. I didn't mean it literally." She looked at Hamilton in the back. He was already asleep. "We're running out of time. How are we going to convince Hamilton to tell us where his dad is hiding?"

"It's simple. We do nothing."

"Nothing?"

"Well, not exactly nothing. Hamilton and I are going to eat pizza and play video games, while you make candles."

"What are you talking about? In the first place, I have absolutely no idea how to make candles. I can barely make popcorn and toast."

"Can you melt wax and pour it into a glass jar?" Nick asked.

"I guess."

"Congratulations. You're a candlemaker. Hamilton doesn't exactly strike me like the sort of guy who's very good at keeping secrets. If we just give him some space . . . and some pizzas, he'll eventually tell us on his own."

Kate shook her head. "It's the dumbest plan I ever heard. I'm not staying up all night making candles while you scarf down pizza."

"How about this. If it works, you let me give you a code name."

"What if it doesn't?"

"Then you get to give me a code name."

"That's not a bet. You'd love to get a code name. Next to stealing things, inventing ridiculous aliases is just about your favorite hobby." Kate narrowed her eyes. "I want something else. Something that will put a lasting smile on my face. I think you know what I'm talking about."

Nick nodded his head. "I do."

"And it better be incredible and satisfying. Not just some little tease."

"I'm not worried," Nick said. "You're not going to win."

10

At 3 A.M., Kate, Nick, and Hamilton were back at the yurt and most of the pizza was gone, Hamilton was outside taking a nature break, and Nick was bleary eyed from playing Call of Duty all night. Kate had just finished making her fifth candle.

"That takes care of Christmas," she said, positioning it beside the other four. "I hope my sister, Megan, likes patchouli."

Nick paused the video game and looked outside. Hamilton was still behind a tree. "Yeesh. He's told me pretty much his whole life story, except where his father is hiding. I'm not sure I can keep this up much longer."

Hamilton walked back into the yurt and plopped himself down in front of the TV. "Thanks for pausing the game. I guess you don't buy Dr Peppers. You just, like, rent them, right, dude?" he said to Nick.

"No problem." Nick pointed in Kate's direction. "My little snuggle muffin spends most of her free time communing with the Earth and protesting the big vitamin conglomerates, so it's nice to have some bro-time once in a while."

Kate rolled her eyes. "I hate to interrupt bro-time, but it's almost sunrise, and I've got a big day of communing and protesting ahead of me. Maybe we should get some sleep?"

"Is it still okay if I crash on your lanai?" Hamilton asked. "It's only for one more night. After that I'm going to Kauai to stay with my dad until things cool down."

Nick glanced at Kate. "Your dad is on Kauai? Is he staying at one of the hotels?"

"No way. He was staying at the Four Seasons in Wailea, but my stepmom, Vicky, showed up there. Now I've got him somewhere where nobody will ever find him."

"How can you be sure?" Nick asked.

Hamilton yawned and put down the video game controller. "No roads, no cell service, totally off the grid. It's paradise for dropouts."

"Sounds awesome. Where is it?"

"Sorry, dude. I'm not supposed to say." Hamilton got up and stretched. "I'm catching the first flight to Lihue. Can you give me a ride to the airport later?"

"Sure." Kate watched him leave the yurt and lie down in the hammock outside. "Well?" she said to Nick once Hamilton was asleep. "Do you have your concession speech already written, or were you just going to wing it?"

"Of course I have my speech ready, and it goes something like this. . . . It feels great to be right. Thanks to my brilliant plan, we know the Kahuna is on Kauai."

"Yeah." Kate made air quotes with her fingers. "'Somewhere where nobody will ever find him.' That's just one step away from you claiming you won because he's somewhere on Planet Earth."

"This is terrific," Nick said. "It's our first fight as a pretend almost married couple. There's really only one thing for us to do. We need to have make-up sex immediately. It's a fact that pretend almost married couples should never go to bed mad."

"You don't have to worry about that. You'll be sleeping in the ice cream truck."

"Your loss," Nick said. "My skills as a thief and a con man are second-rate compared to my make-up sex skills."

There was no doubt in Kate's mind that this was true. And it was an impressive statement to make considering he was possibly the number one thief and con man on the planet.

Kate handed Nick a blanket and pillow and pushed him out of the yurt. "You're going to have to practice your make-up sex skills alone tonight."

At 10 A.M., Kate pulled into the Kahului Airport, parked in front of Departures, and watched Hamilton climb out of the truck. "What time is your flight supposed to arrive on Kauai?"

"Not really sure, dude. Sometime between breakfast and lunch." Hamilton grabbed his Osprey backpack from the rear and slung it over his shoulder. "Mahalo for the ride." He flashed a shaka sign at Nick and Kate. "Catch you later."

Kate waited until Hamilton was inside the terminal before pulling away from the curb. "Did you notice the backpack? I snuck a peek in it earlier. Sleeping bag, tent, hiking shoes, camping stove. He wasn't kidding when he said he was going off the grid."

"According to Wikipedia, seventy percent of Kauai is completely inaccessible. It has over fifty miles of sandy beaches and more rainforest than you could explore in a lifetime. I'm afraid that doesn't narrow the search area down too much."

Kate turned into long-term parking. "One step ahead of you. Dad and Larry are already in the terminal. Hamilton has never seen them before, so they're going to catch the same flight and see if they can follow him once he lands. We'll take a later flight with Cosmo." Kate slouched down into the car seat and put her hands behind her head. "Now, I'm going to relax in this haunted ice cream truck, sit back, and enjoy the moment. I've probably got a good hour before Cosmo gets here and starts talking."

"Yeah. About that. It's going to be a pretty short moment. Cosmo is waiting for us in a Citation Latitude I chartered this morning. It's all fueled up and ready to go at the airport's private FBO. If we leave now, we'll beat Hamilton to Kauai by at least two hours."

Kate sat straight up, eyes wide. "What? We can't afford a private plane. That's not in the budget. We've already destroyed a tour boat on this trip."

"The boat was old, and the operator-owner is dead," Nick said.

"It's unnecessarily extravagant."

"It's the most efficient route." Nick patted Kate on the shoulder. "No need to feel bad about your plan. Your plan was good too."

Kate took hold of the wheel. "Whatever. You're the one who lost the bet and has to pay the piper. And that's a *moment* that I plan on savoring."

"I'm not going to have to worry about it, since I *won* the bet. By the way, what are your thoughts about our code names? I was thinking that I could be the Smuggler and you could be the Snuggler."

Kate pulled out of the parking lot and drove toward the private terminal. "The Smuggler and the Snuggler. Absolutely horrible. It sounds like the title of some lame made-for-TV movie. Lucky for me, I'm not going to have to worry about it, since I won the bet." She parked the truck and walked through the FBO lobby to the waiting Latitude.

"You've got to see this," Cosmo said as soon as Kate walked into the cabin. "The plane is filled with free stuff. Playing cards, granola bars, Oreos, and even cough drops."

Vicky gave Nick and Kate a finger wave. "Don't forget about the cute little bottles of alcohol." She shook her mostly empty glass at Kate, jingling the ice cubes. "FYI, we're out of vodka."

"It's ten A.M."

Vicky took a sip. "I'm in mourning. My no-good husband is alive."

Kate took Nick aside. "What is she doing here? Isn't it bad enough we're dragging Larry along?"

"I don't know," Nick said. "She's not my invited guest."

They looked at Cosmo.

"What?" Cosmo said.

"How did Vicky get on this plane?" Kate asked him.

"You're surprised, right? Okay, but it's all good. She's going to document everything with her selfies."

"This is a covert operation, sort of," Kate said. "We don't want it splashed all over her Instagram page. And she's not part of the team."

"Okay, but it's not my fault. She's sneaky. She followed me. And then she threatened me. And next thing she was on the plane."

Vicky snapped a picture of herself with her empty glass.

"If this goes public, Jessup will mess himself," Kate said.

"So it's not all bad," Nick said. "Everyone buckle up."

Kate and Nick took their seats, and minutes later they were airborne, flying toward Kauai. Kate looked out the window as they passed over Lanai and then Oahu.

"There are four main islands in the Hawaiian chain," Cosmos announced. "Oahu is the most populated. There are more people living there than on all the other islands combined. Kauai is the smallest and the oldest. It's also one of the wettest and greenest. Mount Waialeale gets around four hundred and fifty inches of rain each year."

Vicky leaned over Kate's seat. "You look tired. I'd be tired too if I was sharing a bedroom with Nick."

"We stayed up all night making candles and eating pizzas."

"Pizzas, huh? I like mine with extra sausage," Vicky said. "In my experience, there can never be enough sausage."

Nick nodded. "It was super hard for her to resist me. I had to sleep in my ice cream truck, or who knows what would have happened."

"That's old-school," Cosmo said. "You're a real gentleman."

Vicky blew out a raspberry. "Disappointing. Is that really all that happened?"

"Nick lost a bet, and now he's going to have to satisfy my deepest desire," Kate said.

Nick relaxed in his seat. "It kills me to say it, but Kate actually lost the bet, and now we're all getting awesome code names. Larry is the Weasel and Jake is the Colonel."

The plane started its descent toward Lihue Airport.

"The county seat, Lihue, is on the east side of the island," Cosmo said. "To the north is Hanalei. It's super lush and covered in rainforests and waterfalls. *Jurassic Park* was filmed there. *Jurassic Park* was a mindblower. *Fallen Kingdom* was my second favorite. Blue the velociraptor totally stole that movie. Am I right or am I right?"

Kate watched out the window as the pilot lowered the Latitude's wheels, landed the plane, and taxied to the terminal.

"We have rooms at the Koa Kea Hotel in Poipu," Nick said to Kate. "It's more or less midway between Kokee and Hanalei, so I thought it would be a good location to use as our base camp."

"Great. Let's send Cosmo on ahead, and we'll stay in Lihue in case Dad needs backup." Kate walked off the plane and crossed the tarmac into the open-air terminal. "We'll just need to keep a low profile, so Hamilton doesn't spot us."

An hour later, Vicky and Cosmo were driving south with the luggage. Nick and Kate were waiting near Arrivals, in a rented BMW X5 SUV.

"What gives?" Kate asked. "I rented a Ford Taurus, and the woman working the Avis counter upgrades you to a BMW."

"People just like doing nice things for me. Maybe it's my winning personality."

"I highly doubt it."

Nick took a receipt out of his pocket. "Then maybe it's the stack of FBI vouchers I borrowed from Cosmo. They're great. It's like a blank check signed by Uncle Sam. I figured Jessup wouldn't mind if his two best cops treated themselves once in a while."

"Of course he'll mind. It's taxpayer money."

"I'm a taxpayer."

Kate threw up her hands. "No, you're not. The last time you filed a tax return was never."

"Oh, right. In that case, you're in a heck of a pickle to try to explain it to Jessup. I wouldn't want to be in your shoes."

Kate's new cellphone rang. She took a deep breath and answered. "Hi, Dad, what's up?"

"The good news is we just landed in Lihue, and we're on the same flight as the Kahuna's son."

"And the bad news?"

"So are Horace and Jasper. I don't think they made Larry. They're too busy watching Hamilton. Should I tell the pilot, so the police will meet them at the gate?"

"Is Olga with them?"

"I didn't see her."

Kate paused for a moment. "Let them go for now. They're just the hired hands, and they won't try anything in the middle of an airport. When the plane lands, send Larry to the Koa Kea Hotel, and you follow Hamilton. Nick and I will tail Horace and Jasper. Hopefully, they'll lead us to the Zellenkova woman, and we can get some answers."

Kate and Nick watched Hamilton leave the terminal and settle himself on a bench to wait for the bus headed to Lihue town. Jake joined him on the bench a couple of minutes later. Hamilton gave him a head nod and went back to listening to music on his earbuds.

Kate pointed to the rental car office across the street. Horace was negotiating for a car, while Jasper kept an eye on Hamilton.

"I hope they're better hit men than they are at surveillance. If Hamilton wasn't in a semi-permanent state of extreme mellow, they would have been spotted long ago," Kate said.

A white and green bus rounded the corner and idled up to the stop. Nick and Kate watched as Hamilton and Jake got on. The doors closed behind them, and the bus slowly lumbered past their parking spot. Seconds later, Horace and Jasper pulled out of the rental car parking lot and followed the bus toward an exit.

Kate put the BMW into drive and caught up to Horace and Jasper at the first traffic light. "I'm going to keep pretty close to them. They're concentrating on the bus and aren't going to be paying much attention to who's following them."

The bus drove straight through the intersection onto Ahukini Road, turned right onto the Kuhio Highway, and stopped at a Walmart in the center of town. Half a dozen people got off, and about the same number got on. The doors closed, and the bus continued north on the highway.

"Hamilton is still on the bus," Kate said.

Nick nodded. "There's pretty much just one main road headed north from here. It more or less hugs the coastline, connecting the towns of Kapaa, Anahola, and Kilauea all the way up to Hanalei."

The bus drove into Old Kapaa Town and down a main street that was lined with small stores selling everything from shave ice to ukuleles.

The bus groaned to a stop in front of the Island Hemp and

Cotton Company building. Hamilton got out and walked down the street into Kapaa Body Art. A sign out front advertised henna tattoos and glitter body art. Horace and Jasper parked their car on the other side of the street and waited.

Kate's cellphone rang. "Hi, Dad."

"Hemp and Cotton wasn't a regularly scheduled stop. He asked the bus driver to let him off there," Jake said. "I couldn't get out too without him getting suspicious."

Horace and Jasper got out of the car, crossed the street, and scanned the area before backing into the store. "Have to go," Kate said. "Those two goons just followed Hamilton into the henna salon, and they look like trouble."

"If Hamilton sees us, our plan is blown," Nick said, running across the street with Kate.

"No choice. Better than Horace and Jasper killing him, or someone else." Kate drew her gun, cracked the door, and peeked inside.

Kapaa Body Art was a large one-room studio with four tattoo-parlor chairs, walls lined with tribal tattoo designs, a back office marked "Staff Only," and bookcases filled to the brim with thousands of glass bottles of henna dyes and glitters. Jasper was standing behind a wooden reception desk and brandishing a large serrated knife in the face of the twenty-year-old woman manning the cash register.

"He's not here, Jasper," Kate heard Horace shout from the back room. "The little bastard must have flown the coop."

Jasper dragged his knife along the desktop, leaving a long, deep, jagged scar in its path. "The blond kid who just came in the store a minute ago. Where is he?"

The twenty-year-old tried to back away from Jasper, but he grabbed her shirt and held tight.

"I don't know," she said. "He left with the owner out the rear entrance. They're friends, and she was going to give him a ride somewhere."

Kate aimed her gun at Jasper. "Hi there. Remember me?"

Jasper swung around to face Kate. "Are you kidding me? What does it take to get rid of you?"

"Put down the knife, you idiot, and get your even stupider partner out here right now."

"Hey, Horace!" Jasper yelled. "The cutie who shot us is back, and she said you're stupid."

A couple of hockey pucks slid out from the back office and rolled into the center of the room. Jasper ducked down behind the counter. "Now you've gone and done it," Jasper said from his hiding place. "The only thing Horace likes more than burning things is blowing things up."

Kate and Nick looked at each other and dove for cover behind the tattoo chairs. There was a tremendously loud boom that shook the foundation of the building and a brilliant flash of light.

"Stun grenades," Kate shouted, disoriented and struggling to get her bearings.

Horace stepped out of the back office, and the salon exploded with the sound of automatic gunfire. Nick and Kate took cover next to the reception desk as bullets sprayed the room, decimating everything in their path, exploding the bottles lining the shelves and filling the room with a thick dust cloud of glitter.

"Do you hear that?" Nick asked Kate.

"I don't hear anything. A flash grenade just exploded ten feet away from me."

"I don't hear anything either. I think they've gone."

Kate stood up and scanned the room. The receptionist was crouched behind the desk looking scared but otherwise unharmed. There were bullet holes in every wall and every piece of furniture. Not a single jar remained intact. Henna dye and shards of glass covered the floor.

Kate stared at Nick, and Nick stared at Kate.

"I'm covered from head to toe in glitter, aren't I?" Kate asked. "The reason I'm curious is that you look like you just returned home from the front lines of the war to end all wars, between the fairies and the pixies."

Nick pointed to a spot on his face just below the corner of his mouth and gestured toward Kate.

"That's the only place I got it?" Kate asked, wiping the corner of her mouth with her index finger. "How do I look now?"

"That was actually the only place on your entire body that

didn't have any glitter." He gave Kate a glittery thumbs-up. "Good news. Now that spot is covered too."

Kate scrubbed at her face, adding an additional multicolored film of metallic flakes to the front of her hand. "Better now?"

"Depends on whether you like this look. I think your face actually got even more glittery."

Kate looked down her shirt. "Good grief. It's under my clothes too. How is that even possible?"

The receptionist stood up from behind the desk. "It's impossible to lose. Sticks to everything. I have to take four showers and vacuum my house twice every day when I get home from work."

"And that gets rid of it?" Kate asked.

"Oh no. I'm still covered in glitter. It's just that then I'm so tired I don't care about it anymore."

Kate looked at Nick. "We lost Hamilton, and those two numbskulls escaped, again. I'm covered in glitter, and I'm half-deaf from that flash grenade. I need something good to happen. When is something good going to happen?"

Nick leaned in to Kate and kissed her lightly on her glittery lips.

"What was that about?" she asked.

"I was hoping it was good. It's all I've got right now."

Kate and Nick spent several hours with the Kauai police, filling out reports and giving them descriptions of Horace and Jasper. They were about to leave when the owner returned to the salon and told them she'd spent a couple of hours surfing with Hamilton in Kilauea before dropping him off in a Hanalei coffee shop.

"Ordinarily, I'd go after Hamilton," Kate said to Nick, "but I have to de-glitter."

"Good decision," Nick said. "I'm all about a little flash when needed, but this is ridiculous."

11

It was almost five o'clock by the time Kate, Nick, and Jake checked into their rooms at the Koa Kea.

Kate stepped out of the shower an hour later, put on a hotel bathrobe, and answered her ringing cellphone. "Hi, Nick."

"Are you glitter-free?"

Kate looked at herself in the mirror. Ninety-nine percent better, but her skin and hair still sparkled under the bathroom lights. "Mostly, but my bedroom floor looks like Tinker Bell lives here, and I'm going to have to burn my clothes. How about you?"

"The same. I'm at your door now. I have your luggage."

Kate opened the door, took the suitcase from Nick, plopped it on the bed, and sorted through the contents. The bohemian chic maxi dresses had been replaced with jeans and T-shirts, and the cut-off shorts had been replaced with Fjällräven hiking clothes.

"Thank goodness," Kate said. "I was starting to get used to the overalls. Scary."

"Happy?" Nick asked.

"You have no idea," Kate said.

"Maybe I should stay while you change. Make sure everything fits."

"Maybe you should wait outside and think about how to best fulfill your lost bet to me."

She pushed Nick out of the room, put on a pair of skinny jeans and a white T-shirt, and joined him in the hallway.

"It's easy to find the restaurant," Nick said. "Just follow the trail of glitter footprints from your room to the pool deck to the hotel entrance. The restaurant is in the lobby."

Kate looked around. The three-story boutique hotel was set up in a U shape, surrounding an understated pool and opening to a family-friendly beach where gentle waves lapped the white sand.

"Kauai feels more intimate than Maui," Kate said.

"Yeah, there's a rule on Kauai that nothing is allowed to be built taller than a coconut tree, so you're not going to find any skyscrapers like you do on Oahu."

They walked into the restaurant and sat down with Jake and Cosmo. Vicky and Larry were at the bar.

"You look good with that glitter still in your hair," Cosmo said to Kate. "I'm not supposed to get near glitter on account of all the Uno men are born cursed with abnormal amounts of static electricity, and static is what makes glitter stick to things, and every time I'm near glitter, it ends up in my eye and I get a scratched cornea, and I have to see the ophthalmologist, and he tells me *'Cosmo, for the last time, no more fucking glitter.'* Also, I'm not supposed to get near balloons or wool socks. Do you know why? Static."

Vicky and Larry sat down at the table. "Have you found my husband yet?" Vicky asked Kate. "I heard you lost Hamilton today and demolished a tattoo parlor. Nice work."

"I prefer to think of Hamilton and the Kahuna as temporarily misplaced," Kate said.

Nick pulled a tourist map of Kauai out of his pocket. "Hamilton was last seen in Hanalei. That's where we'll look tomorrow."

Jake looked at the map. "What makes you think he'll still be there?"

"There's nothing past Hanalei. It's the end of the road. It wouldn't make sense for him to go all the way there, unless he was planning on staying in the area."

"Hamilton was ready for some wilderness hiking. Hanalei is remote, but it's hardly off-grid," Jake said.

Kate snagged a passing waiter. "We were thinking of going to Hanalei tomorrow. Are there any good hiking trails?"

"Only the most famous one on Kauai, the Kalalau Trail. It's eleven miles long and follows the Na Pali coastline. I wouldn't recommend you hike more than the first couple miles, though.

After that it becomes one of the most difficult low-altitude hikes in the world. Very dangerous if you don't know what you're doing, and you officially need a permit to camp in the valley."

"How about unofficially?"

"There's kind of a makeshift community of hippies, free spirits, and dropouts living out there on this amazing beach. Every so often, the rangers hike in and try to clean the 'residents' out, but they mostly just scatter into the valley and wait for the rangers to leave."

Kate turned to Nick once the waiter had left. "Didn't Hamilton tell us he'd stashed his dad somewhere with no roads and no cell service? I think his exact words were 'It's paradise for dropouts.'"

Nick smiled. "It feels right. Who's up for a dangerous, illegal camping trip?"

"Now this is more like it," Jake said. "If it wasn't for the two homicidal maniacs trying to kill us, I would think this trip was going to be all glitter and hippies and stoners."

Larry looked from person to person at the table. "In case nobody has noticed, I'm a little accident prone. I say the Kahuna is probably just staying at a hotel. A nice, safe hotel where nobody will get beaten up, drowned, fall off a cliff, or set on fire."

"Jeez, Larry." Vicky held up her thumb to her ear and her pinky to her mouth. "Ring, ring. Hello." She handed the imaginary phone to Larry. "It's for you. It's your ball sack. He says he's tired of being empty and wants to know when you

113

plan to grow a pair." She hung up the phone. "Good grief. If my fifty-year-old husband and my pothead stepson can do it, we can too."

"Great. It's settled," Nick said. "We'll leave Larry in Hanalei where he can snoop around, just in case we're wrong about the Kahuna hiding at Kalalau. The rest of us should plan to check out of the hotel at five A.M., if we want to be at the trailhead by sunrise. We're going to need every bit of daylight if we hope to make it there in one day."

"I'm going to need hiking shoes," Cosmo said. "All I have with me are dress shoes and sneakers."

"We're going to need a lot more than that in the way of provisions if we're going to do this," Kate said. "Tents and food for starters."

"No worries." Nick got up from the table, walked to the front desk, and returned with a luggage cart full of backpacks. "Based on what Hamilton told us on Maui, I figured we might be doing some camping. I asked a friend of mine who works with Hawaii Forest and Trail to drop off six packs and all the gear we'd need for a three-day wilderness hike. We'll have to redistribute some of the gear in Larry's pack since he's not going."

Kate sorted through the packs. Nick had name tags on each of them. "I see packs for the Colonel, the Weasel, the Cosmonator, Tricky Vicky, and the Smuggler, but I don't see mine." She narrowed her eyes. "All that's left is this one marked 'Snuggler.'"

Jake looked at Kate. "First, you're a hippie and now you're a snuggler. You're not turning into some millennial snowflake, are you?"

"She lost a bet with Nick," Cosmo said. "Now he gets to give all of us cool code names. Personally, I love mine. *The Terminator* is one of my favorite movies."

"I didn't lose," Kate said. "Let's settle this once and for all. We need to find a neutral third party and let him decide who won."

"And the decision is final?" Nick asked. "No welching?"

"Absolutely. We just need to find an impartial judge."

Larry raised his hand. "Back in high school, I was Bulgaria in the model UN."

"I guess, in theory, he is kind of a lawyer, per se," Nick said to Kate.

Kate blew out a sigh. "Let's just get it over with."

Larry tented his fingers after he heard both versions. "It's a difficult case. On the one hand, Nick failed to get the precise location of the Kahuna from Hamilton on the night in question. And, on the other hand, one could make an argument that his plan worked, vis-à-vis, you're going on the Kalalau Trail tomorrow morning, where we expect to find the Kahuna."

"So who won?" Kate asked.

Larry untented his fingers and leaned forward. "I have made my decision. You both lost, per se."

"We both lost? That's not possible."

Larry looked doubtful. "Maybe you both won?"

"Good grief. That's no better." Kate took the backpack and stared down at the name tag. "I'm the Snuggler, either way."

The sun was rising just as the caravan of cars transporting Kate, Nick, Cosmo, Jake, and Vicky pulled into Haena State Park and stopped in front of the Kalalau trailhead sign. Nick and Kate got out of their BMW SUV and waited for the others to join them.

"I did some reading last night. In a couple hours, this parking lot will be filled," Nick said. "It's a popular day hike, but almost everybody stops in the first valley and turns around before getting to the really hairy parts."

Vicky joined them at the trailhead. She was dressed in a skintight, low-cut turquoise tank top designed to expose her midriff, brown short-shorts, white socks, and hiking boots. "Tick, tock. Let's get a move on. I want to get some good selfies on the trail before the sun gets too high."

Jake walked through the parking lot and stopped next to Vicky. "What gives? You look like that character, Lara Croft, from my ten-year-old grandson's video game."

Vicky looked down at her clothes. "Thanks. They're from this movie I starred in before I met the Kahuna. I played a beautiful archaeologist who ventures into dangerous ruins around the world in search of priceless artifacts and ding dongs. Spoiler alert. I found them."

Jake shook his head. "I'm surrounded by cuckoos. All I can

say is, I better get to stomp some bad guys pretty soon." He turned and shouted back to Cosmo, who was struggling with his pack in the parking lot. "Let's go. We're burning daylight."

"I think these socks have some wool in them," Cosmo said. "I'm pretty sure I'm breaking out in a rash. I might need Benadryl. Does anyone have Benadryl?"

Jake took the lead, Vicky followed him, Cosmo followed Vicky, and Kate and Nick brought up the rear. They trudged up the steep, muddy trail and through thick green jungle, soggy with rain from the night before.

Kate stopped for a minute to knock off a layer of the heavy red mud sticking to the bottom of her boots. "It's not coming off. This stuff is deadly."

"Yeah," Nick said. "Think of it as a souvenir. The desk clerk said everyone who visits Kauai goes home with at least some of their clothes stained red from the dirt."

"Kauai is the oldest of the Hawaiian Islands," Cosmo said. "The volcanic rock has such a high iron content that, over millions of years, it's literally rusted away and decomposed into red dirt. I read about it in my guidebook. I thought it would come in handy, so I packed it with my requisitions for travel expenses and per diem allowances. I practically know it all by heart already. If you have a question you can ask me. If it's not in my guidebook I can google it, as long as I have cell service and my battery isn't dead. I charge my phone every night so that almost never happens."

A light dusting of rain came and went and came again, before turning into a downpour. Little torrents of water drained through the underbrush and onto the trail, creating a stream of water than ran downhill toward them. Kate could see Vicky and Cosmo a short way off, struggling to stay upright in the soupy mud. Jake was in the distance, rounding a bend and disappearing from her sight.

"Dad's in his element," Kate said. "I don't think we'll see him again until our regroup spot in the first valley."

The trail continued to climb through the rainforest, slowly growing less dense and offering spectacular peekaboo views of the bright blue Pacific Ocean hundreds of feet below.

"We're about halfway to the top," Nick said. "The trail rises to around six hundred feet from sea level in just one mile."

Kate wiped the rain from her face as they caught up to Cosmo. He was lying on his back, trying to right himself, and covered from head to toe in red mud.

"I might have slipped one or two or a hundred times. Are we almost there?" he asked.

"Almost," Nick said. "Only ten and a half miles to go."

"This is an eleven-mile trail," Cosmo said. "We only walked half a mile, so far? Are we at least almost to the top?"

"Absolutely. The good news is that, once we reach the summit, it's all downhill to Hanakapiai Beach. The bad news is after that there are four more valleys to cross and five thousand feet more of total elevation gain before we get to

Kalalau. And, what's waiting for us past Hanakapiai makes this first part look like a walk in the park."

Fifteen minutes later, Kate and Nick were at the summit. Gusty winds coming from the exposed cliffside blew heavy rain at them, seemingly from all directions.

"Even in this weather, it's gorgeous," Kate said, looking out over the cliffs at the ocean.

They started their descent toward the first valley. Once they were back in the rainforest, the winds died down, but the steep trail was quickly becoming a muddy river of red glop.

"This is pretty slow going. I think the way down might be even harder than the way up," Kate said. "Hard to believe Hamilton did this in the dark last night."

"I'm sure he's walked the trail before and is familiar with it," Nick said. "And for that matter, we're not sure he's ahead of us. Or if he stopped halfway and continued on at first light. Have you thought about what you're going to do if you find the Kahuna in the valley? He may not be cooperative. He probably has something to hide if he felt running was a better option than going to the police."

Kate held out her hands to balance herself as she stepped down over a slippery rock ledge. "Olga Zellenkova tried to kill his son. I'm hoping that will be enough to convince him that he needs help."

The rain was slowing to a drizzle and sunlight was beginning to peek through the clouds, revealing previously hidden hilltops and vistas. As the sun heated the wet canopy and grasses surrounding them, the humidity levels quickly skyrocketed, leaving Kate and Nick feeling wetter than they had in the morning downpour.

"Have you checked in with Jessup?" Nick asked. "Your seventy-two hours ended today."

"I called him last night. He's not happy." Kate turned to look back at Nick. "Apparently, somebody has been buying haunted ice cream trucks and expensive bottles of wine using stolen FBI vouchers signed by an Agent Karl Ketchup, Los Angeles branch FBI field office manager."

"It's probably just one of his top cops, having some fun. We cops love pranking each other."

Kate shook her head. "Anyway, between the vouchers, a blown-up tattoo parlor, and a tourist boat sunk to the bottom of the ocean, he told me not to bother coming back from Hawaii without the Kahuna."

"Ouch. What about me?" Nick asked.

"He said you're welcome to come back. He has a room at a federal penitentiary waiting for you."

"I guess we better find the Kahuna."

The path was beginning to flatten as they approached Hanakapiai Beach, and Kate could hear the sound of rushing water in the distance. "You know me," she said. "I wasn't planning on coming back without him anyway."

Nick and Kate rounded a bend. Jake, Cosmo, and Vicky were all standing in front of a fast-moving river of water that emptied into an angry-looking ocean a short distance downstream. A handmade sign by the rocky beach warned not to go near the waves, with an ominous-looking eighty or so tally marks underneath the crude handwriting.

"I don't like the looks of this sign," Cosmo said. "I'm not that good a swimmer. I don't want to become the next hash mark. There's still stuff I have to do. I've been thinking about getting a cat. And I haven't filled out all our vouchers."

Vicky rolled her eyes. "I didn't squeeze myself into this sexy archeologist outfit just to be stopped by a little water. If there's one thing I learned from being a sexy adult film archeologist, it's that you've got to take some risks if you want to find priceless artifacts and ding-dongs."

"I must be losing it," Jake said. "Except for the part about the ding-dongs, she's starting to make sense."

Nick opened his backpack, removed a sixty-meter length of blue nylon climbing rope, and attached one end to a hala tree growing near the bank. "I'm going to swim across with the rope. Once I'm on the other side, I'll secure the other end to another tree, and we can all use it to cross safely."

Kate watched Nick wade into the water. "If you get in trouble, keep holding on to the rope and we'll haul you back in to shore."

"Don't worry. I'm not letting go of the rope. If I get pushed out to sea and get caught in the riptide, the nearest safe shore exit point is six miles away."

After a couple of feet, Nick was in waist-deep water and

fighting to stay upright. He dove in headfirst and started swimming diagonally against the current.

"He's a pretty strong swimmer," Jake said to Kate. "He would smoke most of those guys I worked with in Special Forces."

Nick reached the other side, climbed out of the water, secured his end of the rope to a heliotrope tree, and gave Kate a thumbs-up. "The current is pretty strong," he shouted. "I have rock-climbing carabiners in my pack. Everyone can use them to attach themselves to the rope so they won't get swept away."

Jake snapped a carabiner onto the rope, waded into the water, and pulled himself across.

Vicky and Cosmo each crossed separately until only Kate was left on the opposite shore. She attached the carabiner, strapped herself into Nick's pack, and stepped into the water. By the time she got to the middle, her toes could no longer touch bottom, and the force of the current was immense. "I think the water level is rising," she shouted to Nick.

A massive roar pierced the valley. Kate turned to look upstream. A wall of water and debris was barreling down the mountain toward her at breakneck speed. "Flash flood," Kate shouted, bracing herself for the impact. "Everyone take cover."

The initial impact of the water felt like a car crash and left her breathless. She struggled to keep her head above the swirling vortex and looked to the shore. Vicky and Cosmo had made it to higher ground and were out of the flood's path. Jake and Nick had their arms wrapped around the heliotrope tree, which was now mostly underwater, and were trying their best to make certain the rope stayed secure.

"Hold on," Nick shouted. "We'll get you out as soon as we can."

"I'm not going anywhere," Kate yelled over the roar of the water. She looked over at the opposite shore. The hala tree was bending under the force of the water. Seconds later it was uprooted and swept away, along with Kate, toward the ocean.

Kate collided with a log wedged between two rocks and held tight. The force of the water continued to relentlessly push her toward the crashing waves, just meters away. She watched as debris raced past her into the surf and was quickly swept out to sea by the powerful rip currents.

"I'm not sure how much longer I can hold on to this log," Kate shouted toward shore. She looked over. Jake had tied himself to the heliotrope and was holding on to the rope, but Nick was nowhere to be seen. A tree branch hit Kate, her grip gave way, and she felt herself being sucked, feetfirst, under the log.

Kate felt an arm wrap around her chest and pull her back to the surface. She blew out the water filling her mouth and looked up. Nick was holding her tightly and working to secure the rope around both of them. A minute or so later, the water subsided enough that Jake was finally able to haul them back to shore.

Kate and Nick lay on their backs, exhausted, and watched the water level recede just as quickly as it rose.

"What were you thinking?" Kate said, still holding on to Nick. "You could have drowned."

Nick flashed her a crooked smile. "What can I say? If there's one thing I've learned from sexy archaeologists, it's that you have to take risks for priceless things."

Kate punched him in the arm. "And ding-dongs. Don't forget the ding-dongs."

12

By midmorning, the clouds had dissipated and the bright tropical sun was starting to dry off the rainforest, leaving behind an oppressive humidity that wrapped around Nick, Kate, Cosmo, and Vicky like a wet wool blanket. Jake was far ahead of them.

The group trudged up the steep path through a grove of massive sisal plants with rosettes of giant sword-shaped leaves.

"They look like prehistoric agave plants," Vicky said, touching one of the sisal's leaves. "I'd kill for a Fred Flintstone-sized tequila right now."

The path continued through the sisals, getting progressively more narrow and unkempt as they neared the top of the hill.

Kate stopped and looked back at Nick. "We're clearly past

the tourist turnaround. This is definitely a lot less used than the first section."

At the summit, Jake was waiting for them near a large rock formation.

"I think this is Space Rock. It marks the highest part of the trail," Nick said. "Hoolulu Valley is a short distance downhill. At this point, we're a little less than eight miles from Kalalau Beach."

Kate looked out over the edge of the precipice at the waves crashing into the cliffside, seven hundred feet below. "That's one big drop. I've been a lot of places, but the scenery here is some of the most dramatic I've ever seen."

A couple of miles later, they had walked down the hill, through Hoolulu and Waiahuakua Valleys, and were making yet another steep ascent. Ahead of them, waterfalls tumbled down huge green undulating cliffs into the jungle, and the trail weaved in and out of the rainforest, revealing spectacular views down the Na Pali coastline.

"We're halfway to Kalalau," Nick said. "The next valley is called Hanakoa. It would be a great place to break for lunch and get some rest before we tackle the last five miles of the trail."

Kate, Nick, Jake, Cosmo, and Vicky walked over the summit and down into Hanakoa. The lush rainforest was nestled between two ridges that guarded the green valley like sentries.

"A lot of people break the hike up into two days and stay here overnight," Nick said as they walked along the valley floor, past an unoccupied campsite and onto a narrow side trail.

"Where are we going?" Kate asked as they walked deeper into the valley's interior.

"Pit stop," Nick said. "It's just a short walk."

The side trail opened up to reveal a three-hundred-foot-tall waterfall cascading into an enormous pond. The water was crystal clear and the pond was surrounded by lush jungle and the sounds of songbirds hiding in the canopy.

Kate let out a low whistle. "This is just the pit stop? I can't wait to see the main attraction."

Nick removed his backpack and stripped down to his boxer briefs. "I don't know about everybody else, but I'm going for a swim before lunch," he said, and dove into the water.

Vicky poked Kate with her elbow. "There's your main attraction," she said. "Yum!" She got a camera out of her backpack and took off her turquoise tank top. "I haven't frolicked in at least twenty-four hours. Who's going to take pictures of me frolicking in the water for my Instagram wall?"

Jake had his back to Vicky. "She's topless, isn't she?" he asked Kate.

"Yep."

"I guess I could do it," Cosmo said. "Being as it's for Instagram. Is it hard to frolic?"

Vicky stood with her hands on her hips. "What kind of a question is that? Of course it's hard to frolic! If just anybody could do it, we'd all be having girl-on-girl pillow fights and running slow-motion in bikinis on beaches and accidentally on purpose losing our tops on water park slides, and then there wouldn't be any need for Instagram models. What kind of a world would that be?"

Cosmo took the camera. "I never thought of that. Where do you want to frolic first?"

Kate watched Cosmo go off with Vicky, while Jake returned to the campsite to pull lunch together. Nick was still hanging out near the waterfall. She shucked her clothes down to her sports bra and spandex bikini-cut panties and swam over to Nick.

"I want to thank you for saving my life this morning," Kate said.

"It's what us heroic types do," Nick said. "How grateful are you? Do I get a reward?"

Oh man, Kate thought. Not only did he deserve a reward, but she was in the mood to give him one. Good thing they were in a group and the reward possibilities would be limited.

"What did you have in mind?" Kate asked.

Nick swam closer and pulled her to him. "I like the sports bra. It's a good look for you, but you'd look even better without it."

Kate wrapped her legs around him. "Would that be reward enough?"

"It would be a start."

"Hey, Smuggler and Snuggler," Vicky called from shore,

waving at them. "Let's go. All this frolicking has made me crazy hungry. Jake has lunch ready for us at the campsite."

"We could skip lunch," Nick said to Kate.

Kate unwrapped her legs. "No way. I need food. I'm wasting away in this steamy jungle."

"Get used to it," Nick said. "There's a strong possibility it's only going to get steamier."

At two o'clock, Kate, Nick, Jake, Cosmo, and Vicky stood in front of a sign posted just to the side of the trail's seven-mile marker, reading "Hazardous Cliff, Risk of Serious Injury or Death, Stay Back from Edge."

"They call this the Crawler's Ledge," Nick said, staring straight ahead. "I guess that probably doesn't need any explanation."

Kate looked at the trail in front of them. A barely eighteen-inch-wide dirt path led along the cliff face as far as she could see. On the right side of the path, there was a terrifying drop the length of a football field directly into the Pacific Ocean. On the other side of the path, a wall of rock rose straight out of the ground, extending a good hundred vertical feet above them.

"I don't see any guardrail or handholds," Kate said. "One tiny slip and we're dead."

Cosmo reread the sign. "How are we supposed to stay away from the edge? The entire path is literally the edge.

Whoever wrote this sign is a maniac. Holy crap. Who has some Xanax?"

"It doesn't look so bad," Jake said. He took a few steps out onto the ledge. A thirty-mile-per-hour gust of wind blew in from the open ocean and smashed into the cliff. Jake steadied himself and waited for the breeze to die down. He turned around and looked at Kate. "Okay. It's bad. It's really bad."

"Who doesn't feel comfortable doing this?" Kate asked. "If anybody wants to bail, they can go back to Hanakoa and wait until the rest of us return."

Jake tightened the cinch on his backpack. "Are you kidding? I live for this stuff."

"The Kahuna might be a big dummy, but he's my big dummy," Vicky said. "I'm going."

"I'm kind of the senior agent." Cosmo shrugged. "What kind of a role model would I be if I let the rookie handle all the tough stuff by herself?"

"You think I'm going to let you go off by yourself and have all the fun?" Nick stepped past the sign and started walking. "Let's go find us a kahuna."

Kate followed Nick and carefully made her way along the ledge. Vicky and Cosmo were right behind her. Jake was taking up the rear.

"This seems like a good time for me to mention that I get a teensy bit flatulent when I get nervous," Cosmo said to Jake. "My ex-girlfriend is an amateur psychologist, and she says it all comes from my bottling up my emotions and not crying enough, or was it crying too much? Anyway, it turns out I have a dysfunctional relationship with myself. Bottom line is you might want to keep your distance."

"A mile sounds about right," Jake said. "Maybe a continent."

Another gust of wind knocked into them, and everyone leaned in against the rock wall to their left.

Kate looked at the warning sign, less than three hundred feet back. "At this pace, it's going to take us forever—that is, if we don't fall off the cliff first."

Nick felt his way forward. "Look at it this way. In the past twenty-four hours, we've been shot at by hit men, nearly burned alive, exploded a tattoo parlor, and almost drowned twice. What are the chances of falling off a cliff if all those things didn't kill us?"

The path widened just a little bit in spots, here and there, over the next half mile. "Maybe it's my imagination," Cosmo said. "I think the trail is getting a little easier, or else I'm just getting used to it, or maybe I'm finally running low on, you know, air biscuits."

Nick stopped. "You need to hang on to your air biscuits, because easier is coming to an end."

Kate looked past Nick. The narrow path had gotten narrower. Much narrower. And rocky. And the wind was still gusting.

"Here's a suggestion," Nick said. "There's a reason they call this Crawler's Ledge. Crawl over the rocky spots and sharp bends in the trail if you aren't comfortable upright."

Vicky instantly dropped to hands and knees, reached behind her, and passed Cosmo her cellphone. "This is a great opportunity to take a few belfies for my Instagram page."

"What's a belfie?" Cosmo asked.

"It's a selfie of your butt. It's kind of the go-to selfie for us Instagram models."

"How about that?" Cosmo called back to Jake. "Did you know there was more than one kind of selfie?"

"Kate, switch positions with me," Jake shouted. "This is worse than when I was a prisoner of war in that Vietnamese internment camp."

"There are ten basic types of selfies," Vicky said, concentrating on hand and knee placement. "The I-woke-up-like-this selfie, the fur-baby selfie, the bragging-beach-legs selfie, the bathroom mirror selfie, the food-next-to-your-face selfie, the lazy Sunday selfie, the gym selfie, and the I'm-so-drunk selfie, in addition to belfies and regular selfies, which I call relfies."

"I only take relfies," Cosmo said, struggling to stay on the treacherous path while holding Vicky's phone. "How about you, Jake?"

"That's not all," Vicky said. "There are nine kinds of selfie faces, not including advanced faces and specialty faces. The duck face, the fish gape, the kissy face, the model pout, the flirty half smile, the raised eyebrow, the smize, the squinch, and the sparrow face. You can see how this is adding up."

"Amazing," Cosmo said, snapping a picture of Vicky's butt.

"Nine faces times ten types. That's ninety different selfies in total. How do you keep it all straight?"

"Larry keeps an Excel spreadsheet." She looked back at Cosmo. "Are you getting some good ones? How does my ass look? I bet it looks awesome."

"It looks pretty good. These are the first belfies I've ever taken, so I'm not really an expert. What do you think, Jake? Does Vicky's ass look awesome?"

"I'm going to jump," Jake said. "It'll be less painful."

"I'm not looking for a yes-man. This is important," Vicky said. "Is it big enough? Do I need to do more squats?"

"Nick, Kate, are we almost there?" Jake asked. "Please tell me we're almost there."

"Hold up," Cosmo said. "I'll take another belfie."

Cosmo raised the phone to snap the picture, and a gust of wind hit him and knocked him off balance. He slid off the trail, shrieking and clawing at the scrub brush that lined the ledge. Jake lunged at him and grabbed him by the seat of his pants, snagging Cosmo an instant before he would have gone into a free fall and smashed far below on the rocks and surf. Jake hauled him back over the rock face and onto the hard-packed red dirt.

Everyone stopped while Cosmo lay facedown in the dirt, panting, still holding the phone.

"You saved my life," Cosmo said to Jake.

"Yeah, I acted on instinct," Jake said. "I don't suppose we could have a do-over?"

A quarter mile later, the path moved inland and climbed steeply through the forest. Nick trudged up the hill and looked at his watch. "It's four o'clock. We've been walking for ten hours," he said to Kate.

Jake was ahead of them, standing on a bluff and leaning on a Little Free Library that someone had erected as an informal book exchange for fellow travelers. "You've got to see this," he called back.

Kate, Nick, Vicky, and Cosmo scrambled up to meet Jake on the bluff. It overlooked a beautiful crescent-shaped white sand beach, fronting a lush green valley.

"That's Kalalau at the bottom of the hill," Nick said. "We should be there in less than an hour."

"It's bigger than I thought," Kate said.

Nick scanned the area. "Less than a week ago, our search area was forty million square miles. Now it's more like two. I like our new odds."

The sun had long since set by the time Nick, Kate, and the others reached the bottom of the valley and found an unoccupied space to pitch their tents in the makeshift campground. Kate crawled into her sleeping bag and turned to Nick. "I'm dead tired. Let's get a good night's sleep and start looking for the Kahuna as soon as the sun comes up."

"Are you absolutely one hundred percent sure you're tired?"

Kate opened one eye and glanced at Nick. "Good grief. Go to sleep."

13

Kate woke up to a sunny day and the sound of a flute. She unzipped her tent and peeked outside. A hippie in his midsixties, wearing a Harry Potter robe and Birkenstock sandals, was sitting cross-legged on a nearby rock playing "Puff, the Magic Dragon." Nick and Jake were busy cooking a pot of oatmeal in the fire pit. Cosmo and Vicky were still sleeping.

Kate stretched and sat down next to Nick. "That was one tough eleven hours yesterday. I don't think I've slept so soundly in a year." She looked at the flutist. "What's with Dumbledore on the rock?"

"That's Bob. He told me the robe has a secret pocket meant for a wand where he can store his flute. Plus, he's a wizard."

Kate rolled her eyes. "The scary thing is he's probably going to be the most normal person we meet today."

Bob stopped playing, holstered his flute inside his robe, walked over to them, and plopped himself down on a log. "That oatmeal smells good. May I join you Muggles?"

Nick handed Bob a bowl and a spoon. "Have you been living here a long time?"

"About ten years, I guess." Bob spooned a giant glob of oatmeal into his mouth. "There are thirty or forty of us who live here full-time, but I'm the only wizard. Most everybody else camps for a few days then moves on."

Kate showed Bob a picture of the Kahuna and another of Hamilton. "We're looking for a couple friends of ours. Have you seen them?"

Bob looked at the pictures. "The young one hiked in here yesterday and hung out at the beach playing with Old Reliable for most of the day."

"Who's Old Reliable?" Kate asked.

"Not who. What. It's the communal slingshot we use to chuck coconuts into the ocean on game night."

Kate smiled. "Sounds like fun. And the other man?"

"The older one showed up a week ago. I haven't seen him since, but he's got to be in the valley somewhere."

"Why?"

"Impassable cliffs to the west and south. Impassable ocean to the north." He pointed east, back in the direction of the Kalalau Trail. "That's the only way in and out, and we keep an eye on it in case the park rangers decide to visit. Technically, we're not supposed to be here."

Kate spooned out another bowl of oatmeal for Bob. "Sounds like you know this valley like the back of your hand. What do you think about helping us find our friends?"

"Sounds like a nice break," Bob said. "Every day, it's the same old thing around here. If I have to listen to Naked Gary argue with Naked Susan one more time about what's the better kind of yoga, Hatha or Ashtanga, I'm going to have to up my 'shrooms."

"It's probably better to stay away from yoga entirely if your first name is Naked," Nick said.

"Great point. I'll bring it up during my next audience with the Minister of Magic. How about if I meet you at the Kalalau Valley Trail in thirty minutes. You can't miss it. It's a two-mile spur off the main trail that leads to the back of the valley."

Kate watched Bob disappear into the forest. "I guess we have a tour guide."

"I'll keep an eye on the trail while you're searching the valley," Jake said. "We don't want Hamilton or his father to slip past us."

Nick and Kate finished their breakfasts and loaded some water and food into one of the backpacks.

"When Cosmo and Vicky wake up, I think they should hang out at the beach," Kate said, slinging the pack over her shoulder. "Maybe we'll get lucky and the Kahuna will show up there at some point today."

Kate and Nick backtracked along the same path they'd followed the night before to reach their campsite. Bob was already waiting for them by the Kalalau Valley Trail junction.

"Most of us live near the beach," Bob said as he led them into the forest and down an embankment to a small stream. "But there are three or four people who camp in the valley. One of them will probably have seen your friends if they're here."

Kate and Nick followed Bob across the stream and turned left onto a narrow path that led along the streambed deeper into the rainforest. The path stopped in front of a medium-sized cave embedded in a rocky cliff.

"*Mike!*" Bob shouted into the hole in the rock face.

Nick stared at the cave opening. "Who's Mike?"

"He's kind of the head hermit around here," Bob said.

"Maybe he's not home," Kate said.

Bob shook his head. "It's that he's always all reclusive and solitary before his second cup of coffee." He removed a flashlight from his robe and waved it at the entrance. "*Lumos,*" he said, pushing the on button and illuminating a disheveled thirty-something man with a mop of scraggly brown hair and an even more scraggly looking beard.

"This here's Mike the Hermit," Bob said.

Mike covered his eyes. "Jeez, Bob. How about a little patience? You don't need to blind me." He stepped out of the cave, snatched the flashlight from Bob's hands, and threw it into the forest.

138

"There's a reason why he's a hermit," Bob said. "No social skills."

"I have social skills up my butt," Mike said. "I prefer not to use them. They lead to distractions and annoyances and intrusions . . . like this one. And I hate small talk, so get to the point for this visit."

"We're looking for some friends, and we were hoping you might have seen them," Kate said. She took off her backpack and searched for the photos of Hamilton and the Kahuna. "Just a second. I know they're in here somewhere."

Mike watched Kate rummage through the pack. He gave his head a small shake and turned to Bob. "Did you hear about the new hermit who just moved into the forest? Tanya went over to check him out, and she said his hidey hole was a real pigsty. Moss all over the place, and his berries weren't even sorted. She thinks he drinks, but you didn't hear it from me."

"Tanya is one to talk," Bob said. "She got drunk at the hermit potluck last month and told Grace's boyfriend Stanley she wanted his 'p' in her 'v.' I overheard it firsthand."

"And?"

"Apparently he took her up on it and dipped his wick."

Mike went wide-eyed. "No-o. What did Grace do?"

"She broke up with him. You should have heard the scene they made. She threw him and his goat right out of their cave that same night."

"No loss there," Mike said. "I never liked Stanley. I mean, what's with that burlap sack he goes around wearing? What self-respecting modern-day hermit wears a burlap sack? It's pure showboating."

Kate slid a glance in Nick's direction. "Good thing hermits don't like small talk," she said.

"Gossip isn't small talk," Bob said. "Small talk is polite conversation that doesn't mean anything. Gossip isn't polite."

Kate fished the pictures out of her knapsack and handed them to Mike.

"Sure, I've seen these guys," Mike said. "The older one's been tent camping near the waterfall at the back of the valley. The younger one is there too, but he just showed up yesterday." He gave the pictures to Kate and stuck his hand out palm up. Nick put a twenty-dollar bill in it, and Mike walked back into his cave.

Bob led Kate and Nick through the forest and along a muddy game trail.

"The waterfall is about a mile up this path," Bob said. "It should take us about thirty minutes. The trail gets pretty rough ahead."

Kate pushed through the wet underbrush that was becoming denser with nearly every passing step. Soon the trail was running alongside a small stream strewn with boulders and inviting little swimming holes.

"This is as far as I go," Bob said. "You don't need me anymore. Just follow the creek until you get to the waterfall. You can't miss it."

A half hour later, Nick and Kate stood at the edge of the

jungle and peered through the clearing at a two-hundred-foot waterfall showering down into a crystal clear pool of water below. On the banks of the pool, two identical North Face dome tents had been erected around a makeshift campsite.

"I don't see Hamilton or the Kahuna, but someone is definitely living here," Kate said. "The embers in the fire pit are still smoking."

Nick pointed to a clothesline strung between two hala trees. An assortment of board shirts, T-shirts, socks, and men's underwear were drying in the morning sun. "And it looks like laundry day. If it's Hamilton and his father, they're settled in for the long haul."

A man in his early fifties wearing Volcom board shorts, flip-flops, and a loose-fitting tan hoodie walked out of the forest into the east side of the clearing carrying a load of branches. He dropped them on the ground in front of the fire pit and pulled his salt-and-pepper shoulder-length hair back into a man bun. Hamilton stuck his head out of one of the tents and joined his father by the fire pit.

"Looks like we found the Kahuna," Kate said to Nick.

"All thanks to a wizard, a gossipy hermit, and my brilliant plan," Nick said.

Hamilton and his father watched Nick and Kate cross the clearing and walk into their campsite.

"Hey, I know that dude," Hamilton said to his father,

pointing to Nick. "He's, like, that guy who lives next door and drives an ice cream truck."

Kate showed her FBI credentials to the older man. "Mr. Wylde?"

The man in the tan hoodie had a grim set to his mouth. "'Mr. Wylde' is what my seven-hundred-dollar-per-hour stick-up-his-ass lawyer calls me. Everyone else just calls me the Kahuna or the Big Kahuna or just plain BK if you're in a rush. How did you find me?" He glanced at Hamilton. "Let me guess."

"No way, Dad. I was totally all discreet. The only ones who even knew I was coming to Kauai were this super-chill surfer here and his uptight lady friend. They drove me to the airport."

Kate narrowed her eyes ever so slightly. "I'm not uptight."

"Like, maybe you just got too much going on," Hamilton said. "With the hemp farming and candle making and FBI. Working for the FBI has to be a hella stressful job, what with having to be around the criminal element all day. Stress will take years off your life, dude."

Kate stared at Nick. "Tell me something I don't know." She turned to the Big Kahuna. "A lot of people are looking for you."

"I'm aware," Big Kahuna said. "That's why I'm hiding out here."

"Did Hamilton tell you one of them sent hit men to your Maui farm?"

The Kahuna put his hand on Hamilton's shoulder.

"I was going to get around to it, Dad. I didn't want you to worry. They were just a couple losers."

"Those losers were trying to kill you," Kate said. "If we hadn't stopped them, they would have burned your house, and half of the North Shore, to the ground."

The Kahuna shook his head. "I didn't think they'd go after my family."

"Who are they?" Nick asked.

"I wish I knew. I think someone is stealing intellectual property from Sentience. I was trying to track them down when things got weird."

"'Weird'?"

"People following me. Threatening phone calls in the middle of the night telling me to stop poking around."

"What did you do?"

The Kahuna smiled. "What else? I poked around twice as hard. Then someone almost ran me down in a parking lot, so I decided to take off until I could figure things out."

"Why didn't you call the police?"

"I don't have any proof. Only suspicions."

"Still, we could have helped. We have forensic detectives who specialize in investigating these sorts of crimes," Kate said.

The Kahuna shrugged. "I guess so, but Sentience doesn't make cars or televisions. We develop artificial intelligence algorithms for the robotics industry. All we have is our intellectual property. There are a lot of good people who have invested their entire lives in the company. If it ever got out that our trade secrets were stolen, we could kiss the dream of becoming a publicly traded company goodbye."

"That sounds a little extreme," Nick said. "It would be a scandal, but I doubt it would totally derail the company."

The Kahuna had a hard set to his mouth. "Did I mention that some of the stuff we're working on has military applications?"

Kate's eyebrows raised slightly. "You're working for the military?"

"Not specifically, but AI is just technology. Like most technology, it could make the world a better place or a much more dangerous place. It all depends on how it's used."

Hamilton scratched his head. "Dude, Dad. Haven't you seen *The Matrix* or *Westworld*? Robots always start out all helpful and sexy before they become crazy murdery."

"Holy crap, Hamilton. I am not building a sexy robot army. I'm just creating software so other people can make things like smart houses and self-driving cars."

"And sexy robot armies," Hamilton said.

The Big Kahuna flashed a small grimace in Hamilton's direction. "Look, I don't even know what, if anything, was taken from my computers. Even if they got something, chances are it was encrypted."

"And that's why you faked your own death and flew to Hawaii?" Kate asked.

"I didn't know who I could trust. Whoever broke into my server had to be someone close to me. Besides, it's not exactly the first time I've gone off the grid, so I figured no one would raise too much of a fuss."

Kate looked at Nick, then back at the Kahuna. "With all due respect, I think you might be in over your head," she said. "What if we told you we think Zellenkova Private Equity might be involved?"

"You mean Olga? Not a chance. She's one of my biggest investors. She stands to lose everything."

"How much is 'everything'?" Kate asked.

"Let's just say there are a hundred million reasons why she wants Sentience to go public."

"It's the one reason she *doesn't* want it to go public that interests us," Nick said. "It looks like the CEOs of the companies in which Zellenkova invests have a nasty habit of dying."

"It doesn't make sense. There's got to be some other explanation."

"Zellenkova is probably on Kauai right now with the hit men who showed up at Hamilton's place," Nick said. "She tried to kill your wife's lawyer, Larry. The police are looking for Zellenkova and her two thugs as we speak."

The Kahuna sat down on a rock. "Well, I can't hold that against her. Everybody wants to kill Larry." He sighed. "I guess I can go home to my crazy hot, but mostly crazy, wife. It's only a matter of time until you find and arrest Olga."

"Arresting Olga might not be in our best interest right

now," Kate said. "We want to make sure we catch everyone involved, so we don't want to tip our hand too soon. Someone is murdering Silicon Valley billionaires and possibly stealing military-grade A1 software. I don't see Olga masterminding all that."

Nick nodded. "I agree. I think Olga is just a high-priced grifter working for someone else. Someone who's trying very hard to stay out of the spotlight. We need to give her room to run, and hopefully she'll lead us to her boss."

The Big Kahuna smiled. "At least I don't need to go home to my wife yet."

"The good news is you don't have to go home to your wife," Kate said. "The bad news is she's waiting for you on Kalalau Beach. We need to break camp and get you into protective custody. It isn't safe here."

14

Kate and Nick helped Hamilton and his father break down their camp. They packed up, set off on the long walk back to the beach, and by the time they got to the trailhead it was almost three o'clock.

Jake was waiting for them at the junction. "We've got a big problem. Horace and Jasper showed up with a half dozen other gorillas about an hour ago. They're searching the beach and campground."

Kate looked at Hamilton. "Horace and Jasper are the two goons who tried to burn down your farm on Maui. Looks like they've brought in reinforcements."

"What do you want me to do?" Jake asked. "Is it stomping time?"

"Not yet," Nick said. "We need to flush out their boss, but

first we need to get the Kahuna and Hamilton out of this valley."

"It's not going to be easy," Jake said. "The bad guys are crawling all over the place, and there are a couple helicopters making passes up and down the coast. The locals think it's the park rangers looking for squatters, but if you ask me, they're part of the Horace and Jasper team, scouting the area."

"You, Cosmo, and Vicky should be okay," Kate said. "Horace and Jasper have never seen any of you, so they won't think too much about it if you break camp. We'll hide out in the jungle until dark and wait for you to meet us there. We'll hike out at midnight. With any luck, we'll be back at Haena State Park by noon tomorrow."

"The trail is risky in daylight," Jake said. "I can't see Cosmo and Vicky surviving it at night."

"The only other choice is to hide in the valley and wait for them to find us. And eventually they will find us. There's only one way out, and a night hike is our only option if we want to sneak past Olga's crew and the helicopters."

"We could leave Cosmo and Vicky here," Jake said. "We'll make better time without them."

"It's an option," Kate said, "but it's going to have to be their choice, because there's a good possibility that when Horace and Jasper run out of patience, no one is going to be safe on this beach."

"Point taken," Jake said.

Jake marched back to the beach, and Kate led her group

back into the rainforest. After a quarter mile she found a spot that felt secure, and everyone dropped their packs.

"Don't wander too far away," Kate said. "If you hear me whistle, hide as best you can and stay there until I give an all clear."

Hamilton and the Kahuna went to the stream to refill their water bottles. Nick and Kate sat on the forest floor with their backs against a moss-covered tree trunk.

"I'd kill for a bacon cheeseburger," Kate said.

"I'd kill for another shot at the waterfall scene," Nick said. "We have some time before Jake shows up. There's a private little pond up ahead."

"You can't be serious."

"Why not?"

"We're babysitting those two," she said, pointing toward the two men at the stream. "Plus, there's a small army of mercenaries after us."

"So if there wasn't an army of killers after us, it would be game on?"

"Only if it included a bacon cheeseburger."

"A bacon cheeseburger can't compare to what I have to offer," Nick said.

Kate closed her eyes. "I'm too tired and hungry to process that. You need to come up with a plan to get us out of this mess. Something that doesn't involve Cosmo and Vicky falling off the trail and plunging to their deaths in the middle of the night."

"And?"

"And something that doesn't involve getting me naked."

"I'll try," Nick said, "but fair warning. All my best plans involve you getting naked."

At 11 P.M., Kate heard Jake calling for her near the Valley Trail junction. She made her way out of the dark jungle to the trailhead with Nick, Hamilton, and the Kahuna. Jake was waiting for her there with Bob. "Where are Vicky and Cosmo?"

"They'll be here in a couple minutes. Horace and Jasper are all over the campground. We split up, so we wouldn't draw more attention to ourselves."

"What about Bob?"

Jake smiled. "Before Bob moved to Kalalau and became a wizard, he was a United States Marine. Turns out he's collected a couple souvenirs that might come in handy right about now."

Bob reached under his robe and pulled out a Heckler and Koch M320 military-grade grenade launcher with a night vision scope. "I got it in the First Great Wizarding War. I also got a crate of old plantation-era dynamite, but I'm saving it for a special occasion."

Kate took the M320 from Bob and looked it over. "It's a bit of an overkill, don't you think?"

"Fortunately, that happens to be my favorite kind of killing," Jake said, holding up a seventeen-inch-long, forty-millimeter-in-diameter gray torpedo with two sets of fins.

"That doesn't look like a grenade," Nick said.

"It's a Pike mini-missile. Powered by a rocket motor. Laser guidance system accurate to within five yards. Range of more than a mile. Designed by Raytheon to be used with the M320. Unfortunately, Bob only has this one, so we'll have to make it count."

Kate shook her head. "You promised not to shoot anybody."

"And I'm not going to have to, since there won't be anything left to shoot after this baby blows them into a million pieces." Jake held up his hand. "I know, I know. You don't have to say it. How about if we only use it in an emergency?"

Kate tilted her head back. "Ugh."

"Great." Jake gave her a thumbs-up. "I'll take that as a hard maybe."

The Kahuna looked down the trail toward the campground. "I think somebody's coming. Maybe it's Vicky. Did you tell her I'm here?" he asked Jake.

Jake fiddled with the night vision scope on the M320. "Sure, I did. Right after we had a cup of tea and talked about our feelings."

The Kahuna smiled. "She's a firecracker, but it's not the first time I've gone on an impromptu walkabout. She's usually pretty cool about it."

Hamilton grinned. "Last time she slipped you a Mickey, and when you woke up you were on a Japanese fishing trawler in the middle of the Indian Ocean."

"Best two weeks of my life. I'm going back out with those guys next summer. Like I said, she's a firecracker."

Kate watched as Vicky rounded a corner, just ahead of Cosmo, walked up to the Kahuna, and gave him a big kiss.

"Hey, dummy," Vicky said. "Looks like they found you. Off on another one of your boondoggles?"

"It wasn't that much fun. Someone was trying to kill me."

"Whatever. I maxed out the credit cards and sold your Porsche, so I guess we're even."

Nick put on his backpack. "We should probably get moving. It's going to be a long night."

"How are we going to slip past Horace and Jasper?" Cosmo asked.

Bob took his flute out of his pocket. "I could cast a Confundus Charm on them."

"Would that work?"

"It might. It's a hard spell to master. Maybe I should try a test run." He waved his wand at Hamilton. *"Confundo."*

Everyone stared at Hamilton for a beat.

"Do you feel confused?" Bob asked.

"I don't know," Hamilton said. "About what?"

"Maybe we should go with plan B," Kate said. "One that doesn't involve spells."

Bob looked at Kate. "You could be right. Technically, I'm not really supposed to perform magic in front of Muggles. There's an old game trail through the rainforest that will get you out of the valley as far as Red Hill. After that, there's no choice. You have to follow the Kalalau Trail back to Hanalei."

"Sounds good," Kate said, "or at least as good as it's going to get. Let's go."

Bob led them into the valley and along a muddy narrow path snaking through the dark jungle.

"Everybody turn off your flashlights. I hear people talking," Kate said. "It sounds like Czech."

Nick strained to listen. "I think it's Horace and some other guy I don't recognize. How far away from the main trail are we?"

"Not far. Maybe a hundred feet," Bob said. "This path runs pretty much parallel to the main trail."

"That means no more flashlights until we're past the guards, and we keep the talking to a minimum," Jake said. "He turned on the night vision scope on the M320. "I'll take the lead. Let's stay close together, and I'll look for any hazards."

Kate and the others crept along the pitch-black path, stumbling over roots and rocks, stopping every few minutes whenever they heard the sounds of the patrol coming from the main trail. An hour later, they stepped out of the forest onto the same bluff with its spectacular view over Kalalau Beach that they'd stopped at yesterday. Kate paused in front of the Little Free Library and looked around. The nearly full moon was already high in the sky, illuminating the beach behind them and Crawler's Ledge ahead.

"Red Hill, as promised," Bob said. "This is as far as I go."

Kate and the others walked the length of Red Hill's open expanse and began picking their way along the narrow cliffside trail that would lead them back to civilization. Bob backtracked into the rainforest.

"Look on the bright side," Kate said to Nick. "Maybe it'll be less windy at night."

"I don't think so," Cosmo said. "I hear it howling, just around the next corner. It's a funny sort of *wup, wup* whooshing sound."

"Now I hear it too," Vicky said. "It's sounds like it's getting closer."

Nick and Kate looked at each other.

"That's not wind," Kate said.

A helicopter sped around the corner and streaked past them, continuing down the coast toward Kalalau.

"Do you think they spotted us?" Cosmo asked.

Kate watched the helicopter bank hard right over the ocean and turn back toward Crawler's Ledge. "I'd have to say yes."

Nick looked around. "We're completely exposed on this ledge. There's no place to hide. This is a bad place for this to happen."

Kate and the others watched as the helicopter slowed and hovered just in front of them. A spotlight pierced through the night sky, illuminating them as they stood with their backs to the cliff.

"Everybody down!" Kate yelled.

A spray of bullets ricocheted off the rock walls all around them. The helicopter backed off and repositioned.

Hamilton was on the ground holding his bloodied leg,

while his father knelt beside him. Nick's shirtsleeve was soaked in blood.

Jake shouldered the M320 grenade launcher. "I'm going to overkill the heck out of those guys." He loaded the Pike mini-missile into the M320, aimed the scope directly at the helicopter, and fired. The Pike rocketed away, leaving a small cloud of fire and smoke in its wake, and exploded into the tail of the helicopter a second later.

Kate watched the helicopter as it struggled to stay aloft then began to spin wildly out of control. "It's headed right for us," she said.

She pushed Vicky and Cosmo back down to the ground, and Nick and Jake flattened themselves over Hamilton and the Kahuna. The rotorless helicopter groaned and collided with the face of the cliff, exploding in a giant fireball. Helicopter parts flew in all directions. A large piece of a razor-sharp blade bit into the cliff directly in front of Kate.

Jake stood up and watched the wreckage burning in the sea two hundred feet below. "Outstanding. I'm going to have to get me some more of those Pikes when I get home."

"Not so outstanding," Nick said. He pointed at the path in front of them. "We're missing about a hundred feet of ledge where the helicopter exploded. We're trapped on this side."

Jake pulled a knife out of a sheath on his belt and cut Hamilton's cargo pants off at the knee.

"I have a first aid kit," the Kahuna said, rummaging through his pack, handing it over to Kate.

"I see an entry wound and an exit wound," Kate said. "I don't see any bone fragments. I'm going to do a fast cleanup and pack it with pressure to slow down the bleeding. We need to get out of here. We have to assume Horace and Jasper know we're up here. Even if the helicopter didn't radio them, there's no way they could have missed the explosion."

"We need to get everyone back to the valley," Nick said. "We can hide in the jungle."

Cosmo shook his head. "We'll be trapped there."

"It's better than staying on this cliff."

Kate looked at Nick's blood-soaked sleeve. "How bad is it?"

"Not bad," Nick said. "I just got nicked. It'll keep until we're in a better position."

Hamilton was on his feet, propped up by Nick and Kate.

"Can you walk?" Kate asked him.

"Yeah. It hurts like hell, but I don't feel like I'm going to throw up anymore." He limped a couple of steps, testing out the leg. "I'm going to get mad respect from the guys surfing Peahi. The only thing better than a bullet scar is a shark bite."

They made slow progress back along the ledge toward Red Hill. Afraid to use a flashlight, they crept carefully in the moonlight, crawling when necessary. They reached the perimeter of the red dirt dome, and everyone gave up a sigh of relief. The most dangerous part of the trail was behind them. The relief was short-lived when they reached the overlook. Kate was first in line, and she could see Horace standing near the Little Free Library, scanning the terrain. She motioned for everyone to fall back into the deep shadows created by a massive clump of giant sisal plants.

A forty-something man wearing fatigues and built like a six-foot fireplug was using a machete to poke through the brush at the forest perimeter a short distance from the library.

"There's some old pig path through the forest over here," he said, his voice carrying up the hill to Kate. "Plenty of fresh tracks in the mud, but they're all leading away from the beach. They must have gotten past us this way, but it doesn't look like they've returned yet."

"Keep looking," Horace said. "They can't be far away. I'll keep walking the trail to the top of the dome."

"They're blocking our way to the valley and the rainforest," Kate whispered. "We can't get around them. We're going to have to go over them."

From their hiding spot, Jake aimed the night vision scope down the hill. "More trouble. Jasper's not far behind. He's at the bottom of the hill, maybe a quarter mile away, and he's got two other goons in tow."

"You take Vicky, Hamilton, Cosmo, and the Kahuna into the rainforest," Kate said to Nick. "Dad and I will distract Horace and the other guy long enough for you to rush past them and get away. We'll meet you at the hermit's cave."

Jake put away his scope and unsheathed his knife. "I'll take the big chunky beast with the machete. Give me a minute to get a little closer. I'll have to commando crawl on the downside of the dome. I'll wait for the secret O'Hare family signal before I do anything."

Cosmo watched Jake creep around the sisal and disappear into the night. "What's the secret family signal? Is it a birdcall? I'll bet it's something awesome like an eagle or an ostrich."

"A birdcall? Not exactly. You'll know it when you hear it, and that's when you all run past the bad guys."

Everyone went silent as the sound of hiking boots scuffing along in the dirt got closer, and Horace approached the clump of sisals.

Kate pulled a nine-millimeter Glock from her waistband, stepped out from behind the sisal plant, and shot Horace in the chest.

Nick, Cosmo, Vicky, the Kahuna, and Hamilton froze in horror for a beat before realizing they'd just gotten the signal. Nick shoved Cosmo forward, and they all skirted around Horace and hustled as best they could over the dome.

Horace staggered back from the impact and looked down at his chest in stunned disbelief. "What the . . ."

Kate stared at Horace. No blood. Not a good sign.

Horace narrowed his eyes, charged at Kate, and knocked the gun from her hand. "Body armor under my aloha shirt, girlie," he said. "I'm going to have a bruise. And besides giving me a bruise, I don't like that you tried to kill me." He dragged a tactical knife with a seven-inch blade out of a sheath on his thigh. "I'm going to cut you into a thousand pieces."

"No gun?" Kate asked.

"Yeah, I got a gun, but I thought it would be more fun to gut you like a fish."

"You're an idiot," Kate said, taking a fighting stance, curling her hands into loose fists. "You have your gun tucked under your body armor, don't you? You can't get at it. *And don't call me girlie.*"

"I don't need it," Horace said, rushing at Kate, slashing back and forth with the knife. "And I'll call you whatever I want, *girlie.*"

Kate moved to one side and landed three quick jabs to Horace's face, knocking him back a couple of feet and bloodying his lip.

Horace wiped his mouth with the back of his free hand. "Looks like you can fight, girlie. Had a little training, have we?"

Kate circled him, continuing to throw jabs. One of Horace's knife thrusts caught her on the upper leg, tearing through her pants and drawing a trickle of blood.

Kate looked down at her ripped pants. "What the heck! These Fjällräven pants are expensive. Now I'm going to have to wear a pair of ridiculous hippie overalls until I can get back to L.A."

"I have bad news for you. You're not getting back to L.A," Horace said, continuing to slash at her.

Kate ducked and kicked Horace in the knee. He buckled, fell facedown to the ground, twitched a couple of times, and went still.

Kate toed him. "Horace?"

Horace didn't move. He didn't make a sound. Blood oozed out from under him. Kate turned him over with her foot and saw that he'd partially decapitated himself with his own knife. It was still stuck in his neck.

"Crap," Kate said with a sigh.

She walked to the edge of the overlook and found Jake downhill, standing by what used to be the makeshift library but now seemed to be demolished. She waved and rushed down the Red Hill trail to meet him.

He was holding on to a metal pole. The chunky guy was lying in the middle of a pile of books and the splintered remains of the little wooden box that used to hold them.

"He looks dead," Kate said.

Jake nodded. "I know. Wasn't my intention. Smacked him in the head with the Little Free Library, and he just collapsed. I guess they're not making hired goons like they used to." He looked down at the ground and then at the pole in his hand. "Or libraries. All that's left of it is this pipe. How's your guy?"

"Dead too. Fell on his own knife."

"Jasper and his crew are on the trail, about three minutes away," Jake said. "We should take cover and regroup."

Kate and Jake moved far enough off-site to be hidden but not so far that they couldn't eavesdrop on Jasper.

The three men lumbered up to the library and stood over the man sprawled on the ground.

"Dead?" one of the men asked.

Jasper gave the body a good hard kick and got no response.

"Dead," Jasper said. He scanned the area. No Kahuna. No Horace. He directed one of the men to go to the overlook and report down to him. He stood, hands on hips, waiting for the report.

Kate and Jake silently hid in the underbrush a short distance away.

The man reached the overlook and disappeared for a moment. He reappeared and called down to Jasper.

"Horace is here," he yelled. "Dead. Looks like the stupid Czech blockhead fell on his own knife."

Jasper turned to the man standing next to him. "Call the Remarkables on the sat phone. And we're going to need a new helicopter out here first thing in the morning. Tomorrow we're going into the valley and we're not coming back without bagging a Kahuna."

Kate looked over at Jake. "They have a satellite phone."

"Of course," Jake said. "We have one, too, right?"

"We had one. It went down with the ship in Lahaina, and I didn't get a chance to replace it."

"I don't suppose you have service on your cellphone?"

"No. Not that it matters, because I also don't have any battery left."

"So, we're unable to communicate with anyone to get help?"

"Yep."

"Well, that takes us back to basics, doesn't it?"

15

Kate and Nick stood at the entrance to Mike the Hermit's cave. The sun was beginning to rise over the valley. Jake had left a half hour earlier to check out Jasper's campsite and try to gather a little intelligence. Everyone else was still asleep.

"Rough night?" Nick asked Kate.

"Just a little. Three hours of sleep in a cave isn't all it's cracked up to be."

"We were lucky Mike had a suture kit and some penicillin. I think Hamilton will be fine."

Kate nodded. "It's going to be near impossible to get him out of this valley for the next couple days with his injury. I don't think we have that much time to wait around before Jasper finds us."

"It's going to be impossible, period. The only way out is along Crawler's Ledge, and that's impassable, even if it wasn't being guarded by half a dozen mercenaries."

Cosmo and the hermit joined Kate and Nick at the entrance.

"Where was I?" Cosmo said to Mike. "Oh, yeah. We were talking about hermits. So, I had a hermit crab for a pet when I was six. He was my best friend, and do you know what? His name was Mike too. Isn't that a weird coincidence? You know, because you're both hermits . . . named Mike."

Cosmo paused to catch his breath. "Is your beard itchy? Do you like hermit cookies? Have you ever heard of that band Herman's Hermits? I think they sang that song 'Henry the Eighth.' It goes *'I'm Henry the Eighth, I am. Henry the Eighth I am, I am. Second verse same as the first.'*" He looked expectantly at the hermit. "*'I'm Henry the Eighth, I am. Henry the Eighth I am, I am. Third verse the same as the first.'* If you can't remember the words you can just hum. *'Hmm hmm-hmm hmm hmm, hmm hmm.'*"

"Not that I don't just love having company, but when are you planning on leaving?" Mike asked Kate.

"Just as soon as we can figure a way out of the valley."

Mike cut his eyes to Cosmo. "If I can get you out of the valley, will you take him with you?"

"Maybe," Kate said.

Mike's shoulders slumped a little. "Only maybe? Okay, no matter. There's a back way, but you have to be Spider-Man or Batman or something."

"No problem," Nick said. "We just get Kate suited up in spandex and let her do her thing."

"Ha, that's good," Cosmo said. "Kate in spandex. Like Catwoman with the little pointy black ears. She was awesome. I think about Catwoman a lot when I'm, you know, alone. I mean, some people have a shoe fetish, which I don't understand at all. Not that I'm saying I have a Catwoman fetish, but if I *did* have a fetish it would be Catwoman related. That's okay, right? It's not like I have a Jack Nicholson Joker fetish. That would be sick. Don't you think it would be sick? I hope I'm not insulting anyone who has a Jack Nicholson Joker fetish."

"Okay, moving along," Kate said. "I want to hear more about the back way out of here."

Mike pointed in the direction of the waterfall. "Sometimes we lower supplies from Kalepa Ridge down the mountain to the back of the valley. There's no trail, and it's really steep and really wet, but if you have some rock-climbing experience you might be able to make it up."

"And once we're at Kalepa Ridge?"

"There's an unofficial, unmaintained two-mile trail that leads along the ridge to Kalalau Lookout in Kokee State Park. Then you're back in civilized society, if that's your thing."

"There's no way Hamilton could make it," Kate said. "We'd have to leave him behind."

"Jasper and his thugs are searching for the Kahuna," Nick said. "If we can successfully smuggle him out of the valley, they're not going to stick around to look for Hamilton or anyone else."

Mike the Hermit occupied one of the larger caves in the area. He could stand without stooping. He had a ledge for his sleeping bag, an alcove that held a camp chair, and a tunnel leading to who-knows-where that was filled with endangered hoary bats. He kept his stash of canned goods at the entrance to the tunnel. There was a second chamber to the cave that was never used due to dampness, and this was the space allocated to guests. Vicky, Hamilton, and the Kahuna shuffled out of the cave and blinked in the sudden daylight.

"Ow," Hamilton said. "I feel, like, pain. And I'm wet. I think it rains in there."

Jake stepped out of the dense foliage a short distance from the cave and followed the path to where Nick and Kate were standing.

"Jasper and the others are still at the campground, organizing themselves," he said. "They're going to start searching the valley this morning, and they seem pretty serious about it."

"Mike knows about a backdoor way out," Nick said. "It sounds like it involves some serious climbing, so Kate and I are taking the Kahuna and leaving everyone else behind."

"You're thinking to lure Jasper out of the canyon," Jake said.

"Yeah. We'll drop some bread crumbs."

"And you're leaving me behind to guard the Froot Loops," Jake said. "Outstanding."

Nick slung his backpack over his shoulder and buckled the harness around his waist. "I'm taking the climbing gear and enough food and water for the day. We'll send help as soon as we reach the ranger station at Kokee."

An hour later, Kate, Nick, and the Kahuna were at the waterfall.

"I cut a path leading here that's so obvious even Cosmo could follow it," Nick said, putting the machete back in his pack. "I even dropped the bloody shirt we were using as a tourniquet for Hamilton last night along the way. There's no way Jasper can miss us."

"Great. I love being bait for ruthless killers," Kate said, looking up the cliff. "I can't see the top. All I see is cliff and clouds."

"Kalalau Lookout is four thousand feet above sea level," the Kahuna said. "It's in the clouds most of the time. It's probably raining up there too."

"What elevation are we at now?" Kate asked.

"Around three hundred feet. Three thousand, seven hundred more to go."

Nick removed three climbing harnesses from his pack, passed one to Kate, and helped the Kahuna into another. "How long has it been since you climbed?" he asked Kate.

"I had some military training, but not a lot of opportunities since then."

The Kahuna tugged on the harness. "I've tried rock climbing

a couple times, but I'm more of an ocean than a mountains sort of guy."

Kate watched Nick as he got into his own harness. "How about you?"

"Professional necessity. Back before I became a straight arrow and saw the errors of my ways, taking the stairs wasn't always an option."

Kate rolled her eyes. "Seriously. You do remember that I have a priceless diamond in my pocket right now? Did you steal it from the museum before or after you became a 'straight arrow'?"

"That doesn't count. It was a romantic gesture."

"How about renting my apartment to naked hippies? How about stealing my boss's identity?"

"It was for a good cause. And I didn't steal anyone's identity. I signed as Karl Ketchup, not Karl Jessup."

The first hour of climbing was mostly good old-fashioned scrambling, using the vegetation growing out of the side of the mountain as support to scale the steep embankment. Kate looked down at the thousand-foot drop to the valley floor and then up at the three-thousand-foot nearly vertical cliff left to climb. The trees had all but disappeared and been replaced with wet, mossy walls of dirt and rock. Worse, the slope had gotten progressively steeper to the point where hands and feet alone were no longer an option. Nick had stopped to rest, and was digging through his backpack for climbing rope, camming devices, and carabiners.

He found a crack in the rock face, inserted a cam, and tethered himself to it with the climbing rope. "I'll take the lead and run two ropes, one for you and one for the Kahuna. My rope is two hundred feet long, but I'm going to try to place my cams no more than ten feet apart. That way, if I lose my grip, the most I'll fall is twenty feet. Any further and the risk of injury increases drastically."

Kate nodded. "Sounds like a plan. I'll belay you on the way up. Are you sure you can do this with your injured arm?"

"Yeah, it's down to a dull ache. Good thing I'm such a tough guy."

Nick scrambled up the rock wall while Kate managed the rope, letting out just enough for Nick to continue to climb, but not so much as to leave any slack in the line. Every ten feet, Nick inserted another cam in the cliff and clipped himself in. Finally, there was no more rope to let out, and Nick was perched on a little ledge two hundred feet above Kate and the Kahuna.

Nick attached a Petzl Reverso to the last anchor he'd placed and gave Kate a thumbs-up. "You should be good to go. I'll belay you and the Kahuna on the way up, and I'll keep all the slack out of your lines as you climb."

"You go first," Kate said to the Kahuna. "I'll follow around fifteen feet behind you and remove the cams as I pass them."

By the time Kate and the Kahuna were halfway to Nick,

their progress had slowed to a near standstill. "How are you doing?" Kate asked the Kahuna. "Do you need a break?"

The Kahuna wiped some sweat away from his forehead. "This has got to be one of the most radical things I've ever done. My arms feel like jelly."

"Try to use your legs and back as much as possible. You'll wear yourself out if you try to pull yourself up the whole way."

A gust of wind swept along the mountain, and Kate watched as the Kahuna's grip gave out. He fell away from the cliff and plunged five feet or so before Nick arrested his fall. He swung back and forth on the rope before colliding into the cliff face and finding a handhold.

"Like I said." The Kahuna looked up at Nick and then down at Kate. "Radical."

A half hour later, Kate and the Kahuna joined Nick on the little ledge and sat down to rest.

"Two hundred feet down. Just a little more than two thousand left to go," Kate said, handing the bag containing the camming devices she'd collected on the way up back to Nick.

"Two thousand feet divided by two hundred feet of rope. That means we've got to do this another ten times before we reach the top." The Kahuna looked at his watch. "It's ten A.M. now. At this rate, we won't be done before dark."

"I'm hoping we won't have to lead climb the whole way," Nick said. "It looks to me like the pitch becomes more manageable after another five hundred feet of elevation gain."

JANET EVANOVICH AND PETER EVANOVICH

"And, then we'll be able to scramble up using only hands and feet?"

"I'm hoping so. It seems like there's more red dirt than rock as we get higher. It's going to make finding secure anchor spots for our cams a lot harder."

The Kahuna dug his hand into the crumbly dirt. "What happens if one of the cams fails?"

"Best-case scenario, you fall thirty feet before smacking into a cliff wall."

"That's like falling off a three-story building. What's the worst case?"

"All the cams fail, one after another, like dominoes, and all three of us plummet thousands of feet to the valley floor."

Kate stood up and gathered the rope. "Then we'd better not fall. I'll take the lead on the next two hundred feet." She looked at Nick. "You did the first section in, what, thirty-five minutes?"

"I don't really keep track. More like thirty-three."

"Yeah. I don't keep track, either." She checked her watch and started climbing. "See you soon. Let's say thirty-two minutes from now."

Twenty-nine minutes later, Kate was done with her section. And thirty minutes after that, Nick and the Kahuna joined her at the top.

"Do you have any binoculars with you?" Kate asked Nick.

"Sure." Nick rooted around in his daypack and handed them to Kate. "Why?"

Kate aimed the binoculars toward the base of the mountain. "It looks like we have company." She handed them back to Nick. "You might want to see this."

Nick looked through the eyepiece. Jasper was standing at the base of the waterfall, staring up at them through his own set of binoculars. "I guess they found us."

"What should we do now?" Kate asked.

"No worries. I have a plan." Nick handed Kate back the binoculars. "Could you hold this? I kind of need both hands." He leaned forward over the cliff and gave Jasper the double middle finger.

"That's your plan?"

"How did it work?"

Kate stared through the binoculars. Jasper was waving his arms and shouting instructions to the half dozen men who had joined him at the waterfall. Two of them started climbing. Another two ran off into the forest back in the direction of the beach. "That depends. Was your plan to piss him off?"

Nick gathered up the ropes. "That was just phase one. Phase two is we get the heck out of here . . . in a big hurry."

Kate held up the cams. "You're going to need these."

Nick shook his head. "Not this time. We're about halfway to Kalepa Ridge. It's a good head start, but we're going to have to take some shortcuts if we're going to get to the top as soon as possible."

"Shortcuts like a two-hundred-foot free climb with no

safety net? If you make one mistake, you're dead. I can't let you do that," Kate said.

Nick scrambled up the cliff and was twenty feet above Kate before she could finish objecting. He turned his head and flashed her a crooked grin. "What's the matter? Scared I'm going to break your record?"

The sound of bullets being fired from the valley echoed off the mountain, but Nick kept methodically climbing higher.

"At this distance, firing uphill and into the wind, hitting a target would be a one in million shot," Kate said to the Kahuna. "They're just trying to scare us."

The Kahuna flinched as the sound of more gunfire reverberated through the valley. "They're doing a good job."

Nick continued higher. "Give me some slack," Nick called down from one hundred feet above. Kate let out a little extra rope, and Nick jumped to an adjacent handhold and resumed the climb.

A bullet bit into the red dirt just beneath Nick's feet once he was about fifty feet from finishing the section, sending debris showering down on Kate and the Kahuna. "That was too close," Kate said. "It looks like they're starting to figure out how to compensate for the distance and wind."

The Kahuna brushed some of the fallen dirt off his head. "I'm going with lucky shot. It's the only way I can keep from messing myself."

Kate watched Nick pull himself up onto a ledge and secure the Reverso to the cliff. "Seventeen minutes," he called down.

"It's got to be some kind of a record, if you're into that sort of thing, which I'm not."

Kate checked on the Kahuna's tether and sent him up ahead of her. "If it is, it comes with a big asterisk. It's amazing how fast you can go when you're being chased by killers," she shouted up to Nick as she started to climb.

"I think we're about to test that theory," Nick said. "The two guys Jasper told to follow us up the mountain are catching up. They're almost at the base of the cliff."

Kate looked down at the two men trying to assess the best way up the cliff, and then looked up at Nick. She was already halfway to him. The Kahuna was nearly there. "We're still at least six hundred feet above them. They have a lot of hard climbing to do before they reach us. As long as nothing else goes wrong, we'll be at the top long before them."

The Kahuna pulled himself up onto the ledge and sat down, trying to catch his breath. Kate joined them a minute later and aimed the binoculars down the mountain. "So, you know how I was just saying if nothing else goes wrong, we're looking pretty good?"

Nick and the Kahuna looked at each other. "Yeah," they said in unison.

"Well, something else went wrong," Kate said. "The two guys Jasper sent off into the forest are back. They're carrying a big box, and Jasper looks pretty excited to see it. I've got a really bad feeling about that box."

Kate watched through the binoculars as Jasper unloaded a

base, a bipod mount, a telescopic sight, and a long narrow metal tube. "I think they're either building a telescope or a mortar."

The Kahuna was flat on his back with his eyes closed. "I'm going with telescope. Come on, telescope."

Kate shook her head. "If it's a telescope, they're going to have a heck of a time loading it with the whole crate full of eighty-one-millimeter shells sitting right next to it."

Nick borrowed the binoculars and looked down at Jasper and the box. "Okay, so it's a mortar. How much trouble are we in?"

"It looks like an M252. It's UK designed and used by the U.S. military. I was trained on it when I was a Navy SEAL. It can fire up to sixteen bombs per minute, and it can hit a target more than three miles away. Each round has a kill radius of more than a hundred feet."

"This is really happening. They're going to bomb the mountain." The Kahuna opened his eyes and sat up. "Boy, they really want to kill me. Whatever they stole from Sentience must be big."

Nick looked at Kalepa Ridge. It was still shrouded in fog. "We just need to make it to the cloud cover before they get that thing assembled. How long do we have?"

"Fifteen or twenty minutes, depending on whether they know what they're doing," Kate said.

"Then we should get moving. Same plan as the last section. I'll free-climb. You and the Kahuna can follow once I have ropes in place."

The Kahuna looked up from his sitting position. "I'm completely spent. I don't know if I can climb anymore, period, even with a rope."

"I'm coming with you," Kate said to Nick. "That way the two of us together can pull the Kahuna up the cliff, if we need to."

Nick looked down the cliff. The two mercenaries were climbing and had made considerable progress in a short time. "Okay. No time to argue." He turned to the Kahuna. "If those guys get too close for comfort, start throwing our gear at them. Rope, cams, water bottles, even the backpacks. Anything to slow them down. Anyway, we need to travel light if we hope to get as far away as possible before the shelling starts."

Nick and Kate climbed side by side up the last hundred feet of the cliff. They pulled themselves over the top and lay flat on their backs. "It's still another steep mile uphill to Kalepa Ridge," Nick said, "but at least it looks like there's no more technical climbing."

Nick and Kate had just started pulling the Kahuna up the cliff when they heard a low whistle coming from the valley floor. A few seconds later, an explosion a half mile to the right of Nick and Kate sent a huge chunk of red dirt and rock flying away from the mountain and raining down on the valley.

"That wasn't even close," Nick said. "And it still rattled my fillings."

Kate continued to haul on the Kahuna's rope with all her strength. "That was just a test run. They'll use it to recalibrate the mortar and try again. With every miss, they'll continue to zero in on our position."

Another bomb exploded, this time half a mile to their left and above them, leaving a gaping red hole in the mountain. Nick and Kate looked at each other.

"They overcompensated," Nick said. "The next shell is going to be a lot closer to home."

Kate's hands were burning from the pressure of the rope. "We've got to get out of here. Just keep pulling. He's almost to the top."

The Kahuna threw a couple of cams and his water bottle down the mountain toward the men in pursuit. They bounced off the wall, barely missing their targets, and continued to fall. "Those two thugs are gaining on us," he shouted up to Nick and Kate. "I'm guessing we still have around a three-hundred-foot lead."

Nick and Kate pulled the Kahuna over the top to safety, just as they heard a whistle pass over their heads and disappear into the cloud cover. A second later, another bomb exploded far above them, sending a thick cloud of dust rising through the clouds and giving the fog an eerie reddish hue.

The Kahuna looked over at Kate. "Do you feel the ground rumbling?"

A flash flood of trees, vegetation, rock, and dirt burst through the clouds and slid down the mountain, gathering speed as it went, in a massive river of muddy debris.

"Landslide," Kate shouted. "Take cover."

Nick, Kate, and the Kahuna dove under a large outcropping of rock, dodging the tumbling boulders that were leading the muddy slurry down the mountain.

The Kahuna hunkered down. "It sounds like a freight train."

A medium-sized tree shot off the top of the outcropping like a missile, and flew over the edge of the cliff. The muddy mixture of rock and dirt followed a couple of seconds later, surrounding the outcropping and pouring over the top like a waterfall.

Nick, Kate, and the Kahuna plastered themselves to the wall beneath the outcropping, avoiding being struck by the larger debris, and waited for the onslaught to end. Finally, the last of the boulders sped by them and the mountain was silent.

"That was . . . terrifying," the Kahuna said to Kate. "Does this sort of stuff happen to you often?"

"Unfortunately, all the time," Kate said.

Nick peered over the cliff. "No more bad guys climbing up the mountain. They must have gotten swept away. Thanks, Jasper. That solves that problem."

Another shell whistled through the air and exploded, just a couple of hundred feet below them. Kate looked up the mountain toward Kalepa Ridge. It still seemed an eternity away.

"The shelling is getting closer, and there's nowhere to hide until we reach the fog," Kate said. "It will be a miracle if we survive."

Nick scrambled up the mountain. "I don't believe in miracles. I depend on them."

16

Jake and Cosmo hid in the jungle, silently watching as Jasper stared into the mortar's telescopic sight and directed one of his men to adjust the angle by three degrees.

"Kate and Nick are sitting ducks as long as Jasper has that cannon," Jake whispered.

Cosmo's eyes were wide. "What are we going to do? There are six of them, all armed to the teeth. We'd be mowed down as soon as we stepped out of the rainforest into the field."

Bob emerged through the dense vegetation behind Jake and Cosmo, carrying a big burlap sack on his back. "It sounds like World War III. Everybody in the valley is freaking out. What did I miss?"

"Jasper and his crew are shelling Nick and Kate. Did you bring the stuff?"

Bob plopped the burlap sack onto the ground. "You bet." He opened the bag, revealing at least a hundred sticks of dynamite. He pointed at Jasper and his crew. "Those Death Eaters are destroying the mountain with their dark magic. I was saving these, but I guess this qualifies as a special occasion."

Cosmo removed a stick from the bag. "These look like they're at least a hundred years old."

"One hundred and two," Bob said. "They're from 1917. That's when the sugar plantations gave up trying to farm the valley. I found them in an abandoned storage bunker."

"Will it still work?" Cosmo asked.

"Dynamite is like wine," Jake said. "It only gets better with age." Jake took the stick from Cosmo and sniffed it. "Musty with just a hint of oakiness. Oh yeah. This is the good stuff. Nineteen seventeen was a good year for dynamite."

"What do you mean by 'gets better with age'?" Cosmo asked.

"More dangerous. As it gets older, nitroglycerin becomes more and more unstable. We don't even need a blasting cap with this stuff." Jake held the stick up to the light. "Dynamite sweats over time. Do you see these crystals coating it? A moderate shock should do the trick."

Cosmo inched away from the sack. "I'm not sure a burlap sack is the right way to store unstable dynamite. I'm not even sure there is a right way to store unstable dynamite."

Bob rolled his eyes. "You Muggles worry too much. I already cast a protection spell on it. We're perfectly safe."

Jake put the stick back in the bag. "There you have it. Nothing to worry about."

Jasper launched another shell. A couple of seconds later, the valley reverberated with the sound of it exploding somewhere up the mountain.

"Jasper and his mortar are at least two hundred feet away from us," Cosmos said. "There's no way to get close enough to throw the dynamite without getting shot."

"Yep. Thought of that," Jake said. "I couldn't throw it much further than fifty feet. That's why I asked Hamilton to pick up something to even the odds."

There was a lot of rustling and grunting in the thick vegetation behind them, and Hamilton limped through the foliage with his arms wrapped around a bundle of rubber tubing and cloth.

"Here you go, dude," Hamilton said. "Had a heck of a time convincing the locals to let me take it from the beach. What are you going to do with Old Reliable?"

Jake unwound the tubing and laid it out between two palm trees. "We're going to load it up with unstable dynamite. The bad guys have a cannon, and now we have a giant slingshot."

Cosmo and Bob helped Jake secure the ends of the tubing on the two trees and straighten the big cloth pocket. Jake unloaded half of the dynamite from Bob's sack and carefully placed it in the cloth pocket.

"You've had the most practice with this thing," Jake said to Hamilton. "Want to do the honors?"

Hamilton grinned. "Absolutely, dude. Just give me coordinates. I'm used to chucking coconuts into the ocean. I'll need some help getting the right trajectory."

"The target is straight ahead about two hundred feet. Once you get over the initial vegetation that's giving us cover, you've got an open field," Jake said.

Hamilton used his whole body to pull the pocket back as far as he could. He launched the dynamite, it sailed over the treetops, and arced high into the sky, spinning and turning. The sticks appeared to hover for a split second before beginning their descent. Everyone held their breath in anticipation of the detonation.

Bob removed his flute from his wizard robe and waved it in the direction of the dynamite. *"Reducto."*

The first of the sticks hit the ground about thirty feet short of their target, blasting a huge hole in the earth and sending a cloud of debris into the air. A second later, the explosions cascaded one after another, engulfing Jasper and his crew in a thick haze of black smoke and fire.

"Wow!" Cosmo said. "That's freaking awesome. Do you think we killed them? Did we annihilate them?"

"Doubtful," Jake said. "Too much smoke to see anything." He loaded the next fifty sticks of dynamite into the slingshot. "I get that this isn't an exact science, but we might want to try for a range adjustment. See if you can increase the distance a little."

"I can't do it with this bad leg," Hamilton said. "I can't put my full weight on it."

"I'm on it," Jake said. "Move over and I'll give it a try."

"Keep your feet square and just lean away," Hamilton said.

Jake pulled back and fired off the pocketful of dynamite. Seconds later, the second round of explosions rocked the clearing, unleashing a colossal fireball that rose at least fifty feet into the air.

"I must have hit their ammo," Jake said. "Go figure."

Jake, Hamilton, Cosmo, and Bob stared into the clearing, waiting for the dust to settle. When it finally did, they ventured forward slowly, taking in the destruction in complete silence.

The mortar had been obliterated. Giant craters littered the blackened earth, strewn with all manner of debris and several barely recognizable dead bodies.

"This isn't good," Cosmo said, stopping short of the worst of the carnage. "I didn't think it would be like this. I'm feeling sick. I've never seen anything like this. Maybe in video games but this is different."

Hamilton limped up to stand beside him. "Yeah, it's like *real,* dude."

"We did what was necessary," Jake said, walking through the damaged attack site. "There are three bodies burned beyond recognition. Some others might have been blown up entirely.

There's no way of knowing if Jasper is one of the dead. There's no way of knowing right now who escaped into the rainforest without us seeing them."

"My karma is doodie," Hamilton said, "but at least Nick and Kate and my dad are safe."

Jake looked up the mountain and the clouds hiding Kalepa Ridge, seeing no sign of Nick or Kate. "I hope so. Something tells me it won't last long."

Nick and Kate stared at the fireball rising from the valley floor.

"Looks like we just got our miracle," Nick said. "I wish we still had the binoculars. I left them behind with the rest of our gear."

"Not a miracle," Kate said. "That kind of destruction has to be my dad's handiwork."

The Kahuna somberly took in the scene below him. "So, it's over?"

"We still need to make it off the mountain," Kate said. "Let's keep walking."

Nick, Kate, and the Kahuna continued their slow progress up toward the cloud cover. "We may have gotten rid of Jasper for the time being, but how are we going to flush Olga out of her hole? Without her, we're at a dead end," Kate said to Nick.

"Not exactly a dead end. Last night you told me when

Jasper discovered Horace's dead body on Red Hill he told one of his flunkies to call the Remarkables for reinforcements. And a new helicopter."

"Yep, the Remarkables. Like Mr. Remarkable and his wife, Elastigirl," Kate said.

Nick grinned and shook his head. "You're thinking of *The Incredibles*. The Remarkables are a mountain range and ski resort on the South Island of New Zealand, near Queenstown."

The Kahuna grabbed a shrub and pulled himself up a steep section. "I remember Olga talking about Queenstown. She would go there for vacation a couple times a year."

"That's awfully far to go for a ski trip," Kate said. "Pretty sketchy."

Nick nodded. "Any smuggler worth his salt does the job himself. If I were stealing IP from Silicon Valley, I wouldn't trust it to a courier or even secure email. I'd take it to my buyer in person."

Kate cast a sideways glance in Nick's direction. "And you think Olga's 'buyer' is in Queenstown?"

"It's a theory. We'll need to find Olga to know for sure."

"Even if he is, New Zealand is a big place. What makes you think she'll tell us where to find her boss?"

"We have something she desperately wants." Nick pointed at the Kahuna. "She'll negotiate."

"And if she won't negotiate with you?"

Nick shrugged. "Then we let Jake negotiate."

"Most of Dad's negotiations end with something getting blown up."

"Exactly." Nick smiled. "That's one way to close a deal, I guess."

"We're almost to the clouds," Kate said, slipping on the mud and blinking against the mist that was sifting down on her. "The summit is close." She turned and looked out over the expanse of the valley. From the top of the mountain, the beach looked like a tiny spit of sand a million miles away. A lone helicopter approached Kalalau from the Na Pali Coast and landed on the beach.

"Jasper requested a new helicopter," Nick said. "I'm guessing it just arrived."

Kate walked into the clouds. "We need to hustle."

Fifteen minutes later, the terrain began to level out and the clouds began to recede. Nick pointed to a spot about a hundred feet up the hill where a narrow path wound its way along a ridgeline at the top of the mountain. "That's got to be the trail."

"Finally, some good luck," Kate said. "I don't think we would have found it in that soup."

"It's a fairly short walk to the Kalalau Lookout," Nick said. "There's a parking lot there and tons of tourists, so it shouldn't be a problem finding a ride back to civilization."

By the time Nick, Kate, and the Kahuna reached the trail, the clouds had largely disappeared, and they were able to look over the expanse of the valley and much of the Na Pali Coast. A short walk later they passed through a pedestrian gate onto a road that dead-ended into a parking lot. The sign on the guardrail read "Kalalau Lookout—Elevation 4,000 Feet." Nick, Kate, and the Kahuna walked into the lot and approached a tour bus operator who was getting ready to leave on his run.

"Can we get a ride back to Poipu?" Nick asked. "We're kind of having a rough day."

The bus driver looked them over. They were sopping wet, covered from head to toe in mud. Their clothes were in tatters, and Nick was bleeding from where the stitches had failed in his shoulder wound.

"I've seen a lot of people having bad days," the driver said. "You're in the red zone on the Bad-Day-O-Meter. You can ride along, but sit at the front, right behind me, so you don't drip on the rest of the people. I'm stopping in Poipu anyway."

The tour bus backed out of its parking space and drove down the mountain road, stopping at Kokee State Park Campground to allow the tourists to stretch their legs and explore. Nick and Kate used the hour to inform the park rangers about what had happened over the past two days and to let them know about the people stranded in the valley.

"It sounds like the rangers are used to rescuing people from that hike," Kate said once they were back in their seats. "They promised me that Jake and the others would be back at the hotel before bedtime."

The bus left Kokee and continued on along Waimea Canyon

Road. Kate watched out the window as they navigated seventeen miles of switchbacks down to the little town of Waimea.

"I've never seen a canyon quite like it," Kate said, leaning forward, talking to the driver. "The colors are striking. Red, green, and brown with waterfalls slicing into the canyon walls. If my phone wasn't dead, I'd take a picture."

"It's ten miles long and three thousand feet deep," the driver said. "And you're right. It's spectacular."

The tour bus turned left at the bottom of the Canyon Road and drove along the coast toward Poipu, nineteen miles away.

Kate slouched in her seat and closed her eyes. "I could sleep for the next two days," she said to Nick. "It was hard enough just finding the Kahuna without having to deal with Jasper. I have no idea how they found us so quickly."

"Good question," Nick said. "Somebody had to tell them."

Kate opened her eyes, sat up in her seat, and looked at Nick. "Larry."

"Yeah, that's my guess, too."

"Do you think he's gotten himself kidnapped . . . again?" Kate asked.

"It's a possibility. We'll find out soon enough."

17

Nick and Kate stood in front of the Koa Kea reception desk.
"What do you mean our rooms are being worked on?"
Kate asked the hotel concierge. "It's five P.M. I want to get into my room."

"The plumbing is all stopped up. Somebody dumped a boatload of glitter down the shower drain. It's been backing up into bathrooms all over the hotel."

Kate held out her arms to the concierge. The wet red dirt that covered ninety-nine percent of her body had dried and hardened into a solid, impenetrable mass.

"I really need a shower," Kate said. "It's kind of an emergency."

"There's an oceanfront suite that isn't booked tonight." The hotel concierge checked her computer. "It's already been cleaned by housekeeping. I can let you use it until your rooms are ready. Would that work?"

"Does it come with those little L'Occitane soaps and shampoos?"

The concierge smiled. "I'll have someone drop off an extra batch. You look like you could use them."

"I'm okay waiting until my room is ready," the Kahuna said. "I'll just jump in the ocean and hang out by the beach."

Nick and Kate watched the Kahuna walk down toward the ocean.

"By the way, we're looking for a friend of ours who is staying in the hotel," Kate said to the concierge.

"What's his name?"

"Larry," Nick said. "I'm not sure he has a last name. Looks like a weasel wearing tight, shiny pants. Probably annoying just about everybody in the hotel by this point."

"Oh yeah, Larry," the concierge said, handing Kate the key card. "I saw him this morning. He had breakfast in the hotel restaurant then took off. I don't know where he went."

"At least Larry isn't missing," Kate said as they walked toward their suite.

Nick swiped his key card at the door. "Let's try to find him after we shower. I'm really interested to hear what he's been up to for the past couple days and if he knows how Jasper tracked us down."

Kate stepped into the room and peeked into the bathroom.

"Marble everywhere. Enormous soaking tub and separate steam shower. Little bottles of free shampoo. Why is hotel shampoo better than regular shampoo? Anyway, I've never looked forward to a shower more in my entire life."

Nick looked through the glass shower door. "It has two showerheads."

"Great. I can wash all this mud off twice as fast."

"Or, we could each wash all the mud off at standard speed . . . at the same time."

Kate raised her eyebrow. "You want to take a shower with me?"

Nick stripped off his shirt. "For the sake of efficiency."

Kate felt the rush burn in her chest and swirl through her stomach. "I suppose it's okay as long as it's for the sake of efficiency."

Nick turned on the hot water to both showerheads, dropped his pants, and looked at her. "Are you going to take a shower with your clothes on?"

"No," Kate said. "Just pacing myself."

"Could you pace a little faster?"

Kate stripped off all her clothes. "Don't get any ideas."

"Too late. Pick a showerhead."

They both stepped under the hot water, and Kate watched as the mud fell away from Nick's body and swirled away down the shower drain. Her gaze lingered mid-body and she realized she was caught staring.

"Jinkies," she said, "that's impressive."

Nick took a handful of L'Occitane scented soap and passed the bottle to Kate. "Hot water has this effect on me."

"Are you sure it's just the hot water?"

"There might be other factors," Nick said.

"Like what?"

Nick pulled her close and kissed her. "Like the way you look when you're wet," he said. "Maybe I should help you clean some of those hard-to-reach places." He leaned in to her and ran his hands in circles over her body as he soaped her from her shoulders down. His hands stopped once they came to her stomach. "So, are you sure you're a hundred percent glitter free . . . everywhere?"

Kate drew in a breath as his hand began to move south. "Not a hundred percent."

"Let's make sure. You know, for efficiency's sake."

"Okay," Kate said, "but just so you know, even at maximum, mind-blowing efficiency . . . it's not going to get you off the hook for losing the bet."

After a half hour of searching, Nick and Kate finally found Larry sitting at the hotel bar, sipping a cosmopolitan.

"Larry, my main man," Nick said, sitting down next to him. "A cosmo? Seriously? You do know that's a lady drink."

Larry flinched and jerked his head toward Nick, knocking over the cocktail glass in the process. He jumped down off his barstool and did his best to brush a lime wedge off his wet pants. "I'm okay." He looked from Nick to Kate. "You're back. Where are Vicky, Jake, and Cosmo?"

"It's a long story. They should be here a little later." Kate paused. "Jasper and Horace showed up at Kalalau Beach yesterday. Did you see them passing through Hanalei?"

Larry shook his head. "No. I hung out there all day, just like you told me, but I didn't see anything."

"You didn't see anything? They brought a small army. How could you miss them?"

Larry held up his hands and made a halfhearted effort to look apologetic. "Sorry. Maybe it was when I went to get something to eat." He sat back down on the barstool and looked at Nick. "What's the plan now? Are you taking the Kahuna back to Los Angeles?"

Nick paused and glanced at Kate. "We're checking out tomorrow morning and catching the first available flight to New Zealand," he said to Larry. "Maybe you could talk to the concierge about our options for getting to Queenstown as quickly as possible?"

Larry nodded. "Sure. I'll do it now."

Kate watched Larry leave the bar. "Is it just me or is Larry acting a little weirder than usual? He spent the last two days in Hanalei. It's a little rural town with one road in and one road out. It's kind of unbelievable that he didn't see Jasper and his army roll through."

"And he obviously already knew we'd found the Kahuna."

Kate checked the entrance to the bar to make sure Larry wasn't returning. "How would he know that?"

"Someone told him. It wasn't me, and it wasn't you. My best guess is Olga Zellenkova."

"Do you think he ratted us out to Zellenkova?" Kate asked.

"I'm sure of it. The little weasel is probably on the phone with her right now. In fact, I'm counting on it."

Kate craned her neck, trying to get a peek out into the lobby. "I see him coming back."

Nick and Kate watched as Larry walked into the bar and up to them. "There's a direct flight out of Honolulu to Auckland at ten-fifteen A.M. That's probably our best bet."

"Thanks," Nick said. "We're going back to our rooms to pack. Keep an eye out for Jake and the others." He gave Larry a bro hug and left with Kate.

"If you think he's spying for Olga, why did you tell him we're going to New Zealand? And since when did you become a hugger? And why start with Larry?"

"You've heard the expression 'Keep your friends close and your enemies closer'?"

"Yeah."

"Well, we're sticking like glue to Larry for the next forty-eight hours. He's going to lead us straight to Olga."

"Why would he do that?"

Nick grinned and held up a cellphone.

"You stole Larry's phone when you went in for the hug?"

Nick shrugged. "Buddhists reject the whole idea of ownership. I mean, when you think about it, can anyone really own a cellphone? I figure it's as much mine as it is his, in the grand scheme of the universe."

Kate shook her head. "What are you talking about? You're not a Buddhist. You're a thief."

"Maybe I could be both," Nick said. "I'm like a cake with many layers."

Kate groaned. "I'm pretty sure one of them is baloney."

Nick tapped the screen, the phone came to life and asked for a password. Nick typed in *per se.* "Bingo," Nick said. "We're in." Nick accessed the recent calls on Larry's phone. "Bingo. Again. He made a call to New Zealand three minutes ago when he was alone in the lobby. And I guarantee he wasn't calling the airline."

Kate took the phone from Nick and scanned through Larry's texts from the past couple of days. "Hold on. This one looks like it's from Olga. She apparently left Kauai in a hurry and told Larry to leave messages for her at the New Zealand number he just called. If this is Olga's cell number, we can have local law enforcement in New Zealand ping her phone once we get to Queenstown. We'll be able to track all her movements."

"Only if she's still using that phone. When I was running a con, I used to replace my phone every couple days. If she's as good as I think she is, she won't be that easy to track down."

"At least it's a start." Kate handed the phone back to Nick.

"So, besides being a con man, you're also a master pickpocket. Good to know."

Nick gave Larry's phone to the concierge. "I found this in the bar. Can you put it in lost and found?" He turned back to Kate. "I prefer to think of myself as a fingersmith. One of my many talents."

"Good grief."

"I didn't hear you complaining about my fingersmithing, or my other talents, in the shower."

"I have to give it to you. Your shower talents are impressive. Still, that was a one-time thing." She paused. "Okay. It might be a two-time thing under the right circumstances, but that's it."

"Or we could go back to my room right now and take up where we left off. We were so busy in the shower, we never made it to the Big Show. Everybody knows it doesn't count toward being a one-time thing if you don't make it to the Big Show."

"As much as I would like to participate in the Big Show, it's not going to happen. The fingersmithing shouldn't have happened. We work together. I'm supposed to be managing you and keeping you out of trouble, which, by the way, is an impossible job. The Big Show is shut down until further notice."

"I can live with that. Is *further notice* later tonight?"

Olga Zellenkova settled into her leather seat and looked out the window of her private Gulfstream G550 as it made its final approach into Queenstown Airport in Otago, New Zealand. Jasper was seated on the other side of the aisle, his face completely bandaged to protect the second- and third-degree burns he'd suffered escaping from the inferno at Kalalau.

Jasper struggled to turn his head toward Olga. "What are we going to tell Mr. Neklan?"

"The truth."

"Well, now. That's real honorable-like. But I'm not sure, in this case, it's the best idea, seeing as Mr. Neklan isn't exactly the second-chances type. I've already had a pretty bad week, what with getting shot, falling off waterfalls, and almost getting blown up."

"I guess you should have thought of that before you let a lone-wolf FBI agent, her 'consultant,' an Instagram model, and an old man outplay you."

"That old man must have thrown a hundred sticks of dynamite at me. And Horace got dead."

Olga stared at Jasper. "Horace is going to be the lucky one if we don't figure out a way to deliver the Kahuna to Neklan."

The airplane's wheels touched the ground and taxied to a stop in front of a private terminal on the far side of the airport. "He's waiting for you inside," the pilot said.

Olga and Jasper got off the plane and walked into the building. A heavyset sixty-something man wearing a ten-thousand-dollar bespoke Savile Row suit was waiting in a little office on the other side of the hangar, with two thuggish-looking bodyguards.

"He doesn't look happy," Jasper whispered.

"He basically ran the Czech secret police, the StB, before it was disbanded in 1990. Those guys were never happy, except maybe when they were putting the screws to some poor stiff who was unlucky enough to be declared an enemy of the state."

"And now?"

Olga looked at Jasper. "Now? Now, ex-communist thugs turned oligarchs, like him, *are* the state."

Neklan motioned them inside the office, pulled out a gun from his jacket pocket, and shot Jasper in the chest. He put the gun down on the table, leaned over the dead man, and carefully unwrapped the bandages from Jasper's face. "Now that reminds me of the old days." He examined the blisters and burn marks. "Restraint and discipline. That's what's required when you use fire to get someone's attention. Some of my colleagues, back in the day, didn't have the right temperament to work with fire. They would go too far, destroying nerve endings and, without pain, the whole exercise would become ... counterproductive."

Olga poured herself a cup of coffee and sat down. "Tremendously interesting, but I wish you hadn't shot Jasper. After what happened at Kalalau, we're running low on hired guns."

Neklan shrugged. "At my age, you can't afford the luxury of wasting time on useless projects ... or people." He paused. "Listen to me. I sound like some old man reminiscing about the good old days." He clapped his hands together. "Back to business. What are we going to do about the Kahuna?"

"I have a plan."

Neklan put his hand on Olga's shoulder. "Good. I knew you would. You've always had a knack for making lemons into lemonade. Tell me."

"He's being protected by the FBI agent and her friends. Sending in a team to kill them is going to be messy and wasteful. Let me negotiate."

"With what? They have the Kahuna. They don't want anything from you."

"It's not about wants. Those sorts of things don't motivate people. It's about what people need, and everybody needs something. You just need to find out what those things are and squeeze. I have somebody close to the FBI agent who will work with us. In forty-eight hours, you'll have your Kahuna."

Neklan smiled. "You've always been resourceful, Olga. That's why we work so well together. I've never been much of a student of human nature. That's your specialty." Neklan's grip on Olga's shoulder tightened. "But, squeezing. That I know."

"Trust me," Olga said. "I can be very persuasive. Let me do what I do best."

Neklan released his grip and walked toward the exit. "Jasper didn't have too much luck trying it his way. So now we'll try it yours." He turned around in the doorway to face Olga. "I trust there won't be any more disappointments I'll have to deal with. Get this done, and I'll increase your commission by ten percent."

Olga got a tube out of her clutch. "An additional ten percent. Perfect." She applied the red lipstick to her lips and smiled. "And, here you were, saying just a couple minutes ago that you weren't a student of human need."

18

A state parks service van pulled up to the front entrance of the hotel. Jake, Cosmo, Vicky, and Hamilton got out and walked into the lobby.

"The park rangers told us you made it out with the Kahuna," Cosmo said to Kate. "We got to ride in a helicopter, and they took Hamilton to the hospital to get checked out and he's okay, and I talked to Jessup. He sounds pretty upset, maybe a seven or eight out of ten." Cosmo wiped some sweat from his forehead and caught his breath. "Also, Jake blew up Jasper, we think. He blew up a bunch of people, but there wasn't enough left of any of them to be certain."

"It was pretty awesome, dude," Hamilton said. "And awful, but mostly awesome. I guess it was awfulsome." He looked around the lobby. "I don't see my dad. Is he okay?"

"He's fine. He's down by the beach, waiting for you and Vicky."

"I should probably go collect the big dummy and at least get him to pay off the credit cards before he decides to take off again." Vicky earmuffed Hamilton. "Plus, I might need a little personal attention from the Little Kahuna, if you know what I mean."

Kate watched Vicky and Hamilton walk away.

"We think Olga and her boss are in New Zealand," Kate said to Jake and Cosmo.

"Where'd you get the intel?" Jake asked.

"Nick temporarily came into possession of Larry's cellphone," Kate said. "There were some suspicious-looking calls to New Zealand on it."

"It looks like Larry might be involved with the bad guys," Nick said. "We think he told Olga we were in Kalalau looking for the Kahuna."

"That alone would make Larry not my favorite person," Jake said. "Do we know the extent of the bad guys' badness?"

Kate nodded. "Besides wanting to kill us, they might be responsible for a couple high-profile murders, not to mention stealing military secrets from Sentience."

"So I'm thinking we're going to New Zealand," Jake said, cutting his eyes to Cosmo, daring him to say a word.

"We're going there tomorrow to keep an eye on Larry," Nick said. "We're hoping he'll lead us to Olga, if we play along and give him enough rope."

"Just don't give him too much rope," Jake said. "You don't want him leading them to you. Or using it to hang you." He looked toward the beach. "Are we dragging the motley crew along with us?"

"Unfortunately, yes," Kate said. "I need to keep the Kahuna close, and unless we lock Hamilton and Vicky up in a windowless room I'm afraid they'll create havoc looking for us."

"I vote for the windowless room," Jake said.

"Tempting, but no," Kate said. "I'll go find Vicky, Hamilton, and the Kahuna. They need to know we're taking off first thing in the morning."

"While you do that, I'm going to make our travel arrangements," Nick said to Kate. "You and Jake rally the troops and have them in the lobby ready to go at six A.M."

At 6:30 A.M., a black airport transfer van pulled into the private flights terminal at Lihue Airport and dropped off everyone but Hamilton, who'd elected to pass on New Zealand and catch a commercial flight back to Maui later in the day.

"Is that our plane?" Cosmo asked, following Nick through the terminal. "It's big for a private plane, isn't it? I mean it's not like a 747, but it's still pretty big. What kind of plane is it?"

"It's a Global 6000," Nick said.

"That sounds expensive," Cosmo said. "I'm going to have to fill out a VB710E. That's the form for Extraordinary Expense. The office of accounting hates to see those forms come in. I'm probably going to get a phone call. What will I tell them when they call?"

"Tell them we need to get to Queenstown as quickly as possible," Nick said. "With this plane, we can fly direct and make the trip in around seven hours."

"That's pretty fast," Cosmo said, "but maybe it would be almost as good to make the trip in eight hours with a Global 200. A Global 200 doesn't sound nearly as expensive as a Global 6000."

Kate and Nick sat near the front of the plane. Jake and Cosmo went toward the rear. Vicky and the Kahuna sat side by side in the dining area midplane, across from Larry. Pastries and fresh fruit had been set out on the sideboard next to Vicky, Larry, and the Kahuna.

"Seriously," Kate said to Nick, "how much is this costing Jessup?"

Nick belted himself in for takeoff. "Let's just say the VB710E will be the correct form to use."

"Jessup is going to crap when he sees all the bills. He's going to kill me."

"Which one is it? Is he going to crap, or is he going to kill you?"

"First, he's going to crap, and then he's going to kill me."

Nick grinned. "He's not going to complain if we recover stolen intellectual property worth billions. He can even count the expenses against our commission."

"'Commission'?"

"Five percent is standard, but I'm only asking two and a half since it's our patriotic duty to stop military secrets from falling into the wrong hands. That's only twenty-five million per every billion dollars we save Uncle Sam. When you think about it, it's a bargain."

Kate hooked the shoulder harness into her seatbelt. "How does zero percent sound? And, as a bonus, I'll try my best to keep you out of jail for another year."

"It's going to be hard to feel very patriotic about zero percent."

Kate sighed. "I'm sure you'll find a way."

"To feel patriotic?"

"To steal as much as possible from Olga and her boss before I put them out of business, permanently." Kate got out her earbuds and searched through her playlist. "I've gotten about six hours of sleep total in the past forty-eight hours." She closed her eyes. "Wake me up when we're in Queenstown."

Nick nudged Kate awake. "We're coming into Queenstown. Take a look out the window."

Kate opened her eyes and removed her earbuds. Massive mountains, some with snowy peaks, surrounded a small town built along the shore of a beautiful blue finger lake shaped like the letter z. "Is that Queenstown? It's smaller than I expected."

"It's a resort town. Around sixteen thousand full-time residents, but it swells to capacity when the snow is good. It's the adventure capital of New Zealand. Skiing in the winter. Paragliding in the summer. It's paradise for adrenaline junkies. Commercial bungee jumping was born there."

"All I can see are mountains. Which are the Remarkables?" Kate asked.

"Queenstown is nestled right in the heart of the Southern Alps." Nick pointed at a mountain range across the lake from Queenstown village. "The Remarkables is the one running north to south."

The plane began its descent, threading itself between two mountains and along a narrow azure-blue river. Wind gusts funneling between the mountains pushed the plane around as it approached the runway, which ended on the bank of Lake Wakatipu. On the opposite side of the lake, the city of Queenstown extended from the shoreline up a modest hill, with the almost six-thousand-foot-tall mountain Ben Lomond standing guard just behind.

"I booked us rooms at a hotel on the outskirts of Queenstown," Nick announced as the plane landed and taxied to a stop in front of two identical black Range Rover SUVs idling on the tarmac. "Except for Jake and the Kahuna. Kate arranged for them to stay at a CIA safe house nearby."

Fifteen minutes later, Kate exited the airport and turned west, driving along the lake toward Queenstown. Nick sat next to her, navigating. Cosmo was crammed between Larry and Vicky in back. Jake and the Kahuna turned to the east, away from town, and receded in Kate's rearview mirror.

"This is cozy," Cosmo said. "Most people don't like the middle seat, but I don't mind." He leaned forward and poked his head through the center console between Nick and Kate. "I like being right in the center of the things. Is this going to be a long ride? Sometimes I get carsick." Cosmo turned to Larry. "Do you want to play twenty questions? I'm thinking of a mineral. I'll give you a hint. It's not titanium."

Kate drove through the picturesque town of Queenstown along the main road, lined with cafés, craft breweries, and five-star hotels. Once they'd reached the outskirts of town, the road dipped down to the lake and followed the shoreline.

"I think we're almost at the hotel," Kate said. "The car's navigation system says it's a quarter mile ahead."

Larry leaned forward. "Where are Jake and the Kahuna staying?"

Vicky snapped her fingers several times in Larry's direction. "Earth to Larry. I'm sitting here in New Zealand. What the heck are you doing, sitting there with your thumb up your ass when you should be taking pictures of my southern hemisphere in the actual Southern Hemisphere? I mean, hello. That's Instagram gold."

Larry got out his cellphone. "I almost lost it in the bar last night. Somebody turned it in to lost and found." He snapped a couple of pictures and looked at the photos. "This is good stuff."

Kate turned off the highway, drove up a hill, and parked the Range Rover in front of a large lodge-style building constructed from stone and beechwood, surrounded by a dozen smaller villas built in a similar style.

The hotel manager met them at the door, and a valet unloaded their bags onto a luggage cart and whisked them away.

The manager handed Nick two sets of keys. "Welcome to Queenstown, Mr. Nacky. You're already checked into villas eight and nine. Number nine was the only two-bedroom available."

Nick handed Cosmo the key to villa nine, while Vicky and Larry explored the hotel grounds. "You and Vicky take the two-bedroom and babysit Larry. Don't let him out of your sight."

Cosmo glanced over at Larry in the distance. "Not even when we're sleeping?"

"One of the bedrooms has two twin beds, so you and Larry should room together at night. You and Vicky can take turns watching him during the day."

Cosmo fiddled with the key. "Sounds good. What are you and Kate going to do?"

Nick looked at Kate. "That's a very good question. If it were up to me, I'd take a nice long, steamy shower then go straight to bed."

Kate rolled her eyes. "Nick and I are going to look for Olga. Was your contact at the New Zealand Security Intelligence Service able to track her down from the phone numbers on Larry's phone?"

Cosmo nodded. "The first number you gave me was to a

landline—the Stratosfare Restaurant in Queenstown. The text was from a prepaid cellphone with a Los Angeles area code. Its last known location was the Queenstown Airport, but that was yesterday afternoon. After that the signal went dead."

"She probably ditched the phone," Nick said to Kate. "Now what?"

Kate opened the driver's side door to the Range Rover. "I'm starving. Let's go get something to eat at the Stratosfare. Maybe I'll leave Olga a message too."

Nick and Kate drove back into the center of town, continued up the hill toward the Ben Lomond Scenic Reserve, and, at five o'clock, parked the Range Rover near a small white building with "Skyline" written across it in bright blue letters. "There's no more road. Where's the restaurant?" She got out of the car with Nick and walked up to the white building. "All I see is a cemetery and this gondola lift base station. That's not a good combination."

Nick read a pamphlet posted outside the building. "The restaurant is about halfway up Ben Lomond on the top of Cemetery Hill. There are only two ways to reach it. The ten-minute gondola ride or the two-hour hike."

Kate looked up the mountain at the cars swinging on their cables in the gusty wind. "I hate gondolas. You're in some rusty metal bucket, suspended thousands of feet in the air . . . and someone else is driving."

Nick grinned. "Did I mention that this gondola is the steepest in the Southern Hemisphere?"

"Awfulsome. I can't wait."

Nick bought two tickets and got onto the next cable car with Kate. The gondola climbed steeply up the mountain along a grassy swath of clear-cut forest, set between two banks of tall pine trees. After a couple of minutes, the view opened up to reveal the town of Queenstown below and colorful paragliders windsurfing the thermal currents above.

"This is pretty amazing," Kate said as she looked over the expanse of Lake Wakatipu. "How big is the lake?"

"Forty-eight miles long and up to three miles wide."

Kate looked at the lake, sparkling in the afternoon sun. "The color is mesmerizing." Out of the corner of her eye, Kate saw a woman sail past her window. "Holy cow. Did you just see that?" She looked out the window and down the mountain where the woman dangled unceremoniously from a large rubber band connected to a giant green metal arm that extended from the cliff face above.

"Besides the restaurant, there are commercial bungee jump and paragliding operators at the top of the mountain. There's also an amusement-park-type luge run, and trails that go up to the summit of Ben Lomond," Nick said as the gondola pulled into the station at the top.

Nick and Kate got out of the cable car and made their way to the restaurant built on the edge of the mountain. An observation platform extended well beyond the cliff face and offered nearly 220-degree views over Queenstown, the lake, and the mountains beyond.

Kate entered the restaurant and approached the woman at the hostess stand.

"We don't open for dinner until five-thirty," the woman said. "Were you interested in making a reservation?"

"We're actually looking for a friend who may have been here recently." Kate showed the hostess a picture of Olga. "Have you seen her?"

"Sure. That's Ms. Zellenkova. She dines here all the time. She was here last night with Mr. Neklan."

"Who's Mr. Neklan?"

"Viktor Neklan. He's some European big shot who owns a mansion and a vineyard near Arrowtown. Comes here once in a while with his entourage, makes us wait on him hand and foot, and doesn't even leave a tip."

"Interesting. Did anyone call asking for Olga last night?" Kate asked.

The hostess shook her head. "Not that I know of. You could ask Sarka. She's a waitress here. She's Czech too, so she and Ms. Zellenkova are kind of friendly."

"Is Sarka working tonight?" Nick asked.

The hostess pointed to a slender, midthirties blonde setting tables for the dinner rush. "She's right over there. Do you want me to get her for you?"

Nick shook his head. "Not necessary. We'll leave her a message."

The hostess rummaged around in the stand and handed Nick some scrap paper. "There are pens over by the bar."

Nick went to the bar, wrote a brief message, returned, and handed the paper to the hostess. "Can you give this to Sarka, and ask her to pass it on to Olga?"

The hostess took the paper and looked at it. "It's a stick figure of a woman giving a big bag of money to another stick figure that appears to be a man, and a speech bubble containing the words *Let's make a deal*."

"Clever," Kate said to Nick. "Now what?"

"Now we make a dinner reservation and wait."

19

By eight o'clock, Nick and Kate had eaten their way through half the menu and were working on dessert.

"You're going to be sorry you ordered that Caesar salad," Kate said. "You're not going to have room for a second dessert."

Nick leaned on the table and rested his chin in his hand while he watched Kate shovel cheesecake into her mouth. "This is really impressive. Do you always order two desserts?"

Kate speared another piece. "Doesn't everybody?"

"No. They just wish they did."

Kate shrugged. "You've got to have priorities."

Nick watched Sarka approach their table with Kate's chocolate mousse.

"Showtime. Here comes the Czech waitress," he said to

Kate. "She must have something to say to us, or our regular waitress would be bringing the food."

Sarka put the glass in front of Kate. "Stratosfare's famous Decadent Chocolate Mousse."

Kate looked up. "Is it really decadent? Because that's what sold me on it."

"It's probably my favorite thing on the menu, but I'm a chocolate person." She paused and waited until Kate took a bite. "I also have a message from your friend. She's waiting for you at the top of the luge track. And Mr. Neklan has already paid for your dinner."

Nick got up, while Kate hurriedly spooned mousse into her mouth.

"What a guy," Nick said. "We're crazy-generous tippers, so let's tack on a gratuity of a hundred percent for our waitress. And, what the heck, let's give the nice hostess who seated us some dollars as well."

"Don't forget the pastry chef," Kate said with her mouth full. "This mousse is terrific. Let's give him a car."

Nick slung an arm around Kate. "I like the way you think. We'll also take a mousse to go," Nick said. "I like a midnight snack."

A couple of minutes later, Nick and Kate left the restaurant with their takeout mousse and walked toward the luge run.

Kate looked at the cement track winding its way up the mountain and then disappearing into the night. "She chose the top to meet, and the chairlift looks like it's shut down, so I guess we're walking." Kate started up the hill. "What's the plan?"

"We're going to bluff and pretend we know more than we actually do. Maybe we can get her to reveal a little about why they want the Kahuna and what we're up against. If we're lucky, maybe we can get her to flip on her boss."

After a half hour, Nick and Kate reached the top. Outdoor spotlights blinked on, lighting the luge run and a wooden shack with a sign advertising cart rentals. Three wheeled sleds designed for tourists were stacked up beside the shack.

Olga was waiting for them on a nearby bench. She got up and casually walked over to Nick and Kate. "I was so happy to get your message. It saved me the trouble of tracking you down. I'm assuming you still have the item I need?"

"We do," Nick said. "He's in New Zealand at a safe house right now."

"Excellent. How much do you want?"

Nick shook his head. "I think you have the wrong idea about why we wanted to meet. We came here to find out how much you would want to help us take down Viktor Neklan."

"Why would I do that?"

"There are at least fifty million reasons. That's the commission we're going to get if we deliver Neklan to the U.S. government and recover what you stole from Sentience. If you work with us, we'll cut you in for a third." Nick held up the doggie bag from Stratosfare. "Plus, this delicious chocolate mousse."

Olga laughed. "You think I'd flip for fifteen million dollars? That's nothing compared to what I'm getting from Viktor. Why don't you reconsider? I'm certain that I can match whatever you were expecting from the government, if you bring us a live Kahuna."

"Why alive? All the other CEOs you've stolen from ended up dead," Kate said.

"For the sake of argument, let's assume Viktor and I have been stealing intellectual property from certain Silicon Valley entities and then covering our tracks. And let's assume we had hoped all ventures would work out so easily."

"I'm assuming," Kate said.

"Sadly, assumptions are sometimes wrong," Olga said. "Victor and I find ourselves to be victims of special circumstances. The data we borrowed from Sentience is encrypted, and the buyer's needs are time sensitive."

"Basically, you need the Kahuna's password to unencrypt the files, and we have the Kahuna," Nick said.

"Correct. Plus a certain Asian government would like to purchase him, along with the technology."

Nick raised his eyebrows. "You want to sell the Kahuna?"

Olga shrugged. "The interested party has the resources to decrypt anything, given enough time. If you don't deal, they'll still buy what we have to sell. It will just be for a lot less money. A third, to be precise. One hundred million dollars. Then the only thing left for Viktor to do is to clean up the mess." She pointed at Kate. "That would be you and your friends."

"So, if we don't give you the Kahuna, you'll kill all of us," Kate said. "And, if we do, you'll pay us fifty million."

Olga smiled. "That's the long and short of it." She winked at Nick. "I might even throw in a bonus."

"I do like bonuses," Nick said. "Kate offered to keep me out of jail as a bonus."

Olga pushed a hand through her red hair. "I can probably do better."

"Gee, as tempting as that is," Kate said, "we're not selling you the Kahuna so you can hand him over to some third-world dictator. I think we'll have to stick with our original plan and throw you in a federal penitentiary for the next gazillion years."

Olga smiled. "I thought you might say that."

Five large men wearing black paramilitary outfits and carrying police batons stepped out from the shadows and stood behind her. "That's why I brought along some friends to help persuade you."

"Does that mean my bonus is off the table?" Nick asked.

"I'm afraid so." She took a step closer to them.

Kate pulled her gun and aimed it at Olga. "That's far enough."

There was a pop from somewhere up the mountain, and

the doggie bag exploded in Nick's hand, sending chocolate mousse everywhere.

Olga flicked a glob of mousse off her sleeve. "I have a sniper watching. Put down your gun, and let's have a civilized conversation. You're just making things worse for yourself."

Kate shot one of the men in black and dove behind the shack with Nick. The sniper fired off several rounds at the shack, and the four remaining men in black began to cautiously advance.

"We're going to have to make a run for it," Nick said. "You can probably take out the idiots in black but the sniper would be a hard shot."

"We won't make it ten feet before one of us is shot if we make a run for it."

Nick grabbed a luge cart from the stack behind the shack. "I wasn't talking about that kind of run. On the count of three?"

Kate looked around the shack. The four men were almost on top of them. "Three." She jumped on the cart, while Nick launched her down the track and leapt on behind her.

In seconds, they were rocketing down the run while the sniper's bullets struck the cement in front of and behind them.

"As soon as we turn the corner, we should be out of his field of sight," Kate said.

Nick looked back. "That's great, but we may have another problem."

A bullet whistled past Kate's shoulder. "That didn't come from the sniper," Kate said.

"Nope. We've got company."

Kate turned her head for just a moment. Olga's mercenaries were right behind them in luge carts of their own. Another bullet took out a chunk of the cement barrier just in front of Kate's cart.

"Now they're starting to piss me off. Take over the driving," she said to Nick.

Nick put his arms around Kate and grabbed the steering wheel. Kate spun around so that they were face-to-face with her legs wrapped around him.

"Try to keep this buggy steady," Kate said.

"Yeah, right," Nick said. "Not gonna happen." He pushed Kate's windblown hair out of his face. "This is cozy, but I can't see anything. Move a little to the side."

Kate moved to the right, took aim, and fired off a couple of rounds. Nick steered the cart around a tight corner, Kate waited for the pursuers to come into sight, and fired again, hitting the driver. He lost control of the cart, and it careened wildly, sailing over the side of the track and disappearing into the night.

"One down, three to go," Kate said.

More bullets flew past Nick and Kate as they passed through a corrugated metal tunnel and out the other side.

Kate glanced down. "For the love of Mike. Is that what I think it is poking me down there?"

"That depends. What do you think it is?"

Kate fired off another round of bullets. Another cart rocketed off the track, sending one of the gunmen tumbling out of sight. "Good grief. I think it's getting bigger. It's impossible to shoot bad guys like this. Can't you control that thing?"

"No, I can't control it. Try backing off a half inch."

The cart drove through a series of rumble strips and dippers on the cement track, vibrating the cart and bouncing Kate up and down in Nick's lap. She looked at Nick. "Well, that clearly didn't help your condition, did it?"

"It's not *my* condition. You're pressed against the brake lever."

"Sure. I knew that." She took a quick look down. "What the heck is a brake lever doing in the middle of the sled?"

A fresh barrage of bullets zinged past Kate and Nick.

"They're getting closer," Kate said. "And I think I'm almost out of ammo." She fired her last two rounds, striking the closest of the two carts. The driver swerved violently and his cart turned sideways, causing it to roll over and over until skidding to a stop.

The driver of the wrecked cart scrambled to his feet just as the final gunman's cart screamed around the corner. He held up his hands moments before the two collided, sending both gunmen flying twenty feet through the air and off the side of the mountain.

Nick braked hard, coming to a full stop at the bottom of

the hill just in front of the restaurant. "That was interesting. And, by the way, the brake lever wasn't too far off the mark in terms of . . . you know."

Kate extricated herself from Nick, got off the cart, and looked up the mountain. There was no sign of Olga or any of the gunmen. "Looks like Olga is going to need some new goons."

"It's not over," Nick said. "They'll throw everything they've got at us now."

20

Kate walked around the interior of villa nine, stepping over the broken glass covering the floor and navigating the obstacle course of turned-over furniture. Cosmo, Vicky, and Larry were gone. All that remained was the contents of their luggage, scattered throughout the rooms.

"This is bad," Kate said.

Nick looked at his watch. "It's nine o'clock. We met with Olga only an hour ago. She doesn't waste time."

"Do you think she killed them?"

Nick righted a fallen floor lamp. "No. They're her insurance policy. She won't harm them as long as we have the Kahuna."

Kate stopped and crouched down to examine a splatter of blood on the carpet. "Are you sure? Maybe she's cutting her losses."

"She didn't hesitate to offer us fifty million for the Kahuna. She wouldn't do that unless she and Neklan stood to make big bucks. As long as they think they have the upper hand, they're not going to risk losing their payday. They'll probably let us sweat it out tonight then offer to trade them for the Kahuna in the morning."

"I think we go proactive on this one."

"I agree," Nick said. "The hostess at Stratosfare said that Viktor Neklan owns a winery somewhere near Arrowtown."

"Do you think Olga would be stupid enough to stash them in Neklan's house?"

"No," Nick said. "I was thinking that, when Olga calls, we need something to bargain with, other than the Kahuna."

"Like Viktor Neklan?"

"It might be fun," Nick said.

"He's surrounded by bodyguards. His home is sure to be a fortress."

"Probably impenetrable."

Kate grinned. "We're going to need help from someone whose expertise is causing a little collateral damage and a lot of mayhem."

"I know just the man for the job."

Kate got out her cellphone. "Yep. Dad's going to love this."

Nick found a tourist map of Queenstown and the surrounding Otago region and spread it out on a table. "Arrowtown is a small historic gold-mining town about fifteen miles northeast of Queenstown. Two roads in and out. One runs along the Shotover Gorge and one passes by Lake Hayes."

"Did you say 'gold mining'?"

"The gold ran out sometime in the 1800s, but the town has managed to reinvent itself into an outdoor-lovers' mecca. Hiking and cycling trails. Whitewater rafting. Jet boat rides down the Shotover River for thrill-seeking tourists."

Kate packed up the map and walked with Nick to the Range Rover. "It shouldn't be too hard to find out where Neklan lives. There probably aren't a lot of Czech oligarchs living in the area."

"Arrowtown is a small, tight-knit community," Nick said. "It's hard to keep a secret like that in a town with a population of two thousand. I'm sure one of the locals will know where to find him."

Kate left the hotel grounds, drove back through Queenstown, passed the airport, and continued along the main highway. To her left, Lake Hayes sparkled under the moonlight. To her right, snowcapped mountain peaks were visible. After ten minutes of driving, Kate entered the little village of Arrowtown.

"I'm meeting Dad in the historic district," Kate said, lost in a maze of tree-lined residential streets. "See if you can find it for me."

Nick looked at the Google map on his cellphone. "Take the second left onto Buckingham Street. It's the main road passing through the village center."

Kate turned left and cruised down a street lined with tiny

nineteenth-century miners' cottages that had been restored and converted into galleries, bars, restaurants, and shops. The shops and galleries were dark, but groups of people milled about the small but chic restaurants and bars, occasionally spilling out into the streets.

Nick pointed at a stone building to Kate's left. "There's a black Range Rover parked in front of that wine bar with the blue door. I'm guessing it's Jake."

Kate and Nick parked next to the SUV, walked through the antique double doors into the bar, and paused to let their eyes adjust to the dim lighting. They scanned the stone and wood-paneled interior and found Jake and the Kahuna standing at the bar.

Jake motioned to Kate and waited for her and Nick to join him. "I tried to get him to stay in the safe house, but he insisted on coming along," Jake said, pointing to the Kahuna. He shrugged. "I figured he's got the right."

"They shot my son, stole my company, tried to burn down my farm, blew up a mountain attempting to kill me, and now they've kidnapped my wife. I think I've got karma on my side."

"You got that right." Jake looked around to make sure no one was watching, opened his backpack, and let Kate and Nick peek inside. It was loaded to the brim with C4 plastic explosives. "I appropriated these from the CIA safe house you stashed us in." He zippered the backpack closed. "Ka-boom. Instant karma."

"Holy crap," Kate said. "You have enough to destroy an entire city block. You promised to show some restraint on this mission."

"I promised not to shoot anybody."

Kate held up her hand. "You killed a guy with a library bookcase and blew up half of Kalalau Valley."

"But I didn't shoot anybody," Jake said. "Okay, I shot down a helicopter, and there may have been three to four bad guys flying in it at the time, but technically I didn't shoot any of them."

Kate sighed. "Maybe you, the Kahuna, and your big bag of explosives should wait in the SUV while Nick and I try to do some detective work and see if anybody in the bar knows where to find Viktor Neklan's place."

"Good idea," the Kahuna said. "We should probably guard all the guns Jake brought with him from the safe house anyway."

"Good grief, Dad. Exactly how many guns did you bring?"

"I was in a rush. I didn't count. How many do you think can fit in the back of a Range Rover?" He looked at Kate. "Maybe we should wait outside."

Kate watched Jake and the Kahuna leave the restaurant. She grabbed a barstool next to Nick and waited until the bartender approached them.

"What can I get for you?" the bartender asked.

"We're interested in trying some of the local wines," Nick said. "Are there any made right here in Arrowtown?"

The bartender reached behind him, grabbed a bottle, and poured glasses for Nick and Kate. "This region has some of the best wines in New Zealand. Most of them are made nearby in the Gibbston Valley, like the one you're drinking. There are a couple vineyards near Arrowtown as well, but the biggest one doesn't sell commercially anymore. It was bought a couple years ago by some Czech billionaire who doesn't need the money and just thought it would be cool to own a winery."

"He sounds like a jerk," Kate said.

"Understatement of the year. Nobody around here can blimmin' stand him."

"Where's his winery?" Kate asked.

"Just to the left before you get to Shotover Gorge. He has a ten-thousand-square-foot house and fifty hectares of vineyards that overlook the canyon and river."

"Sounds beautiful. Can the public visit?" Kate asked.

The bartender laughed. "No way. The guy who owns it, Viktor Neklan, is completely paranoid. The place is crawling with security. Cameras everywhere. You couldn't drive past the gate at the highway without being stopped . . . or shot."

Nick finished his wine and dropped a generous amount of money on the bar. "Thanks. Wish we could stay longer, but we'd better be going. We have a big night ahead of us."

"I've seen that look," Kate said once they were outside. "You have some crazy plan to get us into Neklan's estate, don't you?"

Nick flashed Kate a crooked grin. "Let's just say it's going to be awfulsome. But we need to take some chances if we're going to save Vicky and Cosmo, and I'm going to get a happy ending."

Kate punched Nick in the shoulder. "I'm counting on it, big guy." She paused for a beat. "Hold up. What do you mean by 'happy ending'?"

Kate stood, strapped to the front of Nick, on a large wooden platform at the summit of Coronet Peak. She looked out into the night over the expansive valley five thousand feet below. Tiny lights delineated remote farms, small villages, and busy Queenstown twinkling in the distance with vast swaths of darkness in between. One of those tiny lights, shining brightly three miles to the south, was Viktor Neklan's hundred-acre vineyard overlooking Shotover Canyon.

"This is crazy," Kate said. "I can't believe I let you talk me into more stealing."

"Commandeering," Nick said. "We needed transportation for official business, so we commandeered."

Kate swiveled her head to look at the broken-down door to the little hut behind her. The sign on the hut advertised paraglider rentals. "Jessup is going to pitch a fit."

Nick checked their harness, and then checked Jake's. "This is the most expedient way to get past the guards and cameras watching the perimeter of the estate."

"Granted, but Jessup is still going to pitch a fit. And I'm not happy about being strapped to you."

"There were only two paragliders," Nick said. "Someone had to get strapped to someone. And the weight load is more balanced if we're the ones strapped together."

"I suppose you also have a good explanation about why you're in the position to steer."

"I have more paragliding experience than you," Nick said.

Kate blew out a sigh. It was true. Her paragliding experience was limited. She looked over at her father, standing next to her. He was wearing an identical harness, except that he had an enormous duffel bag filled with plastic explosives and assault weapons strapped to his front.

"How extensive is your paragliding experience?" she asked him.

Jake shrugged. "Nick gave me some pointers."

"We're jumping off a cliff at three in the morning and attempting to land in the middle of a vineyard three miles away without getting shot by the throngs of hired killers guarding the place. Seriously? Pointers?"

"I did thousands of parachute jumps before I retired from Special Forces. And it's not your first rodeo either," he said to Kate. "How different can this be?" Jake examined the two handles on either side of his harness, each of which was attached to a bunch of grouped Kevlar lines leading to the elliptical-shaped canopy. "What are these doohickeys called again?" he asked Nick.

"Those are your brake lines. You use them to manipulate the speed and direction of the glider."

"Right, right. I knew that." Jake pointed to a horizontal bar at the base of the chair-shaped harness. "And this thing is my footrest?"

"It's a speed bar. It helps with the steering. Skydiving parachutes are designed to descend. Paragliding allows you to move horizontally as well as vertically. It's possible to travel a hundred miles under the right conditions."

"Gotcha."

Kate smacked her forehead with the palm of her hand. "He's gonna die. I should have sent him with the Kahuna to steal our getaway jet boat when I had the chance."

"Commandeer," Jake said.

Nick gave the carabiners a final tug. "Speaking of the Kahuna, he just texted me. He's got the boat and is waiting upstream from the estate. When we have Neklan, I'll signal him to pick us up and ferry us safely down the Shotover River back to Lake Wakatipu."

"Sounds like a foolproof plan," Kate said. "What could possibly go wrong?"

"Exactly." Nick handed helmets to Kate and Jake. "These are equipped with radio and microphones, so we can keep in contact with each other while we're in the air." He waited for Kate and Jake to put them on and adjust their microphones. "On the count of three, all we have to do is run down this platform and jump off the cliff."

"Outstanding," Jake said. "Three." He bolted forward, inflating the canopy behind him as he ran. Nick and Kate watched as he launched himself off the platform and sailed into the night.

Seconds later, Nick and Kate were airborne as well, following behind Jake as he soared down the mountain and over the valley. "Passing on your right," Nick said into his helmet microphone as he pressed down on the speed bar and flew past Jake.

Kate watched as they sailed past little farms far below. "I can see the highway and the canyon. Neklan's farm should be dead ahead."

Nick pulled on one of the brake handles, and the paraglider shifted direction, cutting through the wind and soaring toward Shotover Gorge. "Let's fly along the gorge and approach the house from the rear," he said into the helmet microphone. "Most of the security is probably focused on the front."

Kate looked down as they raced above the canyon tracing along the Shotover River. "There's the estate. Let's land in the middle of the vineyard. I think we'll be able to hide in the grapevines."

"Roger that," Jake said into the helmet microphone. "I'm right behind you. I'm starting to get the hang of this thing."

Nick began his descent, picking up speed as he went. "Landing is the tricky part. You want to be facing into the wind and start tapping on the brakes once you're around fifteen feet off the ground. Then, gently increase the pressure as you get closer to your landing. Don't go too hard too early, or you'll stall out and fall."

"No problem," Jake said. "I'll be sure to take it easy."

"Perfect. Just make sure the brakes are at one hundred percent once you touch down or you'll be dragged along the ground."

Kate watched as they passed over Neklan's property boundary. The area immediately around the house was surrounded by floodlights and lit up like a Christmas tree. Beneath her, at least a dozen men patrolled the grounds, some with dogs and all of them carrying assault rifles.

"The bartender wasn't kidding when he said Neklan was paranoid," she said to Nick as they passed silently over the guards' heads and drifted toward the vineyard. "He's got an army down there."

"Just as long as he doesn't have an air force."

A small quadcopter aerial drone with a twenty-megapixel camera mounted to its bottom sped past Nick and Kate.

"I guess I spoke too soon," Nick said. "I don't think it saw us, but we're going to have to get down quickly before it makes a second pass."

"How quickly?"

"You don't want to know." Nick flew over the vineyard, pulled hard on one of the brakes, and shifted his entire body weight to that side. "Get ready. You're going to feel some g-force. It can be disorienting."

The glider turned sharply and began a steep downward

corkscrew, with the entire canopy pointing directly at the earth. Kate braced herself as the centrifugal force racked her body.

"Hang on," Nick said. "We're almost there." He released the brake, taking the glider out of its death spiral and touching down on the ground.

Kate jumped out of the harness and helped stash the glider canopy out of sight inside a nearby irrigation cistern.

"That was incredible," she said. "Almost as good as free-falling. Maybe better." She looked around. Jake was nowhere to be seen. "Are you there, Dad?" she said into the helmet microphone.

Kate waited for a moment, listening to the static on the other end. "He's not answering," she said to Nick. "Dad, are you okay?" Ten seconds later, her helmet radio crackled to life. "I'm down, but I totaled the paraglider and had to land at the far end of the vineyard in order to stay away from the drones. I'm probably about half a klick away from your position."

"We'll wait for you."

"Great. I'll hide the remains of the glider, and come to you. Give me five minutes."

Nick picked a handful of grapes, popped one in his mouth, and looked around at the row after row of trellises filled with vines. "This place is state-of-the-art. He must have spent a fortune on some of these upgrades."

A puff of fire shot out of a series of four-foot metal stakes planted in the ground every ten feet along the entire row, illuminating the vineyard for a split second.

"Propane torches," Kate said. "I imagine they're used to prevent frost from damaging the grapes."

"Yeah, it looks like Neklan opted for the high-tech approach. I tinkered with developing a vineyard on my property in France, and I looked into propane. It's expensive to run the lines up and down the rows, but one flip of a switch is all that's needed to save a harvest. And it cuts down on farm labor." Nick pointed at a giant twenty-foot-tall fan poking above an adjacent row of vines. "The propane lines also power those wind machines, which circulate the heat and keep the heavier cold air from settling down on the plants."

Jake pushed his way past an adjacent trellis and stepped into Nick and Kate's row, carrying the duffel bag. His clothes were in tatters, and he had a nasty-looking road rash on his right hip where he'd been dragged along the ground during the landing.

"You look pretty banged up. Are you okay?" Kate asked.

"Never better." Jake dropped the duffel on the ground and smiled. "This is turning out to be the best vacation I've ever had." He opened the duffel and grabbed a couple of fifty-caliber Desert Eagle Mark XIX Action Express semiautomatic handguns before handing the bag to Kate. "I'm calling dibs on these babies. I like to be prepared."

Nick looked at the guns. "For what? A Sherman tank?"

"You never know," Jake said. "My motto is 'Go big or go home.'"

Kate removed a Glock, a stun gun, some extra magazines of ammo, and a couple of flash grenades, then sorted through the rest of the bag, examining the contents. "Where is all the C4 plastic explosive?"

Jake turned around and patted a fanny pack mounted to his rear. "Got this for Christmas from your sister last year. At first I thought it was ridiculous, but it's perfect for holding my explosives. It even has a separate zippered compartment for the detonators."

"Isn't it supposed to be for holding your blood pressure meds and healthy snacks to regulate your blood sugar level?"

Jake blew out a raspberry. "I threw all that crap away."

Kate looked through the vineyard at Neklan's mansion a quarter mile away. "We have to figure out how we're going to get past the guards and dogs."

Nick looked at Jake. "We need a distraction."

"Lucky for you, that's my specialty. How big a distraction?"

"The biggest."

Jake smiled. Another puff of fire shot out of the torches lining the vineyard. "I just might have a couple ideas."

21

Nick and Kate hid at the edge of the vineyard and studied an eight-foot-tall cement enclosure a hundred feet away. A lone gunman leaned against the structure, rubbing his neck to stay awake and looking at his watch every couple of minutes.

"I'm guessing that guarding the vineyard's mechanical pad isn't a plum assignment. He looks like he's just killing time until his shift is done," Nick whispered.

The guard stretched, put down his gun, looked around, walked over to a tree, and unzipped his pants.

"Big mistake," Kate said. "If I were him, I would have held it."

Jake emerged from the shadows just behind the guard,

encircled the man's neck with his right arm, and grasped his own left biceps with his right hand.

"He's got that poor schmuck in a rear naked chokehold," Kate said. "In a few seconds, his brain won't be getting any blood, and then it's game over."

Jake brought his elbows together, applying pressure to the guard's neck from both sides. After a few seconds of struggling, the gunman went limp and Jake lowered the unconscious man to the ground before dragging him behind the walled mechanical pad.

"It's like watching Michelangelo at work," Nick said, "if Michelangelo was an MMA fighter instead of a painter."

Jake poked his head out of the enclosure, gave Nick and Kate a thumbs-up, and motioned them to join him in the enclosure.

Nick scanned the area. "Looks like the coast is clear. Let's go see what he found."

Nick and Kate sprinted out of the vineyard and over to the pad and snuck inside. A dozen five-thousand-gallon tanks of propane filled the space, leaving not a lot of extra room for the three of them to stand. Mounted to the wall was a network of valves and control panels for adjusting the rate and flow of propane to the equipment in the vineyard.

"Did you time me?" Jake asked Kate. He nudged the sleeping guard with his foot. "How many seconds until Tweedledum hit the floor?"

"Seven. Maybe eight."

Jake looked a little disappointed. "I guess I'm out of practice. That's what happens when you retire. You get soft."

"You probably have jet lag," Nick said. "In a day or two, you'll be strangling bad guys like a champ. I'll bet you even set a personal best."

"I like this guy," Jake said, pointing to Nick. He removed what looked like blobs of modeling clay from his fanny pack and plopped them on top of all the tanks, one by one.

Kate raised an eyebrow. "You're going to blow up the propane tanks?"

Jake shook his head as he set blasting caps in each of the blobs of C4. "What do you think this is? Amateur hour? I thought you wanted a big distraction."

Kate looked at Nick. "Bigger than sixty thousand gallons of propane going up in flames?"

Jake turned all the valves to one hundred percent and adjusted the flow rate to "Maximum" on the control panel. A loud hiss of propane filled the air as it was pumped out of the tanks, through the pipes, and into the fields. "Any idiot can blow up a propane tank. I'm going to blow up a vineyard."

"I guess that should get their attention," Nick said. "It's not every day that a vineyard explodes."

Jake removed a remote control from his fanny pack. "We should probably vamoose. We don't want to be anywhere near here when we send an electrical signal to the blasting caps."

Nick and Kate grabbed the unconscious guard and dragged him behind a rock wall a football field away from the equipment pad. Jake joined them thirty seconds later. "I checked all the charges. We're good to go."

Jake handed Kate what looked like a garage remote that had been customized with a single red button in the center labeled "Krakatoa." "It's my lucky detonator. I was going to pass it down to you on your wedding day, but this seems like the right time."

"Boom," Kate said and pressed the red button. A second later, the mechanical pad exploded in a giant fireball. "Good gravy," she yelled over the noise. "They can probably see that from outer space."

Nick looked down. "Do you feel that? The ground's rumbling like an earthquake."

Seconds later the torches in the vineyard began exploding in series, one after another, sending flames in all directions and turning the metal poles into giant propane-powered flamethrowers.

"Holy moly," Nick said as the entire vineyard instantaneously caught fire. "I swear I've seen some crazy stuff, but it doesn't get any crazier than this."

Kate watched as one of the giant propane-powered fans groaned, followed by another and another. "Ooh. That can't be good," she said.

The groaning stopped and only the roar of the fire could be heard. A millisecond later, the wind machines exploded, hurling giant razor-sharp fan blades in every direction, some at least a hundred feet into the air. They reached the top of their trajectories and plummeted back to earth.

Jake grinned as it rained giant fan blades throughout the vineyard. One embedded itself into the earth just behind Neklan's mansion, sending the guards scrambling for cover. "This is turning out even better than I imagined. I've still got it."

Half the guards had run into the fields to fight the inferno. The other half, joined by an assortment of cooks and housekeepers, were frozen in place, staring glassy eyed at the spectacle with open mouths.

"What do you think?" Kate asked Nick.

"I think an entire marching band could waltz in the front door and not be noticed."

"I don't know," Kate said. "It's been a fun evening so far. I really don't want to ruin it by getting shot."

Nick snapped his fingers. "I've got it. Zombies."

"What?"

"The key to getting past a horde of zombies is to act like a zombie so they think you're one of them."

"So, basically, your plan is that we should wander around Neklan's backyard like a couple of disoriented morons in hopes that it will fool the other disoriented morons into ignoring us while we walk into the house and steal their boss?"

"It's not the stupidest idea," Jake said. "There are so many people milling around out there, we just might blend in." He held up one of his guns. "And if it doesn't work, I still have my Desert Eagles."

Nick mussed Kate's hair and smeared some dirt on her face. "Try to look befuddled." He undid the top button on her shirt. "There, now you're perfect."

Kate glanced at her cleavage. "How is that going to help me look befuddled?"

Nick looked down at Kate. "It's not. That's to help befuddle me."

"Good grief." Kate buttoned her shirt and took in the chaotic scene. "What if the zombies don't buy it?"

"They usually eat your brains, but you never can tell with zombies," Nick said.

"Whatever. Let's do it."

Nick, Kate, and Jake left their hiding spot behind the rock wall and meandered around the yard, making a slow, indirect path toward the house. They stopped every so often to look bewildered. Between the fire raging in the vineyard and the propeller blades littering the grounds, no one was paying attention to them as they skirted the perimeter, looking for an entrance to the house.

"There's our way in," Nick said, pointing to an open door.

Kate stepped inside, gun drawn. "It's a commercial kitchen, but it's deserted. Everyone must be outside watching the fire."

A pastry chef walked out of an adjacent room carrying a small tray of croissants and stopped in his tracks. He looked from Nick to Kate to Jake. "Who are you? You're not supposed to be here."

"We're the health inspectors," Nick said. "We're investigating a complaint that your croissants aren't big and buttery enough." He snatched a croissant off the tray and took a bite. "Oh man, this is good." He handed it to Kate. "You'll want in on this."

Kate pushed the rest of it into her mouth. "Okay, we'll let you off with a warning this time," she said to the chef. She took a second croissant from the stunned man and stuffed it into her pocket. "I'm confiscating this, though, for testing down at the lab. By the way, you wouldn't happen to know where we can find Viktor Neklan?"

"He's in his bedroom, waiting for his croissants. It's on the second floor, overlooking the vineyard." He looked at Kate's gun. "Look, I'm just the pastry chef. Personally, I can't stand the guy. He rings me at all hours of the night." The chef pantomimed answering a cellphone. "Stuart, send me up a sandwich with no crusts. Stuart, send me up an ice cream sundae with two cherries. Stuart, send me up a basket of croissants heated to 102 degrees."

The chef pointed at a small door in the corner of the room. "Once the dumbwaiter was broken and he docked me two weeks' pay because his food was late."

"Interesting." Nick walked over to the dumbwaiter and

looked inside. "How many people do you think we could fit in there?"

Kate looked over Nick's shoulder while Jake kept an eye on the chef. "Somewhere between zero and none."

"It leads directly to Viktor Neklan's bedroom. We won't have to risk running into any of his goons."

"I'm not even trying to stuff myself into that death trap," Kate said. "What's plan B?"

Nick took a couple of double-breasted white chef's jackets and a couple of white pleated hats off a nearby coatrack and handed one to Kate. "We disguise ourselves as master chefs, and bring Mr. Neklan his croissants."

Kate put on the coat and hat. "How do I look?"

"Like an FBI agent in a chef's coat. How do I look?"

"Like a criminal in a white hat."

Nick grabbed the tray of croissants and placed it on top of a food trolley, along with an assortment of jellies and a little flower in a vase. "What are you doing?" Kate asked.

Nick adjusted the vase. "Just because we're ruthless kidnappers doesn't mean we can't take a little pride in our presentation."

Kate rolled her eyes. "I'm sure he'll be very impressed. Just before I stun-gun his ass and stuff him under the food cart."

Jake escorted Stuart out the back door, told him to run like the wind and not look back. "What should I do now?" Jake asked Kate.

"Wait here and keep a lookout," Kate said to Jake. "And, don't blow anything else up."

Jake shrugged. "No problem. I'm all out of C4 anyway."

Nick and Kate pushed the cart through the kitchen and out into the hallway. Dim pathway lights led them through the warren of passageways toward the main living area. "I'm guessing that most of Neklan's security is focused on the outside grounds," Kate said. "He never expected anyone to actually break into his house."

They rolled the cart slowly through the mansion, into a foyer and up to an elevator leading to the second floor. Nick pressed the call button and waited. The elevator doors opened, and two men dressed in black fatigues and carrying automatic weapons nodded at Nick and Kate, exited the elevator, and continued on their way.

Nick and Kate pushed the cart onto the elevator, and waited for the doors to close behind them.

"I have to admit," Kate said. "Sometimes your crazy plans actually work."

The elevator slowed to a stop, the doors opened, and Kate stood face-to-face with Olga Zellenkova. The redhead stared openmouthed in surprise at Nick and Kate for a couple of seconds.

"This is a little awkward," Nick said. "You probably don't recognize us on account of we're in disguise, but we're here to kidnap your boss."

Kate reached out toward Olga, grabbed her with both hands, and pulled her into the elevator. She reached into her pocket, pulled out her stun gun, and pressed it to Olga's chest.

Nick watched as Olga twitched and collapsed onto the elevator floor. "Not that she would have told us, but you might have at least asked her where we can find Cosmo and Vicky."

"I was in a rush. Some people are talkers, and some are doers. I'm a doer."

Nick pushed the cart out of the elevator, opened the elevator control panel, ripped out a handful of wires, and watched the doors close behind them. "How long until she wakes up?"

"I gave her a good shock. Her neurons should be scrambled for at least ten minutes."

Nick hid the wires under the food cart. "It will take a while for them to restore power to the elevator. She's stuck there until someone rescues her. Hopefully, that will buy us a little more time."

Kate pointed to an ornate set of double doors at the end of the hallway. "That must be the master bedroom."

Nick and Kate pushed the cart through the door and into Neklan's bedroom. He barely glanced at them. All of his attention was on the large floor-to-ceiling windows overlooking the vineyard and the raging fire.

"Late as usual," he said. "Just leave the food and get out. I'm going to flay the skin off whoever is responsible for this fiasco."

Kate drew her gun and pointed it at Neklan. "You found her. And, also, gross. You've been watching way too much *Game of Thrones.*"

"That's it?" Nick said. "You've got a lot to learn about being a loose-cannon cop with a bad attitude. You just got the drop on the bad guy. This kind of situation calls for a clever one-liner."

"Like what?"

"How about 'Say hello to my little friend'?"

"Already taken. Al Pacino in *Scarface.*"

"Okay," Nick said. "How about 'I have come here to chew bubblegum and kick ass, and I'm all out of bubblegum'?"

"*They Live.* Great movie, but I don't chew gum. I look like an idiot."

"Right. I forgot about that." Nick paused. "'Give my regards to King Tut, asshole'?"

"Kurt Russell in *Stargate.* And that doesn't even make any sense." Kate looked at Neklan. "You don't know King Tut, do you?"

Neklan clenched his fists and glared at Kate.

"You see," Kate said. "He doesn't get it."

"Well, I'm all out of suggestions. Do you have any ideas?"

Kate handed her gun over to Nick. "If you have to shoot him, go for his privates. I know it's probably a tiny little target but it's always a satisfying hit."

"I'm on it," Nick said, taking the gun.

Kate pulled her stun gun out of her pocket, lunged at Neklan, and shot a bunch of volts into him.

Neklan's muscles contracted, but he managed to stay upright. She shot him again, and he collapsed in a heap on the ground.

Nick looked down at Neklan. "What's that he's holding in his hand?"

Kate unclenched his fist and removed a key fob. "Uh-oh. It looks like a panic button." She cracked the master bedroom door and peeked out. Half a dozen men armed with semiautomatic weapons had just crested the stairs and were running down the hallway toward the master bedroom. "We've got company, and we're not getting out the way we came."

Nick grabbed Neklan by the arms and dragged him to the dumbwaiter. "Can you buy me some time?"

Kate removed a flash grenade from her pocket, pulled the pin, slid it along the floor in the direction of the gunmen, and slammed the bedroom door shut. A second later, she heard the explosion. "That should slow them down for a couple minutes. I have one more grenade. If you're going to do something clever, now would be the time."

Nick already had Neklan half stuffed into the dumbwaiter. "I'm trying, but he's like Jell-O. He keeps oozing out," he said, shoving a stray arm into the small compartment. Nick stepped back a step and surveyed his work. "There. Perfect."

Kate looked over. Neklan looked like a store-bought Butterball chicken, ready to explode out of its packaging. "He doesn't fit."

Nick used his entire body weight to shove Neklan deeper

into the opening. "He'll fit. I'm not sure how we'll get him out, but he'll fit." Nick tried to close the dumbwaiter door. "Whoops. Maybe he won't."

Kate ran full speed at the mostly closed door and slammed into it. Neklan groaned and the lock clicked shut. The dumbwaiter was bulging, but it was holding shut. "Easy peasy lemon squeezy," she said, pressing the call button and sending Neklan down to Jake below.

"That takes care of Neklan, but how are we going to get past the goons in the hall?"

Kate opened the bedroom door. The six men in the hallway were still disoriented but beginning to regain their footing. She pulled the pin on the second grenade, tossed it in their direction, slammed the door shut, and waited for the explosion. "That should give us another couple minutes."

Nick looked down the dumbwaiter shaft. "It sounds like Jake is pulling Neklan out."

Kate leaned over Nick's shoulder. "Dad, we could use a little help here," she shouted.

"Roger that," Jake shouted back. "If I were you I'd stand back."

Kate pulled Nick away from the opening as Jake blasted five or six dinner-plate-size holes in the roof of the dumbwaiter. Jake poked his head up through the demolished dumbwaiter ceiling. "Outstanding. I knew the Desert Eagles would come in handy."

Nick lowered Kate into the shaft, allowing her to drop feetfirst for the remaining four feet into the dumbwaiter. She crashed through what remained of its roof and scrambled into the kitchen.

"I'm out," she shouted up to Nick.

There was a full minute of silence above her, and then she heard the doors to the master bedroom bang open followed by the sounds of gunfire. A second later Nick landed on his feet at the bottom of the shaft and jumped out.

"They're in a really bad mood," he said. "I guess their day's not going so well." He tossed a small computer laptop to Jake. "Stash this somewhere. I liberated it from Neklan's bedroom. Maybe we can find out what he stole from Sentience."

Jake stuffed the laptop under his belt. "Their bad day is about to get worse." He held up a gray block of C4. "I thought I was fresh out, but I found this in the secret pocket of my fanny pack." He plopped it down inside the dumbwaiter, together with a blasting cap, and locked the door shut.

Jake grinned at Kate. "Krakatoa," he said, activating the detonator. An explosion blew the dumbwaiter door off its hinges and rattled the whole house.

Kate waited a couple of beats for the dust to clear before she checked out the damage. "The shaft is filled with rubble. Nobody is following us down that," she said. "I'm guessing Neklan's going to need an interior decorator ASAP for his bedroom too."

Nick retrieved a shopping cart full of groceries and dumped its contents onto the floor. "Come on, Viktor. Time to go." He and Jake heaved the still scramble-brained Neklan into the cart.

Kate cracked the door and checked outside for guards. "The coast is clear," she said. "Let's make a run for it."

Nick maneuvered the rickety shopping cart outside into the night air and started off in the direction of the cliffs. "Why do I always choose the one with the crazy wheel?" He looked around as he rolled Viktor down the lawn. "So far so good. Maybe no one will notice us."

"You think that nobody's going to notice a geriatric commando and two people dressed like chefs pushing a two-hundred-pound crime boss through an open field in an old shopping cart?"

An alarm sounded in the house, and guards poured out into the yard, all desperately searching for Neklan and his kidnappers. Amid the chaos, one of them pointed in Nick and Kate's direction and shouted something in Czech to the others. Time stopped for a moment as the rest of the gunmen froze in place and watched Nick, Kate, and Jake sprint toward the cliff with Viktor Neklan bouncing around like a giant rag doll in the speeding cart.

Nick took a quick look over his shoulder at the twenty armed guards now chasing them. He turned the cart over to Kate and Jake and dialed the Kahuna.

The Kahuna answered on the fifth ring. "What's up?"

"Start the boat!" Nick yelled into the phone.

Kate and Jake struggled to keep going over the rough grass. They were aiming for a makeshift ATV path that was cut into a gulch leading down to the Shotover River.

"Did you find Mr. Big?" the Kahuna asked.

"We need more muscle," Kate said to Nick. "We have to get the cart over the high grass at the edge of the path."

"Yes, we found him," Nick shouted at the Kahuna. "Start the boat."

Kate ripped the cell out of Nick's hands. Neklan's bodyguards were maybe thirty seconds behind them. "*Start the freaking boat!*"

"On my way," the Kahuna said and hung up.

The shopping cart cleared the high grass and gained speed as it hurtled down the switchbacks leading to the river.

Viktor Neklan attempted to sit up in the cart. His eyes were unfocused, and his body was slumped. "Stuart, send me up a cheeseburger with three pickles and a sesame seed bun with the sesames on the side," he said to Kate.

"Right away," Kate said. "Just go back to sleep, and I'll bring it right up."

"Sweet," Neklan said.

A red speedboat with "Shotover River Adventures" emblazoned on the side and the Kahuna at the helm whipped around a bend and stopped in the river just in front of a small boat landing at the bottom of the trail. The Kahuna threw a rope over a piling and watched Nick and Kate as they barreled down the path toward him.

"There's our ride," Nick said. "We just have to get to the bottom."

Jake glanced over his shoulder. "They're gaining on us. I don't think we're going to make it as long as we're slowed down with this cart."

"I'm not giving up Neklan. We'll need to take a shortcut," Kate said as they approached a hairpin turn in the switchback path.

Nick looked at Kate and gave her a thumbs up. A second later they launched themselves and the shopping cart full speed over the bank of the canyon and plunged fifty feet into the Shotover River below. Jake, unencumbered by the shopping cart, sprinted down the path toward the boat landing and the waiting jet boat.

Kate struggled to reach the surface of the frigid water as the current dragged her downriver. Next to her, Viktor Neklan popped out of the water, spluttering and flailing his arms. Nick was a little upstream and swimming toward them.

The Kahuna's jet boat raced around the landing and pulled up alongside Nick, Kate, and Neklan just long enough for Jake to fish them out of the water and drag them onto the deck. The Kahuna slammed the throttle into full speed, and the boat rocketed away.

Neklan lay on the deck, breathing heavily. "I'll kill you all."

"Sure. No problem," Kate said, securing his hands and feet with a length of rope. "You can kill us all, just as soon as you return our friends and after you get out of federal prison, which should be somewhere between a hundred and a thousand years from now."

Neklan smiled. "You think you're the first person to threaten me with prison? Good luck."

Jake turned and pointed at a speedboat that was racing toward them. "I imagine that's loaded with Neklan's goons, and it looks to me like they're closing the distance."

"Hold on tight," the Kahuna said, pushing forward on the throttle. "It's about to get gnarly."

The speedboat leapt forward and accelerated through the narrow, winding canyon, creating a huge zigzagging wake of water in its path.

"If we collide with one of the rock walls at this speed, we've pretty much had it," Kate said to Nick.

Gunfire echoed through the canyon, and the boat's wind guard took a hit. The Kahuna swerved to the right. The back of the boat fishtailed and grazed a rock outcropping.

Nick's cellphone rang.

"Are you kidding me?" Kate said. "You're getting a call now? Here?"

Nick answered and switched to speakerphone. "It's Olga," he said. "She's in the boat of maniacs behind us." He turned and waved to Olga.

"You're more resourceful than I thought," Olga said. "Maybe you should stop the boat and we can talk."

"I can't hear you over the gunfire," Nick said. "Speak up."

Olga laughed. "Personally, I hate resorting to violence. There are a lot of other more fun ways to get someone's attention."

"Oh, for the love of Mike," Kate said. She grabbed one of Jake's Desert Eagles and fired off an entire clip of bullets at Olga's speedboat, blasting multiple holes in the hull and setting one of the two engines on fire. The boat turned sideways and flipped over, sending Olga and everyone else flying through the air and into the river.

"She was right. That was fun," Kate said, handing the gun back to Jake.

The sun had just begun to peek over the horizon, the sky far above them was a subtle orange, and the wrecked boat of goons was no longer visible.

Fifteen minutes later Nick and Kate cruised through the calm waters of Lake Wakitpu, looking for a safe place to dock.

The Kahuna glanced back at Viktor Neklan, bound, gagged, and lying on the bottom of the boat. "Well, we've got Mr. Big. Now what?"

"We trade him for Vicky and Cosmo." Kate sighed. "I guess we'll have to take Larry too. I can't see leaving him with Olga after this." She turned to Nick. "It's going to have to be somewhere private. We can't just walk around Queenstown with a hog-tied billionaire."

Nick grinned. "I know just the place. It's going to be epic."

"I know that grin," Kate said, shaking her head. "It's either going to be unnecessarily expensive or unnecessarily dangerous."

Nick shrugged and grinned again. "Why can't it be both?"

22

Kate stepped onto a long, narrow metal platform that extended twenty feet past the cliff face. Behind her, a rutted one-lane dirt road cut through tens of thousands of acres of privately owned land. She reached the end of the platform and stared down at the valley floor, five hundred feet below, and then up at the network of steel cables running from her side of the canyon to the other.

"Why do I feel like I'm about to walk the plank?" she asked Nick. "This doesn't look like any zip line I've ever seen before."

Nick moved next to her and tugged on the cable. "It's not. This one starts with a one-hundred-fifty-foot free fall, followed by a hundred-mile-per-hour swing that catapults you to the other side of the canyon. Lucky for us, it's closed on Tuesdays. We have it all to ourselves."

"Gee, that sounds really terrific. I always wanted to die doing the stupidest thing possible."

Nick grinned. "Everybody and their brother does their prisoner exchanges on a bridge or an airport runway. Where's the fun in that?"

"We're FBI. We're not supposed to be about fun." Kate strained to see the little platform on the other side, nine hundred feet away, where Jake was waiting with Victor Neklan and their getaway car. "So, assuming we don't die in the process, the plan is for Jake to send Neklan up the return line from the bottom while we simultaneously make our escape with Cosmo and Vicky down this one."

"Exactly. If all goes according to plan, we'll all be on the other side with Jake, and Neklan will be over here with Olga."

"It's amazing that Olga is still alive and functioning and willing to make a deal with us after we blew up her boat."

"Not *we*," Nick said. "*You* blew up her boat. Not that it matters. It's unlikely Neklan will put in a claim for destruction of his personal property."

They moved off the platform onto the solid earth.

"Olga isn't going to let us just walk away from this," Nick said. "We need to assume she plans to kill us as soon as she has Neklan. We want to get as much distance as possible between us and them once we have Cosmo and Vicky. And we need to do it fast. Once we're at the bottom and Viktor's at the top, we'll cut the lines. The nearest bridge crossing is at least an hour's drive from here. We'll be long gone by the time they get to the other side to look for us."

A black Cadillac Escalade crested a hill, rumbled along the barely there dirt road toward Nick and Kate, and stopped a couple hundred feet away. Olga Zellenkova got out of the front passenger side. Four of Neklan's black-uniformed, gun-toting mercenaries piled out of the back. Two of the men waited by the car, while the other two walked with Olga toward Nick and Kate.

"So nice to see you again," she said to Nick. "Usually my adventures with men begin at an elegant restaurant. No one has ever taken me to the middle of nowhere to ransom a kidnapped billionaire. I'm probably in the minority, but I think this is much more romantic." She looked at Kate. "But I guess that's why there's chocolate and vanilla. To each his own, am I right?"

Kate was wearing her pleasant-show-no-emotion FBI face. She nodded politely at Olga.

Olga returned the polite nod. "Right, down to business then. I have your friends in the car. I don't see Viktor."

Nick called Jake on his cellphone. "Send him up, at least partway." He handed Olga a pair of binoculars and pointed down the canyon toward the platform on the other side.

Olga focused the binoculars on the platform where Jake was pulling on one end of a rope-and-pulley system. On the other end of the rope, Viktor Neklan was trussed up like a

Thanksgiving turkey and strapped into a black harness. With each of Jake's pulls, he was slowly inching his way up the cable leading across the canyon toward Nick and Kate's platform.

"Far enough," Nick said to Jake. "Let him hang out there for a while."

Olga watched Neklan as he dangled from the cable in the middle of the canyon a hundred feet above the valley floor. "That's certainly not something you see every day." She handed the binoculars back to Nick and winked. "You showed me yours. I guess it's time for me to show you mine."

Kate stuck her finger into her mouth and pretended to gag.

"I saw that," Olga said.

"Sorry," Kate said. "I had something caught in my throat."

Olga waved at the Escalade. The two gunmen opened the rear passenger side door and waited while Vicky and Cosmo got out.

"What's the capital of Thailand?" Vicky asked one of the guards.

"Bangkok?"

"How about that?" Vicky said. "You got it first try." She executed a perfect kick to his johnson, and walked with Cosmo over to Nick and Kate.

"What took you losers so long?" she asked Kate. "I was stuck in some house in the middle of nowhere with no TV, no Internet." She motioned toward the guards. "And these four morons plus Firecrotch over here for company." She paused. "No offense, Firecrotch," she said to Olga.

Olga shrugged.

"What about Larry?" Kate asked. "Where is he?"

Cosmo shook his head and bit his upper lip. "She killed him."

"He might have been a greedy little weasel," Vicky said, "but he didn't deserve to die."

"Oh please," Olga said. "Let's be honest about this. If he said 'per se' one more time, you would have drawn straws to see who got to kill him."

"You're not a nice person," Cosmo said to Olga.

"Thank you," Olga said. "You're very perceptive." She turned her attention back to Nick. "How are we going to do this?"

Nick attached Vicky and Cosmo together in a tandem harness and secured them to the zip line cable. "We'll send Vicky and Cosmo across the canyon first. You can start pulling up your boss once they're safely across."

Vicky and Cosmo positioned themselves at the edge of the platform.

"I don't like the looks of this," Cosmo said, peering down. "Is it scary?"

"No. Not at all," Kate said. "By the way, you brought extra underwear, didn't you?"

"I usually carry extra," Cosmo said. "On account of the, you know, gluten thing. Why?"

Kate pushed Cosmo and Vicky off the edge, and they shrieked nonstop as they plummeted down the rock wall. They reached the end of their free fall and the swing engaged, pushing them in a hundred-mile-per-hour arc toward the other side of the canyon.

Nick watched through the binoculars as Jake pulled them onto the platform on the other side and detached them from the cable. Vicky and Cosmo were still face-to-face, holding on to each other for dear life when Jake pulled them in.

"They're down," Jake said into Kate's phone, "but they can't stop screaming. I think Cosmo has lost it."

Cosmo ripped the phone from Jake's hand. "I love you," he shouted into the phone. "I love Nick. I love Vicky. I love everyone. Holy crap. Who did I leave out?" He released Vicky and gave Jake a hug. "I love you most of all."

"Judas H. Priest," Jake said into the phone. "Get down here ASAP."

Kate watched as the two bodyguards worked feverishly to haul Viktor Neklan to the top of the cliff. He still had another hundred feet or so to go. "On our way," she said. "I don't want to be here when they finally get Neklan topside."

Nick and Kate tethered themselves together in their own tandem harness, walked out onto the platform, and secured themselves to the cable. Olga pulled a gun and followed them out. "I really must insist you stay. I know Viktor will want a word with you. Don't worry. I'm sure he'll send you on your way when he's done. It might be without the cable and harness, but that's life."

Kate and Nick stood motionless, watching as Viktor Neklan was pulled closer and closer to their side of the canyon. About twenty seconds later, the two men hoisted him onto the platform, cut off his restraints, and ripped the gag out of his mouth.

Neklan coughed and spit, then slowly got to his feet and turned to Olga. "Give me the gun. I want to shoot them myself."

"Time to go," Kate said, and she pulled Nick off the platform, into the free fall.

Neklan stumbled to the platform and got off several shots that missed their target. Kate heard a snap, and felt her direction change suddenly. A millisecond later, she and Nick were soaring across the canyon at breakneck speed. She held tight to Nick as more shots were fired.

Nick looked into Kate's eyes and smiled the same crooked grin that always seemed to precede trouble. His lips brushed over hers and settled into a knock-your-socks-off, head-spinning kiss. She was still kissing him when Jake pulled them onto the platform and disconnected the cable.

"Hello." Jake pointed at himself. "Overly protective father standing here." He watched as Nick and Kate continued to kiss for a few more seconds. "Judas H. Priest. Where's Cosmo? I'd rather get hugged than watch this."

Kate let go of Nick, got out of the harness, and looked back across the canyon. "That was pretty off-the-charts amazing."

"Yeah," Nick said. "And the zip line was pretty fantastic too."

It was 7 P.M. by the time Nick and Kate drove Cosmo, Vicky, and Jake back to the CIA safe house on the outskirts of

Arrowtown. Cosmo and Vicky took long, hot showers as soon as they arrived and immediately after collapsed into their beds. Jake went outside to smoke a cigar. The Kahuna was sitting in the kitchen with the laptop Nick had taken from Neklan's bedroom, trying to break through the password protection.

Kate looked over the Kahuna's shoulder. "How's it going?"

The Kahuna cracked his knuckles. "I just booted up the computer in single-user mode," he said and typed in a series of command-line codes.

Kate watched as the Kahuna typed. "Looks mostly like gobbledygook to me."

"I'm trying to reset his password. It should work so long as he hasn't encrypted his computer."

"I doubt he would go to the effort," Kate said. "I'm sure he never thought anybody would be able to get close enough to steal it from him."

"We'll know for certain in a couple seconds." The Kahuna hit one final keystroke then pushed the return key. He turned to look at Kate and smiled. "We're in. Not bad for a fifty-year-old surfer, right?"

"Let's check his emails first," Nick said. "Olga said his buyer was an Asian government official."

"Which country?"

"We might as well start with the usual suspects in high-stakes intellectual property theft," Kate said. "Look for anything connected to China or North Korea."

The Kahuna scanned through the recent emails in Neklan's

sent folder. "There are a dozen or so to a guy named Zhang Wei at the Chinese embassy in Prague." He googled the embassy website. "It looks like he's the ambassador to the Czech Republic."

Kate read through the emails. "Neklan kept most of the details purposefully vague, but he was definitely trying to organize an in-person meeting with Zhang Wei in Prague. They agreed to one price if the software was delivered in an encrypted form and triple that if the Kahuna was delivered to them along with the merchandise."

"That's consistent with what we know so far," Nick said. "When are they supposed to meet?"

Kate looked at Nick. "Tomorrow. At the embassy."

"Do you have any idea what Olga might have stolen from Sentience?" Nick asked.

The Kahuna shrugged. "Sentience develops artificial intelligence software. Mostly it's used for smart houses and self-driving cars and things like that."

"'Mostly'?"

"We don't have any contracts with the Pentagon, but we're very aware that our AI could be used for military applications. Most of Silicon Valley is ethically opposed to using the technology that way, but the Chinese government isn't. Their military has tons of partnerships with private Chinese-owned tech companies."

"I sat in on an FBI briefing on that a couple months ago," Kate said. "U.S. intelligence believes that the Chinese are intent on becoming the dominant power in cyber warfare over the next ten years."

The Kahuna searched through Neklan's computer for anything related to Sentience. "I'm not finding anything in any of the obvious places. Let's see if there are any deleted files."

The Kahuna downloaded a data recovery app onto Neklan's computer. "When a file is moved to the trash, sometimes it's not really gone for good. The name of the file is removed but the underlying information remains, at least until new information is written over it. So if we're lucky we'll have access to anything he recently deleted."

Nick, Kate, and the Kahuna waited while the app scanned Neklan's laptop. After a couple of minutes, all the files capable of being recovered were displayed in a new folder on his desktop. The Kahuna scanned through them one by one. "No. No. No. Wait a minute." He pointed toward the laptop. "I think I just found a memo from Olga."

Nick looked over the Kahuna's shoulder and read the subject line. "What are 'LAWs'?"

"It's an acronym for lethal autonomous weapons," the Kahuna said. "Basically, they're war machines capable of operating on their own. U.S. military policy is that LAWs are legal so long as a human being is the one ultimately making decisions about the use of lethal force. The drone program is an example."

"Sentience was designing killer robots?" Kate asked.

"No. But I'm developing technology that allows machines to think and learn. Sentience's technology will enable us to build things like cars and houses and blenders and vacuum cleaners that could anticipate what you wanted and make decisions for you."

"Sounds like science fiction."

The Kahuna pushed back in his chair. "Kind of. The newest stuff we're doing is light-years ahead of anything else being developed. It could change the world."

"Or destroy it," Nick said, "if the technology was used to create an army of LAWs that can think and learn and make their own decisions. It sounds like a recipe for disaster on a global scale."

The Kahuna grimaced. "That's always been the risk of innovation. One man's unlimited source of free energy is another man's thermonuclear bomb."

Jake walked back into the house. "What did I miss?"

"It looks like Olga and Neklan stole military-grade AI software from the Kahuna, and are selling it to the Chinese ambassador in the Czech Republic tomorrow," Kate said.

"Bummer. What are we going to do about it? Do you have a plan?"

"Sure, I do," Nick said. "I just haven't thought all of it out yet. But we're going to Prague."

23

Kate awoke and stretched while her eyes adjusted to the darkness and the unfamiliar room. She got out of the bed, opened the door to the little stateroom, and walked into the main body of the Bombardier Global 6000 aircraft that Nick had somehow managed to procure in the middle of the night. Jake and the Kahuna were playing cards. Nick was on the satellite phone. Cosmo was hunched over his laptop, feverishly filling out paperwork, and Vicky was sitting across from him, wearing a low-cut size-zero Bavarian barmaid costume, taking selfies.

Cosmo looked up from his laptop. "You packed a lot of costumes," he said to Vicky. "How did you manage to get them all into your suitcase?"

"The trick is skipping nonessential items like underwear,"

Vicky said. "If you want to be a super Instagram model you need to learn to prioritize. Plus, most of my stuff is long on style and short on fabric so it doesn't take up a lot of luggage space."

"I know what you mean," Cosmo said. "It's just like this one time when I skipped packing extras of form J17, Request for More Forms, and you know what happened? You'll never guess." He paused and looked at Vicky. "I ran out of forms. I don't have to tell you what a mess that was. So, you know what I did? I used my last J17 to order more J17s."

Vicky scrunched up her nose and looked at Cosmo.

"I know what you're thinking," Cosmo said, holding up his hand. "That's like using the last of your three genie wishes to wish for more wishes, but that's how I roll. I'm a lone wolf who follows his own rules."

Kate plopped herself down on the seat opposite Nick and waited for him to finish his phone call. "I don't even know how long I slept. How close are we to Prague?"

"It's a twenty-hour flight, not including the hour we spent in Hong Kong refueling." Nick looked at his watch. "Probably another eight hours."

"Do we know where Neklan and Olga are right now?"

"I checked for all the flight plans over the past twenty-four hours between Queenstown, New Zealand, and the Czech Republic," Cosmo said. "As you might imagine, there weren't too many of them. Just us and one other flight, also on a Global 6000."

"That has to be Neklan and Olga. Are they still in the air?" Kate asked.

Cosmo checked FlightAware. "They're supposed to land in a couple hours. Do you think we should alert the authorities to detain them?"

Kate shook her head. "No. The Chinese ambassador already has the stolen IP from Sentience. Our first priority is recovering the data. We can worry about Olga and Neklan later."

"Agreed," Nick said. "Hopefully the data hasn't been transferred out of the embassy yet."

"What do you and my dad have cooked up?"

"What if I told you we could recover the data, steal hundreds of millions from the Chinese government, and put Neklan and Olga out of business permanently?"

Kate held up her hand. "Just a second. What was that second thing?"

"'Put Neklan out of business'?"

"Before that and after 'recover the stolen data.'"

Nick tried giving her the crooked grin. "I don't think there was anything else."

"I distinctly heard you say 'steal hundreds of millions from the Chinese government.'"

"Maybe it's best to think of it as more of a reimbursement for all our expenses. Our time is worth something, and we logged a lot of hours on this assignment."

"And you're thinking this reimbursement of money would get channeled into our secret slush fund?" Kate said.

"Oh boy," Cosmo said. "This could be a problem. I don't have a slush fund form. I'm not sure it exists. I might have to use P184QQ. That's an Unexplainable Acquisitions form."

Kate rolled her eyes. "Let's just hear the plan. I'm sure it's a beaut."

"You worry too much," Nick said. "It's going to go off smooth as butter."

"Humor me."

"The ambassador's eighteen-year-old son just happens to be a heavy-duty Fortnite player, and a superfan of my client Gregory's podcast."

"You mean the one with the sexy actress who specializes in goofing off and pretending to play video games in stretchy yoga pants?"

"Don't sell Betina short," Nick said. "She also cracks jokes in stretchy yoga pants."

"I know her," Cosmo said. "She's so funny. I blorted my pants the last time I watched her on YouTube." He shook his head and chuckled. "Fortnite, more like blortnite. Classic."

Kate and Nick stared at Cosmo for a couple seconds. "Isn't blorting when you blow milk out your nose?" Kate finally said.

Cosmo's eyes darted back and forth. "Oh." He tilted his head back and groaned. "That makes a lot more sense." He grimaced. "It's probably for the best if you don't mention what I just said about me blorting my pants to anyone else. I'm kind of the cool guy around the office."

"Moving on," Kate said. "What are we doing with Gregory and his alter ego?"

Nick grinned. "Gregory, Betina, and his production crew are already on their way to Prague. I've arranged for him to broadcast an episode of his podcast directly from the Chinese embassy. The ambassador's son was very enthusiastic about it."

"And by *production crew*, you mean us?"

"Bingo."

"If it works, that gets us into the embassy. But I seriously doubt the ambassador keeps his stolen military technology in his son's bedroom."

"I called in a favor and used my social media influencer influencer connections to arrange for a distraction," Nick said. "The Colonel is in charge of that phase of the operation." He gave Jake a high five. "Don't worry. It will be a doozy."

"I have no doubt," Kate said. "And, while the entire city of Prague is distracted?"

"We sneak into the ambassador's office with the Kahuna and replace the stolen files with something else."

"I'm almost afraid to ask what."

Vicky held up a DVD. "It's a montage of all my best highlights from back when I was a famous actress. I was saving it in case I received a lifetime achievement award, but this is more important."

Kate looked at the DVD. It was titled *Sticky Vicky: Boner Jams, Volumes One, Two, and Three*. "You're selling a porn video to the Chinese government?"

"And whatever the price is, it's totally worth it," Vicky said. "I guarantee that they won't have any buyer regret, if you know what I mean."

"The Kahuna added an encryption so it will look just like the files stolen from Sentience. It should fool them long enough for us to get away. By the time they break the encryption, it will be too late."

The Kahuna grinned. "I also added a little something that the boys in Sentience R&D developed a couple years ago. It's a virus that will enable us to redirect any wire payments from the ambassador's account to ours."

Kate raised a single eyebrow. "What were your R&D guys planning to do with it?"

"They stole a couple million dollars from me," the Kahuna said, "before I figured out what had happened and shut them down."

"And you didn't turn them in?" Nick asked.

"Are you kidding? I gave them a promotion. Best decision I ever made. In my business, you need people who think outside the box."

"What about Neklan and Olga?" Cosmo asked.

Nick shrugged. "They aren't going to have a lot of hiding places once the Chinese figure out they got scammed by them for hundreds of millions. I'm hoping they'll take their chances with the U.S. justice system rather than with Zhang Wei."

"I wouldn't count on it," Kate said. "Neklan is crazy."

"But Olga isn't. Who knows? Maybe she'll make a deal."

He slung an arm around Kate's shoulders. "Look how great it worked out for you the last time you made a deal with a con man."

Ten hours later, Nick and Kate were in Prague, staring out the window of their room on the third floor of the Four Seasons. The Vltava River flowed below them, and Prague Castle sat at the top of a hill on the other side. They were occupying the three-thousand-square-foot presidential suite. It was decorated in typical Old World European style, complete with red and gold tapestries and a king-size four-poster bed. Jake and the Kahuna were in one corner of the room talking, while Cosmo was watching Vicky take belfies in the Bavarian barmaid costume.

"Where's Gregory and his crew?" Kate asked Nick. "We're supposed to be at the Chinese embassy in less than an hour."

There was a knock on the door, and Kate blew out a sigh of relief when Nick showed Betina into the room.

"Sorry we're late," Betina said. "There was a complication, but Greg will be right up."

Cosmo rushed over to shake Betina's hand. "I'm Cosmo Uno." He paused to catch his breath. "I'm your number one fan. I think it's amazing how you can think of jokes wearing those tight stretchy pants. When my pants are too tight I can't think of anything, except maybe that I need new pants."

Betina smiled at Cosmo. "Thanks, I guess."

"So, what's it like being a movie star?" Cosmo asked. "Do you know Mel Gibson?"

"I might have seen him at Starbucks once."

"Cool. Have you ever seen *Mad Max Beyond Thunderdome*? Do you remember that part where Mel's supposed to fight Blaster and Tina Turner tells him 'Two men enter, one man leaves'?"

"I guess so. It sounds familiar."

Cosmo's upper lip broke out in sweat beads. "It was a pretty great movie, and that was my favorite part. Maybe you could use it sometime on your podcast."

Betina cleared her throat and paused to channel her inner Tina Turner. "Welcome to the Thunderdome. Two men enter, one man leaves."

Cosmo shivered a little and rubbed his arms. "I just got goosies. That was awesome."

"You mentioned a complication," Kate said to Betina. "What kind of complication? We're on a pretty tight schedule."

Betina rolled her eyes. "The complication? You've got to see this for yourself."

Greg walked through the door, coaxing along a little gray-haired woman wearing a blue velour tracksuit and white tennies. "Come on, Grandma. I'm going to be late for work."

"Nice to see you again, Mrs. K," Nick said.

Mrs. Kowowski hit Greg with her purse. "You're always rushing me." She turned to Nick and Kate and looked around the lavish hotel suite. "I wouldn't believe it if I didn't see it with my own eyes. I guess my Gregory is really an international spy after all."

Nick put his hand on Greg's shoulder. "That's right, Mrs. K. Greg's going to help us save the world from a horde of evil Chinese robots."

"Is it that nasty Badger again?"

"You bet," Nick said. "And we're late. We're supposed to meet the rest of the crew by Prague Castle before heading over to the embassy. They're in charge of distracting the Badger while Greg works."

"Well, I'm coming too." She wet her finger with her tongue and wiped some crumbs off Greg's cheek, as he tried unsuccessfully to bat her hand away. "It's not every day that you get to watch your grandson save the world."

"Sure thing, Mrs. K," Nick said as they left the room. "Just be sure to stay out of the way. The Badger can be unpredictable."

Nick, Kate, and the rest of the crew walked out of the hotel and along the Vltava toward the Charles Bridge. It was a bright, sunny day. The cobblestone streets, most with unpronounceable Czech names, were lined with tourists, and the lazy river was filled with little rowboats rented from the nearby boathouse. They turned onto a two-thousand-foot-long, pedestrian-only stone bridge and walked along the alley lined with baroque-style statues of saints guarded by three gothic watchtowers.

Kate looked up the steep hill at the castle on the other side of the river. "Where's the Chinese embassy?"

"Most of the consulates and Czech government buildings, including the Chinese embassy, are on this side of the river near the castle," Nick said as they trudged up the hill lined with restaurants and tourist shops.

They reached a public garden near the top of the hill, and Nick stopped. He pointed to a group of twenty or so millennials, carrying large poster boards and milling around a fountain. "There's our distraction. You're lucky I represent these guys. They're crazy busy with work right now, but they owe me a favor."

Nick and Kate walked over to the group, along with Jake, Cosmo, Vicky, the Kahuna, Greg, Betina, and Mrs. Kowowski. Their leader was standing on a bench, trying to organize them. "Has everybody got their signs and asshats?" he shouted. He pointed to a young woman in the group. "Cheryl, for the last time, put on your asshat and get ready to start chanting."

Nick shook the leader's hand and turned to Kate. "This is Thomas Worth. He's the best counterprotestor protestor in the Western Hemisphere."

Thomas smiled and waved his hand at Nick. "I used to be just a counterprotestor until I met this guy. He really took us to the next level."

"What do you guys protest?" Cosmo asked.

Thomas got within six inches of Cosmo's face, and within seconds he was surrounded by the group. "'Guys'? Do we all look like guys to you? You'd better watch your gender identification labels, buddy." He sniffed Cosmo. "You stink like fear and white male privilege to me."

Cosmo smelled himself. "Are you sure it's not Old Spice?"

"I'll bet he's a card-carrying member of the patriarchy too," Cheryl said. "Let's take his picture and post it on Facebook."

Cosmo looked as if he was about to faint. "Oh lordy. I always knew my toxic masculinity was going to get me in trouble someday."

Cheryl slapped Cosmo on the back and laughed. "Oh man. You should have seen your face. We're just messing with you."

"Here's the thing," Nick said. "There are plenty of protestors and plenty of counterprotestors. You throw a bunch of people protesting the counterprotestors into the mix, put hats that look like butts on their heads, get the whole thing on video, and take it all the way to the YouTube bank."

"But why are they wearing hats that look like butts?" Vicky asked. "I like butts as much as the next person, but they only look good above your legs and below your belly button."

"Marketing," Nick said. "You need a hook if you want people to remember your brand. Something memorable . . . like asshats."

"That makes sense," Cosmo said. "I'd watch a bunch of asshats on YouTube."

Nick checked his watch. "We're supposed to meet the ambassador's son at ten A.M. then begin the podcast half an hour later." He turned to Jake. "You should plan on showing up at the embassy with Thomas and the Asshats around ten forty-five. We'll need a big distraction."

"No problem," Jake said. "I'm sure I can come up with something."

24

Nick and Kate left Jake at the castle with Mrs. Kowowski and the protestors, and led Betina, Greg, Cosmo, Vicky, and the Kahuna through Letná Park and across a highway onto tree-lined Pelléova Avenue. Stone mansions, once the homes of Bohemian aristocrats and now housing mostly consulates and government offices, hid behind iron gates and fences.

"The Chinese embassy is just ahead on the right," Nick said. "The ambassador's son, Zhang Yong, will meet us at the entrance."

The Chinese embassy was housed in a large complex behind a ten-foot-tall fence and a network of security cameras. Zhang Yong was waiting in front of a set of tall green double doors that opened up into a large courtyard and the consulate building.

"No way," he said when he saw Betina. "It's really you. I thought it might have been a prank. I love your podcast."

Nick shook Yong's hand. "I'm Betina's producer, Nicholas Nacky. We're doing a European tour, and we thought it would be cool to film in the Chinese embassy. She has a huge Chinese audience."

Yong nodded his head. "It's an honor. Will I be on the podcast too?"

"Of course," Nick said. "Playing Fortnite with her international fans is the whole point of the tour."

"Awesome. Who are all the other people?"

"Cosmo and Rich are cameramen," Nick said. "Greg is a technical adviser, Kate is my assistant, and Vicky is an Instagram model making a guest appearance on the show."

"Technically, I'm a super Instagram model," Vicky said. "I'm planning a wardrobe malfunction sometime during the taping, so let me know if you hate boobs."

Yong looked at Vicky in her Bavarian barmaid costume. His eyes were the size of dinner plates. "This is going to be the best day of my life."

Yong led Nick, Kate, and the rest of the crew through the green doors and then past two disinterested armed guards. "I'm bringing some friends back to my place to play video games," he said to them.

The guards barely looked up and waved Yong through. "Pretty lax security," Kate whispered to Nick. "I guess they're used to Yong bringing guests into the compound."

Yong walked them through the courtyard up to the front of a mansion with a Chinese flag flying above the front door. "This is the main building. The residential part is on one side and the offices are on another." He led them into the residential section, through a series of hallways lined with Chinese art and artifacts. "That's my dad," he said, pointing to a sixty-something Chinese man wearing a tailored business suit walking toward them.

Zhang Wei walked up to his son, frowned, and said something to him in Chinese.

"Jeez, Dad. Super rude. Can't you at least speak English in front of my friends?"

The ambassador glared at his son. "Who the heck are all these people?"

"Chill out. We're just going to my room to play Fortnite."

Zhang Wei shook his head. "More video games? Would it kill you to get outside and try some sports once in a while?"

Yong put both hands on his head and groaned. "I don't know, Dad. Would it? Is that what you want . . . your son to get killed playing sports? Would that make you love me?"

"We will speak of this later," Zhang Wei said. "I have matters to attend to now." He turned on his heel and walked away down the hall.

"Sorry about that. My dad's kind of a stick-in-the-mud." He led Nick, Kate, and the others into a suite of rooms decorated in a contemporary Western style, complete with an eighty-five-inch television, a comfortable-looking oversized couch, a pool table, and a state-of-the-art gaming chair. He smiled at Betina. "This is my space at the embassy. It's nice, right?" He flopped himself down on the couch. "Make yourself at home."

"Vicky was hoping to get a picture for her Instagram account in your father's office later," Nick said. "Is it in this building?"

"It's on the second floor at the end of the hallway in the other wing, but Dad is super uncool about me bringing my friends there."

"What a shame," Betina said. "It would be epic to film in his office." She winked at Yong. "You never bring girls there?"

Yong grinned sheepishly. "Okay, you got me. I do bring people there once in a while when Dad is out of town." He thought for a moment. "It would be pretty epic, but we can't. Dad had meetings yesterday and again today with some Czech a-hole."

Nick looked at his watch. It read 10:45 A.M. "Let's hope something pulls him away from his work then." An alarm sounded, and a light on the wall blinked yellow. "What's going on?" he asked Yong.

Yong waved his hand dismissively. "Just ignore it. That thing goes off all the time. Probably just a bunch of people outside protesting something or other. You don't have to worry unless it goes from yellow to red."

"What happens then?"

"The embassy is put on lockdown and all the bigwigs, like

my dad, go to hide in the safe room until they get the all clear."

The alarm sounded again, and the light went red.

Yong sat up. "That's not good. I wonder what's happening out there."

Kate looked at Nick. "I wonder."

Zhang Wei, Viktor Neklan, and Olga Zellenkova looked out of the ambassador's floor-to-ceiling windows at the scene in the courtyard just below. A flash mob of around a hundred Dalai Lamas in orange Buddhist robes dancing to the music of *Saturday Night Fever* had stormed the courtyard and were quickly joined by a hundred dancing Mao Zedongs, all dressed in gray pocketed tunic suits.

Wei shook his head. "It must be the 'Free Tibet' crowd again. This is something new for them though," he said, pointing at the group of asshat-wearing twenty-year-olds as they banged on the mansion's front door demanding to see the ambassador.

Thomas tore down the Chinese flag above the door and replaced it with a "Mao Is a Meanie" poster while Cheryl looked up at the ambassador directly above, shouting incomprehensibly about the patriarchy. Meanwhile, the other Asshats continued to protest the Maos, while the Dalai Lamas danced and the astonished guards looked at one another, unsure of what to do. In the chaos, nobody noticed the sixty-something ex-commando sneak through a side door into the consulate.

Thirty seconds later, the fire alarm sounded. Wei shook his head as the red light in the corner of his office started to blink. "Maybe we'd better evacuate until this all gets sorted out."

A group of uniformed guards rushed in and escorted the ambassador and his guests down to the panic room in the basement of the embassy.

"I don't like this," Olga said to Neklan as the panic room door slammed shut behind them, locking them in. "It doesn't feel right."

Neklan sat down on a chair and watched the panic room video monitors showing chaos in the courtyard. "You don't know how to relax," he said to Olga. "When I was running the StB, this was standard protocol for these disturbances. As soon as it's over, we get our money, Wei gets his AI technology, and we're out of here. Then it's time to kill that FBI agent and her friend, but only after we bury everyone else they care about."

"How do I know what you've given me is worth one hundred million?" Wei asked. "It had better be what you promised, or there will be repercussions. There won't be anyplace on Earth for you to hide from the people in my government funding this deal."

"We've done a lot of very profitable business together. I'd think you'd have some trust by now," Neklan said. "Besides, how do I know you'll wire the money, now that you have the technology?"

"Don't worry. You'll have your money."

Neklan stared at Wei. "I'd better. Prague is my town, and I have my own people who specialize in repercussions too."

Wei watched as the mob dispersed as quickly as it had formed, and a few Czech police cars began to arrive at the scene. "You see. It's already over. My men will check the grounds and we'll be out of here in no more than fifteen minutes."

Yong stood at a window in his suite of rooms as he watched the protestors in the courtyard. "It's a flash mob. A pretty good one too." He walked back to the couch and sat down. "My dad is going to have a conniption. By now security has probably got him on lockdown in the basement." He paused. "The fire alarm's going too. Maybe we should head down there."

"I don't smell any smoke. It's probably just a false alarm," Nick said. "I think we should start filming the podcast. With a flash mob in the background, it's sure to go viral."

"You think so?"

"Definitely. Are you in or out?"

Yong grinned. "Okay. Let's do it."

A minute later, Yong was sandwiched between Betina and Vicky on the couch, playing Fortnite, while Greg stood off to the side in a corner of the room giving Betina instructions into her earpiece, and Cosmo filmed it all with a GoPro camera.

Nick, Kate, and the Kahuna walked toward the door.

"Where are you guys going?" Yong asked. He gestured toward the Kahuna. "Besides, isn't he one of the cameramen?"

Vicky squeezed her arms together and her D-cup breasts escaped from her B-cup-sized Bavarian barmaid top. She looked straight into Cosmo's GoPro. "Whoops. It looks like my boobs have accidentally popped out. Whatever will I do now?"

Kate put her hand over her eyes. "Her girls are out, aren't they?" she said to Nick.

"Yep."

Vicky held up her hands. "Oh well. I guess I'll just have to sit here topless." She turned to Yong. "You don't mind, do you?"

Yong's mouth hung open and the controller slipped out of his hands onto the floor. "No. It's okay with me."

"So, we'll see you later," Nick said.

Yong looked from Vicky to Betina and then back to Vicky again. He appeared a little shell-shocked. "It's okay with me."

Nick grinned. "And you don't mind if we go to your dad's office and look around?"

Yong absentmindedly picked up his controller and went back to playing Fortnite with Betina. "Sure. It's okay with me."

Kate, Nick, and the Kahuna snuck out of the room, closed the door behind them, and backtracked through the building toward the business wing of the consulate. The halls were largely deserted, and the few people that hurried past them seemed much more concerned with what was going on outside than inside.

Kate's cellphone buzzed. She stopped for a moment to read the text. "It's Dad. He set off the fire alarms and shut down the video cameras in this section of the building. He says we have around ten minutes before the flash mob dissipates and the police arrive."

"No problemo," the Kahuna said. "I'm used to working under pressure."

A couple of minutes later, they'd made it through the building to a large set of double doors at the end of the hallway on the second floor.

Nick peeked inside. "It's the ambassador's private office," he said. "Right where Yong said it would be. And nobody's home."

The Kahuna followed Nick and Kate inside, sat down at Zhang Wei's desk, and smiled. "He must have been in a hurry. He didn't even log out. This should be even easier than I thought." His fingers moved a mile a minute over the keyboard as he searched first the embassy server and then Zhang Wei's private files for anything that looked like it came from Sentience.

Kate watched the door. "We have five more minutes. Then we'll need to shut this down."

"I think I found something from Sentience," the Kahuna

said. "It's in his private files." He looked up at Kate. "I also found references to stolen data from Kranos and Waterloo."

"Those are the two Silicon Valley companies whose billionaire CEOs died under sketchy circumstances," Nick said.

Kate took a cellphone picture of the screen. "I guess we know for sure how Olga and Neklan have been making their money. They've been investing in companies with sensitive technologies then using their inside connections to steal data and sell it to Zhang Wei."

"I'm lucky they didn't kill me too," the Kahuna said.

Kate put her hand on the Kahuna's shoulder. "Their original plan was to capture you alive and sell you to Wei."

"That would have been ugly," the Kahuna said. He connected a portable hard drive to the ambassador's computer. "I transferred Vicky's DVD to this external drive last night. Now all we have to do is securely delete the Sentience data." He scanned Wei's computer to make sure it was completely gone. "Next, we rename my wife's 'highlight reel' so it looks like the Sentience file I just deleted. And, finally, we upload Vicky's best from the external drive to the computer." He hit return. "Here we go. It will take a couple minutes, but it looks good. They won't know a thing until they break through the encryption."

"Do you hear that?" Kate said. "It's quiet."

Nick listened. "No more fire alarm. I think we're out of time."

"Almost done. Just give me another thirty seconds." The Kahuna put in a different DVD and uploaded the banking virus to Wei's computer. "Okay. We're set. Now the next time Zhang tries to electronically wire any monies, they should be redirected straight to Nick's account. In theory it shouldn't even matter if he has two-factor authentication or some other security protocol, because it will appear to him as though the money is going to the right place."

Kate cracked the door. "The coast is clear. Let's go."

Nick, Kate, and the Kahuna walked back through the consulate to Yong's suite, and sat down. Yong was still sitting between Betina and Vicky, focused like a laser on the game play. The red light on the wall turned yellow and then, a couple minutes later, turned off completely.

Zhang Wei, accompanied by two uniformed guards, walked into the suite and systematically went through each room. Yong waved them away from the TV screen. "They do this every time there's a security breach," he said to Betina. "Just ignore them."

Wei stopped in his tracks when he came to Vicky, and smacked his forehead. "What the heck is going on in here? Why is she half naked?"

Vicky gave him a finger wave. "It's okay. I'm a super Instagram model. Would this be a good time for me to get a selfie with you?"

Wei tilted his head back and said something in Chinese.

"What's he saying?" Nick asked Yong. "He sounds angry."

Yong rolled his eyes. "Who knows? I don't speak crusty old Communist."

The ambassador pointed to the door. "Everybody get out."

Yong put down his controller. "Yeesh. You'd better go, before my dad has a coronary."

Nick, Kate, and the rest of the crew followed Yong through the embassy and out into the courtyard. The "Mao Is a Meanie" sign still hung proudly above the door, but people were milling around and, with the exception of a couple of Czech policemen talking with embassy security, things seemed to be slowly returning to business as usual.

Yong walked them past the armed guards at the entrance and stood with them outside the green door. There was no sign of the Dalai Lamas, Maos, or Asshats. The police cars were starting to disperse, leaving behind a small crowd of onlookers, including a sixty-year-old Clint Eastwood type and an older gray-haired grandma type wearing a blue tracksuit.

Yong rocked back and forth on his feet. "Sorry we had to cut it short. Did you get some good stuff?"

Nick flashed a crooked grin at Yong. "Definitely."

25

Nick, Kate, Jake, and Cosmo sat on a bench at the base of Petrin Hill, just south of Prague Castle. A funicular tram ran up the steep slope, taking passengers to the top, more than three hundred feet above the river, where inviting parks and hidden gardens welcomed tourists and picnicking Prague residents.

Kate took a deep breath and looked at Nick. His eyes were closed, and he was slumped into the bench, enjoying the songbirds and midday sunshine. "When do you think we'll hear something? Waiting around isn't exactly my forte."

Nick opened one eye. "How could you not relax here? It's like a little oasis in the center of the city."

Cosmo looked up the hill. "My guidebook says there's supposed to be a lookout tower and a small castle that houses a mirror maze at the top, but there's a hundred Czech crown admission and I already spent my daily stipend."

"I'll spring for it just as soon as the Chinese government replenishes my offshore bank account. I'm expecting them to send a sizable deposit my way any time now."

Kate narrowed her eyes. "You mean Uncle Sam's way, right?"

"Right. Of course." He paused. "Do you think Uncle Sam would buy me a beach house?"

"It's a little premature to be thinking beach house." Kate watched a group of people get onto the funicular. "We might have stopped Zhang Wei from giving the AI to the Chinese military, but there's no guarantee that Neklan doesn't have a copy of the Sentience data squirreled away somewhere. We need to take him down."

Nick's cellphone buzzed before he could answer. He read the text. "Good news. As of two minutes ago, we're a hundred million dollars richer."

Kate blinked. "A hundred million dollars? I can't even count that high."

"It's a lot of money, but there's only one thing better than a hundred million, and that's two hundred million." Nick dialed Olga Zellenkova on his cellphone. "Plus, the look on Viktor Neklan's face when he realizes we've scammed him twice in the same day."

"Ahoy hoy," Nick said into the phone once Olga picked up.

"Nicolas. I didn't expect to hear from you so soon," Olga said after a silent moment. "What can I do for you?"

"I'm in Prague, and I thought I'd look you up."

"I figured you'd follow us here at some point. I'm just surprised it was so soon. I'm impressed. Unfortunately, my and Viktor's business here is complete. I'm afraid we won't be staying much longer. I'm sure you understand."

"I understand that you have a buyer for the data you stole, but we have the Kahuna," Nick said. "What do you say we make a deal?"

"What kind of deal?"

"We know the Chinese are willing to pay you three hundred million dollars if you deliver the data with the encryption codes and only one hundred million without. We can give you the codes."

"For three hundred million dollars, they'll expect us to throw in a live Kahuna."

"They don't need the Kahuna," Nick said. "They need the codes. From what the Kahuna told us, it's a state-of-the-art encryption that could take years to break, even by the most sophisticated computer scientists. I've seen the file and I'm assured it's totally worth the price. They won't have any buyer regret, if you know what I mean. I'm sure you'll persuade them."

"And what do you want in return?"

"We split the extra two hundred million down the middle. One hundred million for you and one hundred million for me."

"I'm not sure Viktor will agree," Olga said.

"I think he will. It's more than fair. Without our codes,

he won't get a penny over the hundred. I could call up the Chinese right now and try to make a deal without him."

"Let me ask Viktor." She put Nick on hold and returned thirty seconds later. "We have a deal. Where do you want to meet?"

"I think a nice public park this time. How about the top of Petrin, by the lookout tower? You have fifteen minutes. After that, we're gone."

"I'm not sure we can get there by then," Olga said.

"You mean you won't have time to plan an ambush, don't you?"

Nick could hear Olga smiling through the phone. "I guess we're getting to know each other pretty well." She paused. "Viktor and I will see you in fifteen. Ciao."

Nick, Kate, Jake, and Cosmo made their way to the top of Petrin Hill.

"International wires can take a while from when they're initiated until the transfer is recorded in the receiving bank, but the more time that passes, the more suspicious Neklan will get," Nick said. "He'll be as mad as a hornet and twice as dangerous once he figures out what we did."

Kate looked around the park. "Dad, you stake out one end of the park near the lookout tower and, Cosmo, you position yourself at the other near the mirror maze. Nick and I will wait for Olga in the middle."

"What are we looking for?" Cosmo asked.

"Anything suspicious."

"You mean like Neklan's armed mercenaries closing in on our positions?" Jake said. "Don't worry. We've got your back."

Ten minutes later, Olga Zellenkova and Viktor Neklan stepped off the funicular tram and walked over to Nick and Kate.

"I'm giving you your money," Viktor said, "but that doesn't mean I'm not still coming for you once this is done."

"We'll take our chances," Kate said.

Neklan shrugged. "Just so we understand each other." He turned to Olga. "Let's do this and get out of here."

Olga dialed the Chinese embassy on her cellphone and asked for the ambassador. "I'm here with the gentleman we spoke about," she said once Zhang Wei picked up the call. "He has the encryption codes you need."

"Here's what we need in return," Nick said. "The ambassador wires half the money now. Once we know it's in our accounts, we send him the encryption codes. When he confirms the merchandise is decrypted, he wires us the other half of the money."

Neklan narrowed his eyes. "Whose account is the money getting wired to, mine or yours?"

Nick provided a routing and account number to Olga. "Ask the ambassador to wire my half to this account and your half to your account. That way we can both be sure there's no monkey business."

Olga took the paper from Nick and looked at Neklan.

"It's acceptable," Neklan said, "if it's okay with Zhang too."

Olga spoke over the phone to Zhang, and then to Nick and Neklan. "The money is on its way. What shall we do to pass the time until we confirm it safely arrived?"

"What else?" Nick sat down and made himself comfortable. "We wait."

Kate felt as if her heart was about to explode as the minutes passed. Finally, Nick's cellphone buzzed and he checked his texts. "Good news. The wire arrived." He borrowed Olga's phone and typed the encryption code. "Give this to Zhang."

Neklan checked his banking information on his cellphone. "Why hasn't my share arrived yet?"

"Hold on, Viktor. Sometimes it takes longer to show up, depending on the bank." Olga looked back at her phone, sent the text, and put Zhang on speakerphone. "Can you open the file now, Wei?"

There was a moment of silence on the other end of the phone, followed by cursing in Chinese. "Is this a joke?"

Everybody listened to the sounds of Vicky moaning as her highlight reel DVD played in the background of the phone call. "I thought I asked for the pizza with extra sausage," Vicky's voice said. "I like a lot of sausage, if you know what I mean."

"Surprise," Nick said as Olga and Neklan stared at the phone in disbelief. "You're surprised, aren't you? I can tell just by looking at you." He held up his hands and shook them, jazz hands style. "Surprise."

"You have two hundred million dollars of the People's

Republic's money?" Zhang said. "All I have is some porn video. Where is the technology you promised? The generals who I promised this to are going to kill us both."

Neklan checked his bank account again. "Where's my money? It's still not here. What's going on, Zellenkova?"

"About that," Nick said. "I stole it." He looked at Olga and Neklan. "This is the part where I gloat." He flashed them a crooked grin. "Oh man, gloating is so much better when it's face-to-face. Maybe we can get Zhang on FaceTime so I can gloat with him too."

Olga listened to Zhang curse over the phone for a few more seconds then hung up. "It's over, Viktor. The Chinese will never stop looking for us. It's better to be in a nice, cozy American prison than dead."

"Speak for yourself," Viktor said. He drew a switchblade out of his pocket, stuck it into Olga's stomach, and twisted the blade. She collapsed to the ground and used both hands to try to stop the blood oozing out.

Neklan motioned toward the lookout tower. One of the men in the crowd of tourists drew a semiautomatic gun. The crowd screamed and scattered as he aimed in Kate and Nick's direction. The gunman got off one wild shot before Jake was on top of him. He wrestled the weapon from the mercenary, got him in a chokehold, and dropped the unconscious gunman to the ground five seconds later.

Neklan drew a pistol and took off running past Cosmo and into the little castle housing the mirror maze. Cosmo glanced back at Nick and Kate. "Two men enter, one man leaves," he shouted and followed Neklan.

Nick and Kate sprinted to the castle and ran inside. "Cosmo?" Kate shouted. She looked around. The room was decorated with thousands of faux gothic arches and full-length mirrors. Out of the corner of her eye, she spotted Cosmo and Neklan wrestling with each other. She turned and moved toward them, before realizing it was just a reflection coming from somewhere else within the maze. She watched as Neklan disengaged from Cosmo, took a step back, and fired off a couple shots, striking Cosmo in the leg, shattering several mirrors, and scattering the other people in the room as they ran for cover.

Nick and Kate ran to Cosmo. "Are you okay?" Nick asked, kneeling beside him. He ripped off a piece of his shirt and wrapped it around the bloody leg.

Cosmo moaned as Nick tightened the tourniquet. "He ran into the next room. Don't let him get away."

"Go," Nick said to Kate. "I'll get his bleeding under control."

Kate bolted through the doorway and looked around the room. It was filled with funhouse mirrors and decorated liberally with wax figures of famous historical figures. A sign on the wall asked patrons not to touch, as they were on loan for the next month. Kate ducked as a bullet whistled past her, striking wax Dracula and knocking him off his moorings.

"For the love of Mike. This is crazy, Neklan. Everybody knows you need a wooden stake to kill Dracula. Just give up."

Neklan stepped from behind Napoleon and fired off another shot. "Not until I kill every last one of you." He stumbled backward, tripping over a wax pharaoh and falling just as he fired his weapon. A massive mirror hanging above the room shattered into a thousand pieces as the bullet struck it, sending shards of glass raining down over the entire room. Kate hid under Dracula until the onslaught was over and then pushed him aside. She walked over to Neklan. He was lying on his back, impaled by a giant, ragged shard. Next to him was the wax replica of an Egyptian king he had stumbled over. Nick and Jake rushed into the room and stood next to Kate.

Nick looked down at Neklan and the wax dummy, then over at Kate. "You should just go ahead and say it," he said to her.

Kate squelched a grimace. "Give my regards to King Tut, asshole?"

Cosmo hobbled into the room and joined them by Neklan's body. "Welcome to the Thunderdome. Two men enter, one man leaves?"

"Both good. But not perfect," Nick said.

Jake removed a cigar from his front shirt pocket, put it in his mouth, and smiled at each of them. "I love it when a plan comes together."

26

Twenty-four hours later, Kate opened her apartment door, relieved to find it professionally cleaned and no sign of naked hippies except a single watercolor painting on the wall, presumably left as payment. Nick had predictably disappeared as soon as the plane landed. True to his word, all the scammed money had been deposited into the FBI accounts, which Jessup had informed her might just barely cover all the damages and lawsuits from the past week. Olga was sitting in a prison hospital, recuperating from her injuries and awaiting her arraignment, eager to help dismantle what remained of Neklan's operation in exchange for anything less than life in a maximum-security penitentiary.

Kate walked into her bedroom, dead tired, and found Nick sitting on her bed, watching an old episode of *The Andy Griffith Show* on her television. "Jinkies. How many times do I have to tell you . . . boundaries."

"Give me a break. I just lost two hundred million dollars."

Kate crawled onto the bed with Nick. "That must be pretty tough for a reformed smuggler like you to handle."

"Not really. Mr. Freezy arrives in Los Angeles later this week, compliments of Uncle Sam and one of Cosmo's vouchers. Fortunes come and fortunes go, but haunted ice cream trucks don't come along every day." He flashed her a crooked grin. "Why don't you check your closet? I may have left a souvenir from Hawaii there for you too."

Kate opened her closet. Her FBI windbreaker was still relegated to the back, but there, in the very front, was a giant four-foot-long and one-foot-wide Toblerone. A red satin ribbon was wrapped around it with a card attached addressed to "The Snuggler."

"Is that big enough?" Nick asked. "Does it meet your expectations?"

"It surpasses my expectations. Best bet ever."

"I'm not conceding that I lost the bet, but I was pretty sure you would expect a Toblerone when the case was wrapped up."

"It's a tradition," Kate said.

"There's something else in the closet," Nick said.

A freshly laundered pair of denim overalls hung behind the Toblerone. Kate took them off the hanger, disappeared into the bathroom, and returned wearing nothing else. "Is this what you had in mind?"

Nick drew Kate close. "You know that one-time, maybe two-time thing we talked about back in Hawaii?"

Kate pressed herself against Nick. "Yeah."

"Well, get ready. The Big Show is about to start, and I hear it might last all night."

HAVE YOU DISCOVERED

JANET EVANOVICH'S

STEPHANIE PLUM SERIES?

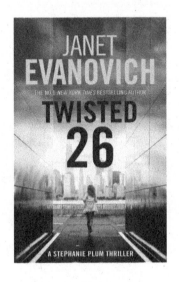

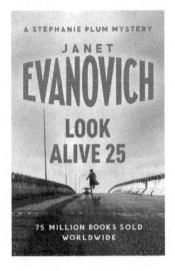

**IF YOU LOVED *THE BIG KAHUNA*,
THEN LOOK NO FURTHER
FOR YOUR NEXT
FOX AND O'HARE ADVENTURE . . .**

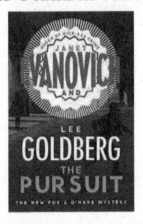

**Diamonds, castles and rocket-propelled grenade
launchers: a typical Nick Fox date.**

International conman and expert thief Nick Fox has
been kidnapped from right under his FBI handler's nose.
Fortunately for him, he's been taken by a gang of thieves
who want his expertise. Unfortunately for the thieves,
his FBI handler is Kate O'Hare, and there's more than a
professional connection between her and Nick.

A diamond vault is the first target, but soon Nick and
Kate have both joined the gang and are chasing around the
Paris sewers in an attempt to prevent a biological weapon
being unleashed. All that stands between them and a
global terror event are Kate's formidable weapons
skills and Nick's well-honed charms . . .

DON'T MISS THE
NEW NOVEL IN
THE STEPHANIE PLUM SERIES!

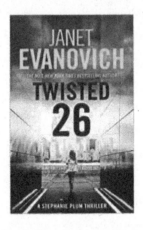

This isn't just another case. This is family.

Grandma Mazur has decided to get married again – this
time to a local gangster named Jimmy Rosolli. If Stephanie
has her doubts about this marriage, she doesn't have to
worry for long, because the groom drops dead of a heart
attack 45 minutes after saying, "I do."

A sad day for Grandma Mazur turns into something far
more dangerous when Jimmy's former "business partners"
are convinced that his new widow is keeping the keys to
a financial windfall all to herself. But the one thing these
wise guys didn't count on was the widow's bounty hunter
granddaughter, who'll do anything to save her.

REVIEW

JOIN STEPHANIE PLUM ON HER
LATEST ADVENTURES . . .

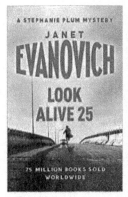 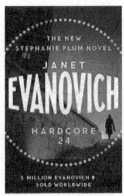 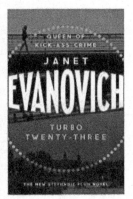

HAVE YOU DISCOVERED
ALL OF JANET EVANOVICH'S BOOKS?

THE STEPHANIE PLUM SERIES . . .

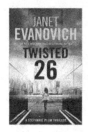  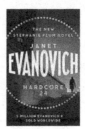 

THE FOX AND O'HARE SERIES . . .

   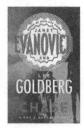

THE LIZZY AND DIESEL SERIES . . .

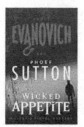  

THE KNIGHT AND MOON SERIES . . .

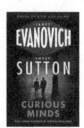 

Join JANET EVANOVICH
on social media!

JanetEvanovich

@janetevanovich

janetevanovich

JanetEvanovichOfficial

Visit EVANOVICH.COM and
sign up for Janet's e-newsletter!